MY ENEMY'S FACE

Hey Elia!
Sure hope you
enjoy the book.
Thanks for reading!
Jerry

Terry Moran
Margaret Lewis Moran

Elia —
Thanks for
wanting to read
our book! Love
working with you!
Margaret

TRP
TotalRecallPress.com
www.totalrecallpress.com

TotalRecall Publications, Inc.
1103 Middlecreek
Friendswood, Texas 77546
281-992-3131   281-482-5390 Fax
www.totalrecallpress.com

ISBN   978-1-59095-660-1
UPC   6-43977-26605-7 -5

Printed in the United States of America with simultaneously printings in Australia, Canada, and United Kingdom.
FIRST EDITION
1   2   3   4   5   6   7   8   9   10

To Grace Lewis and Jo Moran Sayers, our greatest encouragers, and to Ryan, Mitchell and Taylor who bring us joy every day.

In memory of our dads, Bob Moran and Richard Lewis.

Thank you Laschinski Emerson, for your help in validating our account of the pain caused by racism.

Thank you to Anne Jaeger and Sara Baker for your help in the editing process.

About the Author

Terry Moran made a career in law enforcement for 28 years before retiring from Federal service with the FBI and DOE in 2008. He lived in Alabama from 1961 to 1967 where his father was a Special Agent with the FBI. Terry remembers his father working multiple civil rights cases involving members of the Ku Klux Klan. After retiring he works closely with people needing high level security clearances.

Margaret Moran, a native of Knoxville, Tennessee, attended the University of Tennessee and graduated with a degree in Graphic Design. Margaret has taught Art and Photography to both elementary and high school students for 18 years.

Terry and Margaret met at the University of Tennessee and were married in 1981. They lived in Nashville, TN, and Oklahoma City, OK, before coming home to Knoxville. Terry and Margaret have three sons, Ryan, Mitchell, and Taylor.

About the Book

Billy Ray Sawyer is the All American kid. The high school football hero from the "right" side of the tracks is son of the powerful and wealthy Mayor who has raised Billy Ray to accept his racist and narrow-minded ways in 1960s Alabama. Noah Franklin is the polar opposite of Billy Ray. A black son of poor parents, Noah doesn't have racist bone in his body until the Government forces integration. Billy Ray and Noah clash on the first day of school, and through what can only be explained as an Act of God, are forced to live their lives through the other's eyes. Both their spirits and faith are tested through triumphs and failures in a community not ready for change or unity. Hate turns into friendship, as the two boys try to deal with their new circumstances. In an ultimate act of sacrifice, one will be forced to lay down his life to save the other. In an act of love, the other races against time to save him.

Noah's heart throbbed in rhythm with his pounding feet. He had the sensation of his worst nightmares, the ones in which he wanted to run, but his legs wouldn't move. Branches ripped and tore at his face, his arms, and his legs. The sweat, produced as much from his terror as from the dark and humid Alabama night, pooled into his wounds, the saltiness burning deep within his skin. He was smothering. Every breath was a struggle. Mindlessly, his legs churned forward. He knew he had to keep moving. He had to save his friend. He had to save himself.

~ 1 ~

The stifling summer of 1965 was one spent like any other for Noah Franklin. Every morning he would awaken to bacon sizzling on the stove, and biscuits casting their tempting aroma to everyone lucky enough to be nearby. The mixture of the scents was like heaven to Noah. If only there would be enough to satisfy the craving created by the smell. There was only enough to tease the taste buds, to tickle the stomach. Ahh, but it was worth it. Noah's mama made the best biscuits in town.

After the meager breakfast, Noah set out to do his chores. He and his younger brother, Moses, spent the day propelling an ax through mammoth logs. Over and over the ax rose and fell. They would fall into a rhythm, Noah and Moses, and sometimes they'd break into a song. They joked about heading to Detroit City and making it big in Motown.

"I'd best protect these hands. No more choppin' wood for me! Gotta save my fingers for all them autographs I'll be a' signin'." Moses sat down on a log waiting to be split and held up his hands, rotating them to observe both sides.

With a short shove, Noah had Moses sprawled on the ground, his feet sticking straight up into the air. "I'll be sure to get you some white dainty little gloves to protect them precious little hands a' yours. Until then, get your lazy butt back up and do some work."

"No fun, big brother. You are no fun at all."

Adam was the oldest of the three Franklin sons, but Noah acted the part of the first born. Noah seemed to have been born with an attitude of working to his highest ability, even when the work was as mundane as chopping wood. Noah never rested, and rarely, if at all, did he complain about anything. He refused to buy into the self-pity excuse. He accepted his lot in life and made the best of it. But being black and poor in small town northern Alabama in these racially torn times challenged his sanity daily.

Noah Franklin was seventeen years old, an age when most young men are primed for rebellion, especially in a life of extreme poverty as the Franklins were. The hours of labor had produced a body as solid as a rock. And years of living in a family of exceptional faith had made him a true child of God.

Emma and James Franklin had raised their boys with love, discipline, and an attitude of being grateful for God's blessings. Some would not see their life in light of blessings. The family home was small, a two bedroom shack. It was surrounded by tall, skinny pine trees at the end of a long dirt and gravel road at the far and poor end of Webber, Alabama. Twenty other dilapidated houses shared the same street. They were cramped together, as if someone had thrown a handful of seed out onto the hard packed Alabama clay, and up popped the small ramshackle huts. Most of the children in this area wore the same dirty clothes day in and day out. Most went without shoes or made the old ones fit by cutting out the toes. It was a hard life, and one most would not be able to escape in their lifetime.

The two had married in 1941, when both were just nineteen. Several months later, Pearl Harbor was bombed. Raised by God-fearing parents who instilled in him a love for his country, James did his duty by joining the Army. He was sent away to fight the war and returned a decorated soldier. He was welcomed home by Emma and Adam, his newborn son. He was also welcomed home by blatant discrimination. James hoped that two years of meritorious service and risking his life for America would change the ugliness of separate bathrooms and water fountains. He was wrong.

Once a gifted baseball player, his dream was to coach the sport. A dream was all it would be because the only jobs for black men in Webber, Alabama were found at the local steel mill or odd labor jobs provided by well-to-do white people. It didn't matter if you were a decorated soldier or a deviant. The pay was minimal. You either accepted the hard labor or moved somewhere else. If you didn't want the work, there was somebody standing behind you in line that would. The fear of their children going hungry was enough to convince them it was the best, and only thing to do.

While James fought gallantly for God and country, Emma, pregnant with her first child, found full time work as a housekeeper for Robert and Dorothy Grace Sawyer, the richest and most powerful family in Webber. The family of Sawyers had first earned their celebrity when Robert's great-great grandfather was a hero in the War of 1812. In every generation since that time, a Sawyer made his mark in the Alabama history books. Robert and Dorothy Grace's son, Joshua, also came home from World War II a decorated hero. His homecoming included a small band, a parade, a large crowd, and the governor there to shake his hand. Mary Edith Chaney, well known as the prettiest girl in town, was waiting for him too. The tall brunette with milky white skin and long willowy legs had long ago caught the attention of Joshua. It was not long before the two were married and a new powerful generation of Sawyers began.

For twenty years, six days a week, Emma woke before the sun rose, took care of her own family's needs, then walked five miles from the box she called home to the Sawyer's Antebellum mansion. She cooked, cleaned, scrubbed, mopped, washed and dried until her fingers were numb. Then after the Sawyer's supper dishes were cleaned and put away, Emma made the long trek back to her home. Never once did either Sawyer offer to drive her home. They believed they were doing her a favor by just letting her work. They did not owe her a thing.

Robert and Dorothy Grace treated Emma well, but with a definite air of social separation. Still, she grew quite fond of them over the years. When the older couple died tragically in an automobile accident in 1963, Joshua and Mary Edith moved into the family mansion and were kind enough to continue her employment. Joshua was now the Mayor of Webber and perhaps the most powerful Sawyer yet. Joshua was grown when Emma began working for his parents and she had rarely been around him, save for family dinners when Joshua and Mary Edith would visit.

Billy Ray Sawyer, Joshua and Mary Edith's son, was tall, with dark hair and blue-eyes. Like Noah, his body was rock hard, but not from chopping wood and physical labor. Billy

Ray didn't have to work. His physique came from good genes and the weight room at Webber High. The girls in town thought he was gorgeous. Most of the boys wanted to be him. Emma thought he was snobbish, disrespectful, lazy, and needed a good switchin'. After two years in their employment, Emma never felt close to the family. She was a lowly paid servant. Nothing more.

On this hot August day, Emma could see her two boys chopping wood from a quarter of a mile away down the dry, dusty road. With no electricity, the family depended on a large supply of firewood to keep them warm in the winter. She paused and reflected. "Lord, thank you for giving me three fine, healthy boys. They are a mama's dream. I don't deserve what you give me. And I'd rather have them three sons than all the Sawyer money and that Billy good for nothin' Ray." Emma looked skyward. "Forgive me Lord. That wasn't very kind." She paused and smirked. "But it's the truth and you know it."

From the corner of his eye, Noah spotted his mother walking toward them with a small napkin full of leftovers from the Sawyer house. He paused, set his ax upon the log he was working on and with his left hand, wiped the sweat from his brow. "Hey! There's Mama!"

"Don't stop on account a' me! Hello, Moses, honey!" She said as she turned into their property. She walked up the creaking stairs, careful through habit, of stepping over the missing board on step number two. She turned and shouted to Noah. "Happy Birthday, Baby!"

"Thanks, Mama." Noah leaped completely over the set of stairs and gave his mom a strong bear hug.

"You're a good boy, Noah. Hooooweee! A smelly one, but a good one." They both shared a chuckle. Noah smelled his armpits as if to test her truthfulness. He pretended to faint. "Supper'll be ready shortly."

Disappearing behind the screen door, the boys heard her turn on the kitchen faucet and begin singing, "How Great Thou Art." The boys snickered quietly to themselves.

"Reckon she's the next Diana Ross?" asked Moses.

"Yeah. And we can be the Supremes," Noah answered. Then the two broke into a chorus of "Stop in the Name of Love" in their best female voices.

Emma peered out the window. "You boys better stick with choppin' wood. You'll make more money than with that slightly off key singin' a yourn," Emma teased.

"That ain't true 'cause we ain't gettin' a plug nickel for doin' this," Moses managed to say below his breath.

"I heard that, and if you keep belly achin', I'll find more for ya' to do."

Noah and Moses looked at each other and laughed. "Got the dang ears of an elephant," Noah joked.

"I heard that, too."

Suddenly, the front door burst open, slamming into the wall beside it and breaking the jovial mood inside and out.

"James Adam Franklin! What in tarnation is wrong with you comin' in my house like a bunch a wild hogs. Now you go back out and open that door properly. Now!" Emma said sternly.

Adam, Emma and James' firstborn, went back out, but stayed on the front porch. He was in no mood to test the waters with his mother. He knew from experience he would not win. His anger needed to subside before he came back inside.

"What has gotten into that boy lately?" Emma's furrowed brow hid an even deeper fear within.

"Who you mad at today?" Noah inquired, as he leaned against the peeling paint of the front porch railing.

"Ain't fair, Noah! It just ain't fair."

"What ain't?"

"This!" Adam stretched his arms toward the house and then to their neighbor's on all sides. "All this! Ain't fair! What'd we do? Huh? What'd we do to deserve this?" He slapped his arms to his side. Adam was a big man, muscular from years of hard work. His hard life made him look and act older than his twenty years. Adam felt cheated out of his best years. "Look at this place, Noah. It's falling down! Every day it rots a little more. Five of us livin' in this God forsaken shack. Pop did his duty fightin' the white man's war and this is how they repay him. And me? I can't even get a job pickin' up their trash!"

"You didn't get the job? Sorry, Adam."

"This Mr. Jennings. He looked at me like I wasn't fit to tie his shoes, but still told me they had a job. Right about then this white man come in to that office and asked about the job. The boss-man looked at me and told me the job had been filled. Told me to come back in a month or two." Adam looked at the ground and shook his head. "I ain't stupid, Noah. I know what they done."

"You'll get a job, Adam. You just gotta keep tryin'.

"You're young and stupid, boy! You just don't get it do you?" Adam peered deeply into Noah's eyes. Noah couldn't help but see the emptiness in the eyes that stared back. "We are black! We ain't goin' nowhere. Not me. Not you. Not Moses. Just like Pop and his daddy and his daddy before him. Face it Noah. You are poor, you're a nigga' and that's all you'll ever be worth. Nobody's gonna give you nothin'. This is Whitey's world! He takes everything and gives nothin' back. Figures as long as we live out here, stay out of his way, then he'll tolerate us, but that's it. If we want somethin', we gotta take it."

"Suppa's ready!" Emma hollered from inside the house. Her cheerful voice broke the chilling air between the two brothers for an instant, like a ray of sunshine bursting through storm clouds. Everything seemed bearable when she was around.

Noah, hurting from what Adam said, tossed one last comment Adam's way. "It ain't true, Adam. All that stuff you say. It ain't true. Things are gonna change. I know they are."

"You just keep dreamin', brother. Just keep dreamin'". Adam poked Noah in the chest for emphasis. "But deep down you know I'm right." The three brothers entered the kitchen. Noah made sure the door didn't slam behind him.

"Moses, this new kitchen table is a work of art! I do believe you may have some carpentry skills just like our Savior!" Emma was being kind as the table built from plywood and some old vegetable crates pilfered from the trash of the local grocery store, looked as if it would fall apart if you looked at it the wrong way. Still, it would do. Their old kitchen table had been given to them by the kind-hearted Dorothy Grace Sawyer when they bought a new one for their home. Emma had been so proud, the table being the nicest piece of furniture she had ever owned. Unfortunately, it was reclaimed when Mary Edith Sawyer needed a table for her bridge parties. Emma was hurt, but she never let on. The table Moses built would hold a bowl of potatoes as well as any table would, Emma reasoned.

"What do I smell? What heavenly food do I smell?" James Franklin walked into the kitchen, bent over and gave his precious wife a kiss on her right cheek.

"Why, James Franklin. We were going to start without you. I thought you said you were working late."

"Well, my darlin'. When I thought about it, I decided that working an hour or two over and makin' a few extra dollars was not worth the thought of missin' your meat loaf. No sir. Not in a million years."

Emma knew it was a lie. James had been excited all week about the extra cash. Something must have happened, but she was not about to question him in front of the boys. She looked at the love of her life. He was tall, still ruggedly handsome and the kindest, gentlest man she had ever met. She was proud to be his wife.

James quickly washed his hands at the kitchen sink and grabbed a ragged towel to dry them. He sat down at the table and the family joined hands. "Dear Lord," James began. "We are so mighty grateful for all you have given us this day. Continue to bless my dear wife whose loving hands prepared this meal. Bless our three sons who bring us joy every day. And on this very special day, bless Noah, who on this day seventeen years ago, entered our lives. Be with him all the days of his life. Bless this food to nourish our bodies. In your Son's Holy Name we pray. Amen."

"Amen," the rest of the family said in unison.

"And now, I do believe someone has a gift somewhere," Emma said, reaching for something hidden under her chair.

"Now, Mama, don't. I know we can't..."

"You hush up young Noah and be thankful for what you get. Now you open this up, ya' hear. I've been about to bust to give it to ya'."

Noah took the small box with the string ribbon and shook it by his ear. "I think it's a new car! How'd you get it in this tiny box?" Grabbing one end of the string, he tugged until it was off. Then he slowly opened the present, pulling out a small object wrapped in white tissue paper. When the paper was pulled away, a small, shiny silver cross lay in the palm of his hand. His name, in all capital letters, was engraved into it. He stared silently for a minute. "Wow. I couldn't have asked for a better gift. Thanks Momma, Pop." He slipped the cross into his tattered overall pocket. "I'll keep it in my pocket always."

"And when you need the good Lord's help, pull it out and look at it then squeeze it tight. It will be there to remind you there ain't nothin' you can't face that God can't help you through. That's the truth, son," James offered.

"Okay, okay. Great gift. Can we eat?" Adam sighed impatiently.

Emma shot her eldest a half serious frown and then began passing the bowls of food. Judging by the clinks and scrapes of utensils on the ceramic bowls, and the ensuing silence, she knew this dinner would be history in a matter of minutes. She smiled for a moment and counted her blessings.

After dinner, Emma walked to the kitchen cabinet with

something wrapped in a napkin. "Wouldn't be a birthday without birthday cake. Or tea cakes at least!" She ceremoniously unwrapped two tea cakes she had made for the Sawyers, but had been too brown for Mrs. Sawyer's taste. She gave a whole one to Noah, the birthday boy, and split the other one between Adam and Moses. The boys gobbled them up in a minute and she was afraid they would lick the crumbs off the table.

"Moses, see what we got in the mail, today, will ya?" James asked as he leaned back in his chair. Moses gathered the few pieces of mail from the table by the door. He thumbed through them.

"Pop, this letter is from the Webber School Board. Wonder what they want?"

"Open it up Pop." Noah sat on the arm of the chair next to James. He was as curious as the rest of them as to the letter's content.

"Let's see," James began, holding the letter out at arm's length. "Well, I'll be. I don't know what to make of this. I just don't know."

"What Pop? What's it say?" Moses couldn't stand the suspense.

Noah was already reading the letter over his father's shoulder. "They're integratin'. The high school anyway. I'm gonna have to go to Webber High."

James read, "This is to advise you that effective September 8, 1965, all children entering grades ten through twelve in Webber will be required to report to Webber High School, and so on and so forth. It says down at the bottom they'll send a bus to pick you up down at the crossroads."

Moses, entering the ninth grade would not be affected. "Does this mean that Noah's going to a school with white folks?" He shook his head. "Don't think I'd like that very much. Un-uh, wouldn't like that at all."

Noah grinned. "I'll be fine, Moses. White folks is just like us. Just a different color. That's all." Deep inside though, there was a sick feeling in his belly.

"You think the white teachers' gonna be fair to the colored kids? Ya'll gonna get blamed for anything bad that happens. You just watch. It's bad news I'm tellin' ya'. Bad news." Adam had to throw his two cents into the pot.

"I don't know, Adam. I think it's a step in the right direction." Emma was being her typical positive self. "We all know that Jefferson High was just about to fall apart anyway. I've never been too satisfied with it. I don't think you ever received the kind of education you deserved, Adam. It may just open up a whole new world for Noah and Moses." She slowly turned to James, fear showing in her wrinkled eyes.

~ **2** ~

Billy Ray Sawyer leaned back, propped his feet up on the wicker table, and laced his fingers on top of his head. He closed his blue eyes and took a deep breath, smelling the newly clipped lawn that wrapped around the huge antebellum estate he called home. The large, wraparound porch with its ceiling fans whirling above, did a fair job of cutting down the heat of this August morning.

Fortune shined on this seventeen year old. Born an only child into a wealthy and politically prominent family, Billy Ray never had to go without. His grandfather built a small fortune from his privately owned business, the Webber Brick Company. Half of Alabama bought their brick from him. When he and his wife were killed in an automobile accident, Joshua Sawyer, Billy Ray's father, inherited everything.

The name Sawyer in Alabama was a lot like the name Rockefeller in New York, or Kennedy in Massachusetts. The name provided easy entry into the job of Mayor of Webber. In fact, Joshua was enjoying his fourth term. At one time he was pressed to run for governor, which would have suited his inflated ego, but Mary Edith refused to move to Montgomery.

Mayor Sawyer was enraged with the prospect of integration at the local high school. He fought it in every avenue he could think of. However, even his money and influence was not enough to stop the federal government from sticking its nose where it didn't belong.

Billy Ray was the proverbial "Big Man on Campus". He was the best looking, charming, and athletic boy in the county. He knew it, too. Billy Ray was sick at the prospect of the "coloreds", as he had been taught to call them in public, coming in and taking over his school. He and his buddies spent many an afternoon, since the decision to integrate, coming up with ways to "run 'em off".

"You don't expect me, Billy Ray Sawyer, to sit in the same room with some colored and actually be able to learn somethin'?"

His brow furrowed as he thought about it again. The familiar squeak of the screen door shook him out of his bad mood as he saw his dear Mama bring out a silver tray with a cold glass of iced lemonade and some warm tea cakes made by Emma, their maid. The aroma could only be described as heavenly.

"Here ya go darlin'," Mary Edith cooed to her beloved son. In her eyes, he was perfection. "Hope this'll chase some of this bad ole' heat away. These tea cakes are a little brown. I'll speak to Emma."

"Naw, Mama. They're fine, really." He held the cold glass to his forehead before taking a huge gulp. "This lemonade is great! Hits the spot."

The roar of a 1957 Mustang convertible made both their heads turn as it zipped up the oak lined driveway leading to the mansion. His father, Billy Ray thought, looked ridiculous and out of place in such a sporty car. A Ford Mustang was not for some short, balding, pudgy man who barely fit behind the wheel. It was a car for someone young, and full of life. Like himself.

The tires skidded to a halt, kicking up a cloud of dust, causing the Mayor to have a coughing fit. Billy Ray chuckled to himself as he watched his dad twist his body right and left to extract himself from the small front seat.

"Hey, Daddy! You look pretty cool in that car. Mama, you better watch out," he said with a wink at his mother. "That car's a chick mobile if I've ever seen one. He'll be fightin' the ladies off with a stick, ya know."

"Good try, son," Mayor Sawyer snapped back, pretending not to be flattered. A quick glance in the rear view mirror reminded himself how attractive he thought he was for his age. "But I'll be needin' this baby tonight for a meetin'. You can take your truck."

Joshua paused a moment before tossing the keys in Billy Ray's direction with a "just kidding" look on his face. "You be careful, ya' hear? And it better not have a single scratch on it when you get back!"

"Yes, sir! I'll treat it like it's my own! Thanks, Daddy!"

"Billy Ray, come up to my office for a minute before you run off. I need to talk to ya'".

"Sure, Daddy, what's up?"

The two walked into the foyer with its twelve foot ceiling. The walls were dressed top to bottom in a floral design wallpaper Mary Edith heard Jackie Kennedy had used in the White House. The marble floors echoed with their footsteps as they approached the six foot wide spiral staircase leading up to the second floor. Massive oil paintings lined the walls and the carpet covering the steps was straight from the orient, hand woven. At the top of the stairs, a balcony overlooked the main den, full of antiques and art suited for a museum.

They turned into the library. The walls were lined with mahogany bookshelves with intricate carvings of oak leaves and acorns adorning the rare antique manuscripts, very few of which had ever been read.

Mary Edith donned her gardening gloves and tended her roses as she heard bits and pieces of the conversation coming through the open window. She sighed as she heard her husband go into a tirade over the upcoming integration. The last thing she heard before her husband slammed the window shut was if there was a southern bone left in his body, he would do whatever it took to stop the government traitors who were trying to ruin his sacred homeland. And her son's repetitive, "Yes, sirs."

~ 3 ~

None of the students arriving at Webber High School seemed to notice the thickening layer of dark and ominous clouds building in the sky. Nor did they notice the strange purple hue that blended in with the grey, which moved in a slow, barely perceptible counter clockwise rotation. The white students of Webber High were much more interested in what the others were wearing, who had changed the most over the summer, and what prospects of love were waiting to bloom. None of this, however, could compare with the buzz about the new students moments away from arriving at their previously all white school. The bus carrying kids from the other side of town rumbled towards them, the wheels crunching the loose gravel beneath them. New, dark faces, peered out of the dirty windows. Ones, for the first time in history, that would mingle among the white faces in Webber, Alabama.

Billy Ray, newly riled by his father's angry sentiments, sauntered to the front of the crowd to get a better look. He knew that most eyes were on him...the girls, dreaming he'd look their way, the boys wanting to be cool enough to be his friend. He loved the attention, and savored it for just a moment. Motioning towards the approaching bus, he remarked, "It's just like a bad accident. You know it's gruesome, but you just have to look." He smiled at the chuckles and approving nodding of heads.

The old yellow school bus squeaked hideously as it came to a stop, and the door opened with a squeak and a sound resembling releasing steam. None of the bus riders wanted to be the first one off. They may have all stayed on, had Otis, the bus driver, fully equipped with red, frizzy sideburns and a shirt whose buttons threatened to pop off at any second, hadn't hollered out, "Get off the bus, you'ns. Don't ferget your lunches, or belongin's neither. I ain't brangin' nothin' back, ya heah? Go on now, I ain't got all day!" Actually he did. He was about to go home and snooze on his front porch, breaking only for lunch. A few moments before 3:00, he would jerk out of his slumber, climb the steps into the bus, and head back to pick up the kids.

Slowly, the students rose and began filing down the aisle of the bus, and down the couple of steps to depart their last sanction of safety. The first student stopped on the bottom step, happy to remain there as long as possible until the pressure from the others behind him popped him out like a champagne cork. He landed flat on his face. The gawking Webber High students roared with laughter.

"What's wrong, boy?" Billy Ray could not resist saying. "Can't walk and think at the same time?"

The crowd exploded into laughter as the embarrassed tenth grader pulled himself up. He kept his eyes on the ground. A few of the white students left, not wanting to be a part of the harassment. One by one, the newcomers stepped from the bus and slowly started up the long sidewalk to their school.

Billy Ray and his best friends, Red and Davy Lee, immensely enjoying the moment, searched for their next victim. A small girl, clutching her notebook tightly against her chest, hurried toward the doors. Red, smelling the fear in her like a wild dog, said, "Welcome, Aunt Jemima!"   With one quick swipe, he knocked the notebook out of her hands. As it hit the sidewalk, the silver rings popped open and at least fifty sheets of notebook paper promptly fell out. She squatted down quickly and started gathering them up.

Noah, a few steps behind her, bent down to retrieve her notebook. A swift kick from Davy Lee scooted the notebook out of his reach. With narrowed eyes, Noah glanced at him and reached again for the notebook. Davy Lee's foot came back for another swipe and was intercepted by Noah's strong grip. One upward flip caused Davy Lee to lose his balance, and he landed butt first on the concrete amongst the scattered blue-lined paper. A unanimous gasp was followed by an extremely uncomfortable silence.

Billy Ray, as tall, but not as muscular as Noah, looked on in astonishment at his embarrassed friend on the ground. He moved slowly toward and then stopped only inches from Noah's face. "You just made yourself one huge mistake, boy!" He gave Noah a strong shove in the chest, pushing him off balance for an instant.

"You is as stupid as you is ugly!" Red spat, staying a safe distance away.

Noah handed the girl her notebook, and most of the paper. The group hurried for the safety of the school building. Davy Lee pushed himself up off the ground and dusted the dirt from his pants. He glared at Noah, and silently vowed revenge.

"Hey, boy! I ain't through with you!" Noah turned to see a

glaring Billy Ray approaching. "You bettah' apologize!"

Noah, wanting badly to slug this guy, turned towards the school doorway.

"I said, you need to apologize to my buddy!" Billy Ray paused. "On your knees, *boy*. Get on your knees and beg for his forgiveness. If you don't, you'll be on your knees anyway, beggin' for mercy!" Billy Ray smiled and looked at his friends for their approval.

"I don't think he knows English, Billy Ray. You know, they've been goin' to the nigga' school so they ain't been learnin' much," Davy Lee offered. "Maybe you need to speak Swahili. Anybody know Swahili around heah?"

Billy Ray placed an index finger on Noah's chest. He poked as hard as he could to emphasize each word. "Get.... on.... your...knees....now.... you... ignorant... ni..."

The last word was interrupted by a large hand on Billy Ray's shoulder. Richard Lewis, the school's principal, had come out and observed some of the altercation. He knew there would be trouble. He just had not expected it this soon.

"Billy Ray Sawyer, good to see you. How was your summer, son?"

Sawyer. Noah knew the name, as everyone did. The mayor's son. His mother's employer. Although Emma had worked for the mayor and his wife for over two years now, and many years before that for his grandparents, there had never been a reason nor an opportunity for Noah to meet the couple or their son.

With a glance towards the very uncomfortable new students, Mr. Lewis said, "Someone will show you folks to the auditorium where I will join you in a few minutes to answer any questions and give you your schedules. Now, Billy Ray, I'm glad to see you trying to make friends with one of the new students."

"Just havin' a little fun, sir. Makin' 'em feel welcome and all."

"Uh-huh." Mr. Lewis nodded and peered over his glasses. "I think I have a better way for you to help them feel welcome, son."

After the assembly, Billy Ray found himself the tour guide for a group of new students. Like baby ducks following their mother, the group stopped on cue when Billy Ray stopped in front of the rest rooms.

"This is your bathroom. It's the only one you can use. The one downstairs is for whites only. There'll be a sign posted, for those of you that can read." He snickered to himself, proud that he had turned his "punishment" into another opportunity for harassment. "Don't use the water fountain at all. You can wait till lunch or when you get home."

It was Noah's luck to be placed in Billy Ray's group. Billy Ray chose every opportunity to trip, push, or poke Noah when he had the chance. He was trying hard to get a reaction out of him. He knew if Noah reacted violently, it would be Noah, not himself, that would be in trouble.

"Okay, you go to your first class. Bell's about to ring". Then aside to Noah, Billy Ray said, "Best be on your toes, boy. I'll be watchin' you. You gonna get it for pickin' on my buddy. My daddy always told me your kind was nothin' but trouble".

Noah wanted to react, wanted to land his fist square into

Billy Ray's smug face. But he also knew he would be the one in trouble. There was, too, his mother's voice in the back of his head reciting the golden rule. Refusing to back down, he stood toe to toe, face to face with Billy Ray. He glared for a moment, just to get his point across that he wasn't afraid of the golden boy, and then turned and headed to class.

The rest of the morning went by uneventfully, and Noah was beginning to relax a little. His teachers, for the most part, were nice and more accepting than he expected. It was in fifth period History that things began to unravel.

Noah chose an empty desk near the back of the room, laid down his notebook and other textbooks he had collected during the day. As he sat down, his desk was sent toppling by the student sitting behind him. Noah had the misfortune to have chosen the desk in front of Billy Ray Sawyer.

Like a stalking cat watches an unwary bird, Billy Ray eyed Noah as he reached for the desk to upright it. Billy Ray timed his next kick to the moment Noah had it back in place. This time it hit the desk in front of him hard, causing a bulky offensive lineman on the football team to turn and glare at Noah.

"Sorry," Noah said, taking the blame.

This time Billy Ray propped his feet on top of the desk and replied, "Seat's taken."

Noah eyed Billy Ray for a second and then jerked the desk to its proper position. Billy Ray's legs flew back, causing him to spill over backwards and crash down onto the brown and white squared linoleum.

A collective inhalation of breath broke the silence. The other students could not believe that "the" Billy Ray Sawyer had been humiliated.

"Mr. Sawyer, are we having a problem?" asked Mrs. Breckley, the history teacher, who had been at the front of the classroom during the altercation but had not heard or seen a thing until Billy Ray landed on the floor. A young and idealistic woman with auburn hair fixed in the popular bouffant style of the day, was brilliant in history but not always conscious of things going on around her. Some of the students had been known to play cards in her class, and one had even climbed out the window during one of her lectures without her noticing.

"No, ma'am," Billy Ray replied, forcing a smile.

Satisfied, Mrs. Breckley turned and began to write on the chalk board.

Billy Ray climbed back into his chair and whispered in Noah's ear, "You itchin' ta' die, boy? Lemme' tell you something. This is our school. It's our town. Ain't no uppity colored gonna change that. I don't care what the state says. I don't care what the FBI says. I don't even care what President Lyndon B. Johnson himself says. This is Webber, Alabama. This is my town. My family owns it. You got that? You better learn it real quick or you just might find a rope around the cocky nigga neck a' yours."

"What's the problem here?" a bulky kid with a friendly face sitting in front of Noah said, as he twisted around.

Billy Ray nodded at Mike Boswell, his protective left tackle on the football team. "I was just tellin' our nigga' friend here about the school rules."

"Wasn't talkin' to you, Billy Ray." Mike looked at Noah and

offered him another place to sit. "There's an open desk in front of me if you want it."

Both Noah and Billy Ray appeared shocked.

"Nigger lover," someone shouted across the room.

"Hey! That's enough!" Mrs. Breckley admonished. "I will not have that kind of language in my room. Is that clear?"

"What's this fella' ever done to you, Billy Ray, ceptin' stand up for himself? You're bein' a real jerk," Mike continued.

Billy Ray was not used to being talked to like this and for once in his life was speechless.

"That's alright," Noah answered Mike. "I'm fine right here. I'm sure he don't mean no harm."

"Speak for yourself, *boy*," Billy Ray replied, emphasizing the word boy.

"Dang, Billy Ray, what's crawled up your butt and died?" Mike asked sarcastically.

"Are you blind, Mike? Or are you just stupid? The boy is black. He ain't like you and me. He's a nigga'. He ain't...he ain't a person, man. What the hell is wrong with you anyway?"

Tears welled up in Noah's eyes. The words stung and cut his soul like a knife. He'd known prejudice before, but never this close, and never this harsh. He also felt something that he'd never felt so intensely before. Hatred.

The last bell sounded, heralding the end of the worst day of his life. In the hallway, Noah instinctively looked both ways. He flinched when a hand touched his shoulder. It was his new guardian angel, Mike Boswell. "You alright, man?" Mike asked Noah.

"Yeah. I'm fine."

"Listen, man. What's your name anyway?"

"Noah. Noah Franklin."

Mike put his hand on Noah's shoulder. "Listen, Noah. Them boys is harmless. They're just stupid, that's all. They all been brought up with stupid ideas. I'm sorry we're like that sometimes. They're just havin' a little fun at your expense. That don't make it right, but I'm sure they got it outta' their system. Tomorrow will be better. I'm sure a' that." Mike smiled at Noah and released his tight grip from his shoulder. "Listen, for whatever it means, I think God made us all the same. He just colored us different for a little variety. That's all."

Noah snickered slightly. "You sound a lot like my momma."

Mike grinned. "You want I should walk you to your bus?"

"Naaaah," Noah answered. "I'll be fine."

"You sure? Cause I don't mind."

"I'm sure. Like you said. I'm sure they got it outta' their system. Thanks though."

"No sweat, man. I'll see you tomorrow." Mike turned and raised his hand high in the air to wave goodbye as his massive body lumbered down the thinning halls until he was out of sight.

Second guessing himself on Mike's offer, Noah felt hesitant to leave through the front doors so he doubled back and left the building through the rear entrance. It was deserted and eerily quiet. The gray clouds above continued their strange counterclockwise rotation. Noah again searched for any signs of his tormentors. Seeing no one, he headed around the basketball courts and to the side of the school building away from most of the crowds to catch his bus.

Suddenly, like a spider pounces on its prey, Billy Ray lunged directly in Noah's path. They stood toe to toe, like hand to hand combatants on a battlefield. Noah was prepared to fight this time. Then, out of the bushes, Billy Ray's buddies, Red and Davy Lee, circled around him. Noah looked for Mike. He looked for anyone.

"Mike ain't here. You're on your own now, boy. You gotta' fight your own battles," Billy Ray grinned at his conspirators.

"Look man, I don't want no trouble," Noah said as he slowly raised his hands defensively, expecting an attack any second.

"You shoulda' thought of that this mornin' before you kept tryin' to embarrass us," Red barked, spit shooting from his lips.

The thugs laughed and shoved each other. Noah tried his best to watch all three but before he could react, Red grabbed Noah's arms and pinned them behind his back. Noah's books careened to the ground. Noah struggled until Davy Lee joined in to help hold him steady for Billy Ray, who swiftly moved into position to begin the pummeling. Noah's strong legs pushed backwards taking Red and Davy Lee with him, but he was unable to break free. Just as Billy Ray lunged at him, Noah mustered just enough strength to lift both his legs shoulder high. With all the power he could summon, Noah kicked Billy Ray squarely on both sides of his chest with the souls of his feet, and in the process knocking every ounce of breath from his lungs. Billy Ray flew backwards and landed ten feet away, gasping for every bit of air he could find.

Without thinking, Red and Davy Lee released their grasp on

Noah and rushed to Billy Ray's side. "Billy Ray! You alright?" Red shouted.

Billy Ray held his chest, struggling for a breath. When he finally could draw in oxygen, he pointed and shouted as best he could, "Get him! He's getting away! Get him!"

Noah rounded the school building just in time to see his bus pulling away. His heart sank. He looked all around and saw a thick stand of woods lining one side of the school. He bolted in that direction.

"The woods! He went to the woods!" screamed Red.

Noah heard them yell and knew they had seen him.

Billy Ray felt as if he'd been kicked by a mule, but his emotions at this moment were too strong to be held back by a broken rib or two. He pulled himself up and tore into the woods well behind his two friends. But eventually, they met up and trudged quietly into the woods. They knew Noah was out there. They could sense it, almost smell the fear. Neither of them knew what they would do once they found him, but now it had become almost animalistic. The hunt had begun.

It was so quiet they could hear the pounding of their own hearts. The thick stand of pines, willows and oaks cast eerie shadows in every direction. A small snap of a twig brought chills up their collective spines.

Billy Ray waved his arm up and down, instructing the others to stay quiet. The three of them inched towards the sound. Red, quivering like a leaf in a rainstorm, reached down to move a branch out of the way. A frightened raccoon bolted out from under some brush, scratching Red's ankle as it made its escape.

"It bit me! It bit me!" Red screamed. "Is it poisonous? I'm gonna' die! I'm gonna' die!" he whaled.

"Shut up!" Billy Ray hissed. "It was just a scared coon, you idiot.   God, you're such an idiot!"   Billy Ray winced and wrapped one arm around his aching ribs.

Noah, less than twenty feet away, saw this as his opportunity to flee. But the others heard him and quickly bolted after him like a pack of wild dogs.

His legs burning from exhaustion, Noah leapt over a fallen tree. Looking back constantly, he prayed his predators would give up. He successfully dodged a patch of briars, but was smacked hard on his ear by a low lying branch. Blood oozing down his neck, he somehow managed the strength to keep moving.

Billy Ray's heart pounded so hard he thought it would explode inside his chest. But he refused to give up the chase. His dignity had taken two blows in one day, and he was going to teach this boy a lesson. He'd never been challenged before by anyone, much less a black, and he was astonished when Noah refused to be intimidated. What kept him going more than anything was the thought of how his father would react if he didn't get the upper hand.

The pack had closed the margin of distance between them and their prey to less than twenty feet. His legs tiring fast, Noah noticed a creek bed directly in front of him. He didn't believe his fatigued legs could make the leap across, but he had no choice but to try. With the power of a gazelle's thighs, Noah pushed off the edge of the creek bed. Arms and legs flailing, he cleared the rushing water by two feet. Relief flooded through him. It was over, at least for today. Noah straightened up, wiped his sweaty brow and took a deep breath. He turned and was immediately ambushed on the side of his head by a branch the size of a two by four. Dazed, he found himself on the ground with blood pouring from his head and nose. Across the creek he could hear Billy Ray screaming, "Don't touch him! He's mine!"

Two other boys, Bull Ryan and Rooster Pickens, had heard the commotion, and unbeknownst to everyone else, had joined in the chase from the other side of the woods. Rooster found the branch and laid in wait for Noah to cross the creek.

Noah sat up and tried to rub the blood from his eyes. He was quickly shoved back to earth with somebody's foot. His vision was blurred. A pair of hands twisted his ankle so far he thought his bone would snap. He screamed out in pain as he could feel and hear the tendons pop.

"You ain't goin' nowhere, boy! Get off him Rooster. I got him. He's mine," Billy Ray shouted his instructions. He knelt beside Noah then leaned in real close, his mouth almost touching Noah's ear. "Down on the ground, boy. Right where you belong". Billy Ray stood up and gave Noah a hard kick in the ribs. "Don't feel so good does it?" Billy Ray kicked him again.

Noah buckled and tucked his body in close to keep from being kicked again.

"You think you learned your lesson now, boy? Where you are on the food chain."

Billy Ray's friends watched, unsure of what to do. They began to question whether the fun had gone too far. Each boy took a step backwards, as if to detach themselves from the situation.

"I think you need to apologize for what you done today," Billy Ray ordered Noah.

Even if he wanted to, Noah didn't have the strength to answer.

Using his foot, Billy Ray flipped Noah on his stomach and shoved his face into the dirt. Noah struggled for air.

"Hey, Billy Ray. I think he's learned his lesson, man," Davy Lee said nervously. He had not expected such a violent reaction from his lifelong friend.

"Yeah. Let's get outta' here," Red agreed.

"I ain't quite through yet." Billy Ray gripped the back of Noah's neck and pushed his face back into the dirt, almost cutting off his air supply.

"Don't kill him, Billy Ray!" Rooster shouted. He was frightened at Billy Ray's behavior, as was everyone.

Suddenly, a crack of thunder, without lightning, darkened the woods completely for a split second. A jolt of electricity shot through both Noah and Billy Ray. Billy Ray was pitched forcibly off Noah's back.

The other boys fled. Dazed, Billy Ray picked himself up and followed. Noah reached into his pocket and squeezed his cross as he fell into unconsciousness.

It was completely dark, except for the moon's luminescent glow when Noah woke. He was stiff from head to toe. His ankle radiated pain with every beat of his heart. The sound of footsteps on dry twigs made Noah bolt upright.

"You out here?" a distant voice called out.

Noah's eyes were swollen and he couldn't make an identification of the person holding a flashlight about thirty feet away. Whoever it was glowed with a radiance Noah had never seen before. The beam stopped on his beaten face and caused him to throw his hand in front of his eyes, even though he never saw a flashlight. "Grab hold of my neck."

Noah felt one arm slither under his back and another under his legs. Instinctively, he pushed away and rolled down a small embankment. He winced when his lame ankle hit a rock. Looking upward, he saw the glow of light find him again.

The blurry but bright figure bent down and hoisted Noah up over his broad, strong shoulders. Strangely, Noah did not resist.

Somewhere along the wooded path, Noah lost consciousness in the arms of the stranger.

Inside the small shack, Emma sat wringing her hands together. James, Adam and Moses were off looking for Noah. The Sheriff suggested that maybe Noah had run off and because of that, neither he nor any of his deputies would join in any search.

A noise on the porch made Emma spring up and open the creaky front door. There lay Noah, dirty with a layer of dried blood crusting on his face and hands. The retreating flashlight beam bobbed up and down beside a shadowy figure before disappearing into the woods.

Miles away, Billy Ray lay in bed and winced with every breath. He had no idea the force of Noah's kick had fractured three of his ribs. Lying on his side, knees tucked firmly to his chest, he tried breathing very shallow. Thoughts of hate and guilt flooded his mind. One minute he hated Noah and everything he stood for. The next, guilt took over. What if he'd killed him. He was only having a little fun but got carried away. He hoped the black kid was alive. A knock at his door interrupted his thoughts.

"Son. Can I come in?"

"Yes, sir."

Mayor Sawyer sat down on the foot of Billy Ray's bed. "You alright?"

"Yes, sir. I'm fine," Billy Ray answered in a pained tone, suggesting he wasn't fine at all.

"You don't sound alright."

"I'm okay, daddy. Just don't feel real good right now."

"Heard there was some trouble at school today. Heard some of the coloreds started some trouble with you and some of your friends."

Billy Ray turned away, not knowing what or how much to tell his father.

"Look at me, boy! Don't you turn away from me!"

Billy Ray obeyed.

"Did one of those nigras jump you?"

Billy Ray stared at his father. He was scared to answer.

"Answer me!" Mayor Sawyer shouted.

"Yes, sir." Billy Ray was almost crying because of the pain. It hurt to breathe. It hurt to talk.

"Yes sir, what? What happened out there Billy Ray?"

Billy Ray looked up into his father's dark eyes. "They jumped me, daddy. A whole pack of 'em. They jumped me."

"Who jumped you, Billy Ray? I want names and I want 'em now!"

"Don't know, daddy. I..I..I didn't get a good look at 'em. It was dark."

Mayor Sawyer's face turned beat red with anger. He stood up on the side of the bed and gripped Billy Ray's shoulder. "Don't you worry, son. Somebody'll pay for this. I promise you that."

Billy Ray clutched his chest and pulled the blanket up, uncomfortable with his lie.

A sudden wind whipped open his window, blowing down the confederate flag he had tacked to his wall.

~ 4 ~

Noah woke up in his bed, having been carried there by his father when they returned from the search. The family had been relieved to find him, but distressed to find their son beaten so badly. Emma vowed to take Noah out of the school.

Noah's injuries were not bad, considering the beating he had taken. He was sore, for sure, and would walk with a limp, but would be back to normal in a few days. He stretched and felt every bone and muscle in his body. But nature called and he slowly made his way to the outhouse, his eyes barely open.

The sun was rising, but it was still early. Noah cringed at the thought of getting up and going to school, but he knew that the Sawyer kid would win if he didn't show up. He slipped back into bed, though, for another fifteen minutes of blessed comfort.

"That you, Noah?"

"Yeah, Moses. It's me. Sorry I woke you up."

"You okay? Can't believe what happened to you. You sure had Momma worried."

"I had me worried, too," Noah joked.

The sun came through the window in a sharp beam, reflecting off Noah's head.

"Noah?" Moses squinted at the mirage caused by the sun.

"Yeah? What's wrong?" Noah saw the strange expression

on Moses' face and sat up on one elbow.

Moses' eyes widened.

"What's wrong? You okay? You're scarin' me!" Noah said.

Moses could not speak. He slowly reached for his brother Adam in the bed next to him.

Adam mumbled and angrily pushed Moses' hand away. Moses poked him harder and Adam lifted up and rubbed his eyes. Moses pointed at Noah.

"Come on, Moses, what's wrong with you?" Noah asked.

"Who the hell are you? What the hell are you doin' here?" Adam reached for something to strike the intruder with, but found nothing but a shoe. He lifted it up threateningly.

"What are you talkin' about? Have you gone crazy?" Noah couldn't understand his brother's reactions. Then he caught a glimpse of his hands. They were white. He turned them over, in shock, forgetting everything for the moment.

Adam raised the shoe again, ready to throw it. "Where's our brother? What'd you do with Noah?"

Noah ignored the threat and bolted to a cracked mirror over the dresser in the small room. What he saw in the reflection turned his stomach. The face of Billy Ray Sawyer stared back at him.

"What?! No!" Noah rubbed his face as if the white in the mirror would rub off.

"He's crazy!" Moses said.

"Gotta be crazy! Bet he was out drinkin' last night."

Noah wheeled towards his brothers and then back at the mirror. "I don't understand!"

Suddenly Adam thought it was funny that a white boy

would be standing in a black family's home.

"You better explain what you're doin' here. And tell us where our brother is. We can take care of you and ain't nobody gonna find your body out here, if you know what I mean. Start talkin.'"

With his face drained of blood, Noah quietly said, "I'm Noah, I swear. I don't know what happened. What happened?" He stared into the mirror again and rubbed again.

Deciding to play along, and looking forward to beating up a white boy, Adam said, "When's your birthday, brother?"

"What? When's my birthday?"

"Yeah, *Noah*, when's your birthday?"

Moses pointed at Noah from a safe distance. "See, he don't even know his own birthday."

"I do! It's August... August 19th...1948. It was last month!"

Adam and Moses looked at each other. Moses said, "When's mine?"

"February 23rd! And Adam yours is November 2nd!"

The brothers looked at each other again.

"It's me! I swear!"

"What did you get for your birthday?"

"This...this..." Noah rummaged in the pocket of his overalls. "This cross!" He pulled out the silver cross and held it up.

"Where we goin' for our singin' career?" Moses tested.

"What? Oh..Oh. Motown!"

"This is too weird. How are we supposed to believe you?" Moses asked.

"Moses! You're soundin' just as crazy! Don't tell me you believe this weirdo?"

"All I know," Noah said as he pointed into the mirror, "is the boy I'm lookin' at right now is the boy who whupped me yesterday."

"I'm gettin' Momma and Daddy!" Moses said, and leaped off the bed.

"No! You can't! They got enough problems. I gotta think. I gotta find Sawyer." Noah grabbed what he needed from the room and decided to walk the few miles to the school. How could he explain a white boy getting on the bus? "Tell Momma I feel great and wanted to walk to school. Keep your mouths shut about this! Don't tell them anything!" He climbed out the window and limped down the dirt road to find his answers.

The aroma of bacon frying wafted into Billy Ray's bedroom and found his nostrils. Inhaling deeply, Billy Ray smiled, forgetting for a moment the events of the first day of school. He stretched, and contemplated how long he could lay there before he absolutely had to get up. The moment his arms reached above his head, the reality of the day before came crashing down on him in the form of excruciating pain in his ribcage. He slowly reached for the fresh towel his mother had laid on the chair beside the bed. One tender step at a time, he made his way to the bathroom. He knocked over a small vase of yellow flowers on his way.

Mary Edith, on her way to make sure her son had risen, called through the door. "Sweetie? You okay? What happened?"

"Sorry, Momma. Just knocked over a vase. Didn't break, though." He reached up and rubbed his throat, clearing it.

Mary Edith was already down in the kitchen where Joshua enjoyed a cup of coffee.

"Billy Ray sounds funny this mornin'," Mary Edith remarked while topping off Joshua's coffee.

"He's seventeen, Mary Edith. His voice is still changin.'"

Billy Ray, keeping his eyes closed as if he could catch a few winks while walking across his room, reached in and turned on the shower. Feeling the spray with his hand and waiting for just the right temperature, he stepped in. Grabbing the shampoo bottle, he squeezed some into his hand, and then transferred it to his head. As soon as his hands touched his scalp he jerked them back. He gingerly touched it again. he felt a rough texture in place of his smooth locks. "What the..." he mumbled and then caught a glimpse of himself in the chrome handle of the shower. He leaned in closer.

Bounding out of the shower and to the mirror, Billy Ray stood with eyes wide open. Lather from the shampoo streamed down his face, as he stared at the dark face in front of him. Instinct made him turn around with a fist raised, momentarily thinking someone was in the bathroom with him. He turned again towards the mirror, and like Noah, rubbed his skin as if he could remove the brown from his face. He spun away, his heart racing. Then slowly, he turned to face his enemy. Only now, the enemy's face was his own.

Billy Ray sat down on the edge of the bathtub, stunned by what he had seen. After what seemed to be an eternity, he returned to the shower to rinse the shampoo from his hair. He let the water run over his head, but he would not touch it. He stayed in the shower until long after it ran cold, praying it was a bizarre nightmare. After staring at his hands countless times, he realized they were not going to change, and this nightmare was not a dream.

Panic ensued and he realized that his parents would have him arrested if they saw him in their house the way he was. He pulled on his clothes, careful not to irritate his ribs, and tried to slip down the steps as quietly as he could. He grabbed the keys from the foyer table and as slowly as he could, turned the door knob. He opened the door just wide enough for him to slip out, and then ran to his truck, grimacing as each step reminded him of his aching ribs. He hopped in, slammed the door, and spun gravel as he sped out of his driveway. Out of habit, or perhaps not knowing what else to do, he pulled into the school parking lot. He immediately realized his mistake.

"Hey! What 'cha doin' drivin' Billy Ray's truck? He'd never let a darkie sit in it, much less drive it." Cathy Johnson walked to the driver's side with her arms crossed, holding her books to her chest.

Billy Ray had dated Cathy once and still thought she was one of the best looking girls at Webber High. He was embarrassed for her to see him like this, even though he knew she would not recognize him. For the first time in his life, he was speechless.

"You know, he'll kill you if he catches you sittin' there." She waited for a response. "You're either very brave or very stupid. I'm guessin' the latter." With that, she flipped her long brown hair as she spun and walked away.

Still embarrassed, he looked down at his clothes. His starched button down oxford shirt and the pressed khakis would cause stares. None of the black students could afford the clothes he was wearing. He would be in trouble sitting in his truck, and likewise if he got out.

"Takin' a little joy ride, there?" Red jerked open the truck's driver side door and pulled Billy Ray out by his shirt sleeve. Billy Ray plummeted to the asphalt and grabbed his ribcage.

"Didn't learn your lesson yesterday? Do we need a reminder? Billy Ray's gonna kill you!" Rooster came up beside Red.

"What the hell are you doin' with them clothes? You steal them too? Find 'em in Billy Ray's truck?" Davy Lee decided to join in the fun.

"He ain't talkin'. He's a stupid one, this boy is, ain't ya, boy?" Red cajoled.

Billy Ray's short tempered nature took over and he burst forward at his friend, smashing him up against the truck. His fist braced for a forceful blow when a hand grabbed it from behind.

"Billy Ray, just in time! We found this nigga in your truck, probably lookin' for things to steal. Let's take care of him, huh Billy Ray?" Red shouted, secretly relieved that Billy Ray had arrived to save the day.

"No! Leave him alone!" Noah said sternly.

The other boys could not believe their ears.

"What's the matter with you, Billy Ray? We was protectin' you! This boy was in your truck, and looks like he stole your clothes, too!"

"I told him he could drive it. And we switched clothes. I thought it would be funny. Pretty funny, huh?" Noah said, trying to sound calm and collected, which he was neither.

Billy Ray stared at Noah, or himself. He felt nauseous. He turned around clutching his ribs again. He didn't want to look at his friends, or his own likeness. He had never felt so confused and unsure of himself in his life.

Davy Lee piped in, "What about yesterday? The way he attacked you?"

"You mean the way *you* attacked *him*. He did nothing to you. I, he, was defending himself and you all know it!"

The boys looked at each other in disbelief.

"You're actin' weird, Billy Ray," said Red.

"I'll see ya' in class," Noah said and waved them off. The friends looked at each other, shrugged, and then headed up the hill towards the school. They occasionally looked back, wondering what had come over the king of the high school.

Noah then looked in Billy Ray's direction, but couldn't yet bring himself to look at him. "Reckon we need to talk."

Billy Ray was filled with a myriad of conflicting emotions. He was confused, hurt, grateful, scared to death, and then the strongest emotion rose to the surface. He grabbed Noah by the front of the overalls and pulled him within inches of his face. Through gritted teeth, Billy Ray snarled, "What the hell did you do to me, boy? Is this some kind of voodoo your people practice? Is it? Then you best take the spell off me right now 'fore I tear you to pieces. My daddy will have your whole family thrown in jail. Now do somethin' about this ... NOW!"

"I don't know any more than you do! Do you think I like havin' your ugly face? And your redneck friends? And do you think I wanted to protect you just now? I should have let them have you. 'Cept it'd be my face they'd be messin' with!" Noah pushed Billy Ray back, threw his hand up and paced across the parking lot.

Billy Ray thought about hitting Noah right then and there, but couldn't bring himself to hit his own face. Instead, he went with his only instinct and that was to run. He got back into his pick-up truck, and once again peeled out, kicking up dust under the wheels.

Noah knew that he could not face anyone today. He headed away from the school, on foot, knowing he had to figure this whole bizarre situation out. After walking about ten minutes down the road, he turned right and cut through the woods. If he remembered correctly, there was a small lake just a mile or two from the road. He couldn't take a chance on some truant officer finding him and bringing him in for skipping school.

It took about an hour to navigate the woods and find the lake he was looking for. He pushed the last branch out of the way and stepped into the clearing. About fifty feet away was the end of a dirt road, and at the end of that was Billy Ray sitting on the tailgate of his red truck. Noah felt that sick feeling you get when you are about to be forced to do something you really don't want to do. He thought about turning around and ducking back into the woods, but Billy Ray caught sight of him. Not knowing anything better to do, he approached this boy that looked like himself.

"You followin' me? Haven't your ruined my life enough without comin' to rub it in?" Noah didn't figure it would do any good to deny, or even speak to him.

Silence ensued for what seemed like an hour. Finally, Billy

Ray spoke again.

"I guess... I guess I should... be ... well, I'm glad you showed up when you did. I don't think my ribs could've taken another beatin'." After another awkward silence, Billy Ray added, "I don't even know your name. I guess they said it in class, but honestly, I didn't listen."

"Name's Noah. Noah Franklin. My momma works for your family."

"Whoa! You're Emma's boy?"

"Yeah."

"She's mentioned you before. Guess I never paid it much attention. When we got the letter about you people invadin' our school, she said you'd be comin'. What'd the gov'ment need to go and mess up our lives? You people need to learn with your kind, and we need to learn with our own kind."

Ignoring the obvious slam, Noah forced himself to talk to this jerk. "Listen, I don't know what happened to us. But I've been thinkin'. It won't do us any good to run away. If they find us, we'll be in a lot of trouble. So, we, well, just for now, I think we need to live at each other's houses..."

"Yeah, right! You think I'm gonna let you step foot in my house? You may look white right now, but you's a nigga. The only nigga in my house is one that works for my momma and daddy. You cannot and will not take my place in my own house!"

"So how's your momma and daddy gonna take to you, lookin' like you do, waltzin' in and settin' at your table, eatin' their food, and better yet callin' them Momma and Daddy?"

"I'll tell 'em what happened, that you put some kind of

voodoo spell or hex on me. They'll understand, and then they'll run you and your family out of town. My daddy's the most powerful man in town. He'll fix it. He can fix anything'!"

"They'll never believe you. My momma says yo' daddy hates colored folk, and is one of the most hateful men she's ever known."

"He just knows the way God made the races, and whites is better. The master race he calls it. It's just the way it is. Always has been , always will."

"You're an idiot, you know that? But I do know that you're at least smart enough to realize you can't go in your house lookin' like... well... lookin' like me."

"So what are you suggestin'? That I let you live my life and I go live in Niggaville? Ain't happenin'!"

"We have to change clothes, too. You can't wear those clothes, and I can't wear these."

Billy Ray threw a stone he'd been turning around in his hand into the lake. A blue heron sprang from deep brush growing up in the lake, making them both jump. Somehow he knew that this made sense, but he just couldn't stomach the thought.

"We'll figure this out," Noah started. "While I was walkin' out here, I was doin' some thinkin'. I think it's from God. I think everything that happens is part of his plan. We may never know why, but we can know there's a reason for it. So 'till we go back to normal, we're gonna have to make the best of it."

"The *best* of it? The *best* of it? Don't go be tellin' me God's behind this. *My* God wouldn't do this. *My* God does not have a sick sense of humor!"

"You got any better ideas? Man, right now, we don't have a choice. You're gonna have to take my name and live in my home for a while. I'll be you. And trust me, do you think it's gonna be easy to be the school racist? And live in a house where my momma works for people who think she's just above the family dog? Thing is, we don't have a choice."

Billy Ray fired a hate-filled look towards Noah. "No way, man. I ain't wearin' them dirty rags you call clothes. A Sawyer wouldn't get caught dead in them butt ugly overalls."

Noah stepped towards Billy Ray. "Like I said, we ain't got a choice. I know it and you know it too."

Sitting in fifth period History class, Noah fidgeted in his new clothes. His feet were cramped by the tight fitting brown leather penny loafers. Billy Ray felt like his skin would crawl off in the mud caked overalls. He felt confined, so he pulled and stretched in attempts to make them a little less awkward. He stuffed both hands in the oversized pockets and pushed downward to make a little more room. Feeling something deep inside the pocket, Billy Ray pulled out the cross Noah's mother had given him for his birthday. Billy Ray looked at it and rolled his eyes. He looked back at Noah on the next row and held it out, offering to give it back to him. Noah wanted it and started to take it but refused, almost hoping it just possibly might remind Billy Ray of something he really needed. In a barely audible voice, Noah told Billy Ray to keep it, that he needed it more than him. Billy Ray shook his head and stuffed it back into his pocket. Both were completely uncomfortable in their new identities. They sat, silently staring ahead, not hearing one word the teacher was saying.

The principal interrupted the class, saying he needed to see Billy Ray in his office. Instinctively, Billy Ray stood up. The class erupted laughing, but it wasn't until he heard someone mutter a racial slur that he remembered and quickly sat down, pretending to stretch. He glanced at Noah, who slowly rose from his desk and walked out the door with the principal.

Noah was greeted in the principal's office by a large man with graying hair and an off-white suit barely fitting in the leather chair across from a large desk. He knew this was the Honorable Mayor Joshua Sawyer. A bead of sweat pooled in the center of Noah's forehead, and then blazed a path down to the tip of his nose. It hung there for an instant before he wiped it way with the back of his hand.

"Son, how are ya'?" The Mayor didn't try standing, but slapped at Noah's arm.

"Fine, I guess, sir." This was almost unbearable. Here he was, standing in the principal's office, talking to the mayor of his town, and pretending to be his white son. The sweat beaded once again on his forehead.

"Sir?" Mayor Sawyer looked at Noah with a slight grin. "You don't look so fine, Billy Ray. You're sweatin' like a ni...". The mayor glanced at Principal Lewis and realized he had to be more guarded in his choice of words. "You don't look so good, boy. I believe maybe it's the stress caused by the little fracas yesterday. Am I right?"

"No, sir."

"You've never been bashful before, Billy Ray. Tell Mr. Lewis here about how you was jumped yesterday by that group of, uh..new students. Tell 'em about that."

Noah thought as quickly as he could. "Oh, that. Yeah. Well, we was playin' a little pick-up basketball game with some of the new students and it got a little rough. I got fouled and took a spill on the pavement. That's all. Stupid of me I guess." Inside Noah cringed at his outlandish story.

Mayor Sawyer's jaw dropped. He cocked his head to one side. "What? That's not what you told me last night, son. You told me you boys were attacked by one of the new colored boys here." Mayor Sawyer glanced toward Principal Lewis and said angrily, "and if this is true, I will have the Sheriff over here so fast it'll make your head spin. I will. I may not be able to stop this ridiculous idea of integration, but I will not tolerate sacrificing the safety of our children for the sake of some radical left wing politicians. Am I making myself clear?" This last point was driven home with the shaking of a plump finger at the principal's face.

"Mayor Sawyer, I would never knowingly allow violence at this school. You know that. But I'm sure if Billy Ray tells us it was just a friendly game of basketball, well, then I'm sure that's just what it was. To be honest with you, I'm a bit surprised, seein' as how your son *welcomed* the students as they arrived. Nonetheless, Billy Ray, I'm proud of you for putting aside your differences and working toward unity here at Webber High. You should be doubly proud Mayor Sawyer." Principal Lewis had to bite his tongue to keep from smiling.

Red faced, Mayor Sawyer pushed the chair's arms with his own and wedged himself out of the seat. "Lewis," he said nodding toward the principal. "Billy Ray, we'll continue this discussion after school." He angrily pushed on his hat and brushed past Noah on his way out.

"I reckon I'll be headin' back to class now, sir," Noah addressed Principal Lewis.

"Thank you, Billy Ray," Principal Lewis said, taken aback by Billy Ray's politeness. He smiled as he watched who he thought was Billy Ray Sawyer walk down the hallway.

~ 5 ~

In Webber, Alabama, high school football wasn't just a sport. It was a passion, a religion to some. You couldn't just love the game, you lived it. The players were the heroes of the town, and on Friday nights, the town shut down so that everyone could attend. Like thoroughbreds trained to one day run in the Kentucky Derby, young white boys in the town started wearing their pads as early as five years old, with the dream of playing on Webber High's football team and then one day to fame and glory with the Crimson Tide of Alabama or maybe even the Auburn War Eagles.

Billy Ray Sawyer was one of the best the town had raised in nearly thirty years. Even as a junior in high school, he had received well over a hundred letters from Universities around the country. Only one was ever considered. Although he had not officially signed a letter of intent with the University of Alabama, everyone knew it would be his choice. His blood ran Crimson red.

He was the school quarterback, their captain, their leader. And now, only a few days away from the first big game of the season, he was now a color that was not even allowed on the team. Billy Ray was sure this thing was just temporary, but thought it best to talk to his coach. Very quietly, he treaded down the concrete steps which led to the locker room and the coach's office. He put his hand on the door knob and then drew it back quickly. His heart was racing. In all his confident filled life, he had never felt so lost.

He knocked first.

"Door's open," Coach Mabry grunted.

Billy Ray cracked the door open. He wasn't quite ready to spring his new identity on the coach just yet. "Uhhh, Coach Mabry. It's me. Billy Ray."

"Come on in, son. Door's open."

"That's alright. I just have a minute Coach. Just wanted to tell ya' somethin' real quick." Billy Ray heard Coach Mabry bounce out of his squeaky seat and walk toward the door. "Uhh..I hurt my ankle yesterday and I can't make practice. See ya, Coach!"

"Hold on, Sawyer. Lemme see that ankle." Coach Mabry sounded pretty calm, but panic soon built. The thought of losing his star quarterback could spell disaster. He tugged at the doorknob while Billy Ray held the other side tight so the door wouldn't open. "Sawyer! What the hell you doin' son? I'm in no mood to play games!" His previous calm now dissipated. "And what the hell you doin' going and getting yourself injured right before we play? I've told you boys a thousand times, no practicing or playing outside official practices."

"I know, Coach. And I'm sorry. Give me a day or two and I'll be fine. But I really gotta go now."

Coach Mabry pulled the door hard but Billy Ray had already let go. The door banged hard into his side. "Sawyer!"

Billy Ray had disappeared around a corner.

Noah climbed inside Billy Ray's shiny new pickup and sunk deeply into the plush seats. He couldn't help feeling a little guilty as he ran his hand along the interior. He'd never even gotten so far as to dream about owning a vehicle as nice as this. Now, at least for a while, it was his. He backed up slowly out of the parking space, nervous about making the tiniest scratch, a ding, even getting it the slightest bit dirty. As he turned to make sure his path was clear, he saw Billy Ray walking towards the school bus. Their eyes met for a moment and Noah felt a strange compassion for his enemy. This boy, yesterday the meanest and quite possibly, the cockiest person on the face of the earth, now looked more like a whipped puppy. Noah almost smiled, but caught a glare from Billy Ray as he quickly stepped onto the bus.

Billy Ray sat by himself, confusing Noah's friends by not speaking to them. He stared out the window as they passed by affluent homes, his own among them. He fought a tear that started to pool in his right eye. He refused to let anyone see him like that. He pressed his head towards the window and it bounced in rhythm as the paved road soon turned to dirt. For a moment, he forgot about himself as he saw children with no shoes and barely wearing rags, playing by the side of the road. He saw houses, if you could call them that, with paint long worn away, and shutters half on. He figured one of these houses would fit in his bedroom. A few of the students filed off as the bus came to a halt.

The bus traveled a little further down the dirt road and stopped again.

"Everybody off!" Otis shouted.

Billy Ray looked around. He saw the road ahead and it did not end. He stood and made his way toward Otis. "What are you stopping for? You don't expect us to walk the rest of the way do ya'"?

Those left on the bus were shocked at what they heard. They could not believe that Noah was questioning a white man.

Otis sneered at Billy Ray. "You talkin' ta' me, boy?"

"I don't see nobody else drivin' the bus," Billy Ray said very boldly. "That road goes right through. Ain't no reason you can't take us the rest of the way."

The students stared wide-eyed, waiting for Otis to backhand Noah.

Otis smiled. "Don't you get on your high horse, boy."

"It's cause they're colored, ain't it?" Billy Ray could not believe his own ears. Those words couldn't have just come from his own mouth. Suddenly, it was he who felt persecution, just one day after he had persecuted another for that very reason.

Otis laughed. "Look, boy. I ain't got nothin' personal 'gainst you and your kind. I can't drive you the rest of the way cause just up ahead the road washes out and I ain't got enough room to turn the bus around. Now if'n you ask my opinion, the reason this road ain't paved *is* cause your colored. If'n the mayor liked you folks a bit better, he'd probably pave this road. But I gotta be honest, I don't think that's somethin' that's gonna happen in your lifetime."

Billy Ray looked at the dirt road ahead, at the students and then Otis. He didn't want to believe it, but he knew it was true. He stepped off the bus onto the half dirt, half mud road, and began slopping his way down the brown mucky road.

Suddenly with all that had happened, Billy Ray's most pressing problem was that he had no idea which house was Noah's. The houses all looked alike. They were all dilapidated. Falling down. Small. In dire need of repair and paint. It was a totally depressing, new feeling for this town's golden boy, star quarterback, hero. And now, in the blink of an eye, a nobody.

He found an old tin can and kicked it aimlessly as he ambled down the soft gushy muck. The "ting" sound it made with every kick was a temporary reprieve. It was something to do that didn't require him to think. Billy Ray was tired of thinking. The sponge was full.

"Noah, honey! How'd your day go? Are you feeling better?"

The familiar voice was the nicest thing he'd heard all day. He looked up from his tin can game to see Emma sweeping the front porch. She waved at him for the first time since he'd known her. "Hey, Emma! Man is it good to see you!" he called out with a wave of his own.

Emma crossed her hands over the broom and looked at him suspiciously. "Since when you stop callin' me Momma? Is that somethin' they teachin' you in that fancy new school of yourn? Cause if it is, I don't like it. I worked too hard bein' a mama to lose that title so quickly. Now come on over here and give yo' mama a big o' hug."

"Sorry...Mama. Don't know what I was thinkin'." Billy Ray found it difficult to say those words. He berated himself silently for letting his guard down. He didn't want to but gave Emma an awkward hug. Emma planted a big wet kiss on his cheek. He didn't like that at all. He rubbed it off with the back of his hand when she turned away to sweep the rest of the porch.

"Mrs. Sawyer gave me the afternoon off. Wasn't that kind of her? The Mayor was takin' the missus and Billy Ray out to some high falutin' restaurant. Wonder what they even serve at those places? I can't even imagine somebody else fixin' my food and bringin' it right to the table. Can't imagine why anybody would spend that kind of money on eatin' out when you can eat just as good at home. Lordy mercy, I just don't understand people's ways sometimes."

"I've always enjoyed it. I love eatin' out."

Emma turned. "What'd you say, son?"

His guard let down once again, Billy Ray snapped back to reality and was fast on his feet. "Nuthin'. I was just sayin' you do that for us every day, mama. I like the way you serve us. That's all I'm sayin'."

Emma smiled. "I do it because I love you. You're my family. Wouldn't have it no other way." Emma gently swatted Billy Ray on his behind with her broom. "Now you get yourself inside and find a chore or two to do. Supper'll be ready for too long."

Surprised at his own reaction, Billy Ray smiled. But it ended just as fast as it began when he stepped inside the tiny shack. Everything was immaculate and it was obvious that Emma did a wonderful job with what she had. But that was what struck him. What she had. What the Franklins had, was nothing.

───────────────────

Across town, Noah gripped the steering wheel of Billy Ray's truck as if he thought it would disappear before his very eyes. He wanted to savor every moment. He knew he would never own anything as nice as this truck. His family's own home and the property it sat on probably wasn't even worth as much. Truth was, Noah had never driven a vehicle except for one time when his cousin let him drive their tractor. He drove slowly, making sure he didn't put a scratch on the magnificent machine. After getting used to the brakes and steering, it wasn't as hard as he thought it would be.

Driving down the oak lined street, he recognized the Sawyer mansion immediately. Everybody in town knew where the Mayor lived and he knew it even better because his mother worked there. He's just never been allowed inside. Panic struck as he pulled the car into the driveway.

Tiptoeing cautiously up the steps, he had the feeling that he was doing something terribly wrong. After all, a black person never walked into a white man's home through the front door. He would go through the back door if he was there to do work. Noah stood a good five minutes at the door before timidly knocking.

Mary Edith answered. "Billy Ray? Sugar? Are you alright? Was the door stuck?" She jiggled the knob to see if there was a problem.

"Oh. No, ma'am." Noah wasn't sure what to do. He knew Mrs. Sawyer would see him as Billy Ray, but he just couldn't act the part. Not yet anyway.

"Come on in this house. And don't snack too much cause your daddy is takin' us out on the town tonight. We're goin' the The Great Oaks for dinner." Mary Edith seemed to squeal this last part. Noah had no idea what The Great Oaks was, but he knew it must be good because it certainly had Mrs. Sawyer in a tither.

Noah walked inside the mansion and his jaw about dropped to the solid marble floor. He had never, ever, seen a more beautiful home. His mama had told him about it many times, but his imagination was not even close to the real image. He felt unbelievably lucky and just as much out of place. He closed the front door behind him and then opened it. He closed it again, all the while staring at the hinges. It didn't creak. "It stays on its hinges," he mumbled softly.

Mary Edith narrowed her eyes. "Sugar baby. Are you alright? Have you got a fever? Do I need to take your temperature?"

Noah smiled. "I'm fine."

Three hours later, Noah was sitting in the four star restaurant. The Great Oaks was in an old renovated Civil War mansion. Two story tall white columns adorned the front porch. A lady in an elegant mint green gown with pearls and long, white gloves, walked Joshua and Mary Edith Sawyer and Noah Franklin through a maze of tables. Each one was covered with a white tablecloth, silver cutlery, a lit candle and a single red rosebud held carefully in a crystal cut glass vase.

The Mayor and his family were seated. Noah noticed the designs dancing over the table cloth as the flickering candle lit the cuts in the vase. He started to pinch himself, but decided that if this was a dream, he was not quite ready to wake up.

Noah stuck one finger inside the collar of his shirt, trying to pull the tightly tied tie as far away from his neck as possible. Earlier, when Mrs. Sawyer had instructed him to wear a tie, he had feigned a sprained wrist to get out of tying it. Mary Edith obliged and got it so tight it nearly choked him.

The menu before him had a confusing list of items, most of which he had never heard of. He had never had a choice. At home, you ate what Emma cooked. No questions. It didn't matter anyway. When the waitress came, Mayor Sawyer announced that they would have their regulars. Noah folded his menu and handed it to the waitress. He wondered what his regular was.

A large green leaf salad, full of carrot strips, cucumbers, tomatoes, and little bread cubes was set before Noah. A little disappointed in the lack of meat, Noah was nevertheless impressed with what was there. That much salad would have been enough for his entire family. But salads were rare in the Franklin home. He bent his head to ask a blessing but was nudged by Mary Edith underneath the table.

"That's not necessary in public, darling," she said, as if she was embarrassed.

"You gettin' religion, Billy Ray?" Mayor Sawyer chuckled. "Sunday mornin's enough for us. Just enough to keep the good Lord on our side. No need to overdo it, right honey?" He jiggled the ice in his Bourbon and Coke, like he was making some kind of point. "No need bein' radical and all, if you know what I mean."

"Mama always taught us..." Noah began, and then caught himself.

"What, sweetheart? What did I always teach you?" Mary Edith said, a bit of tomato dangling from her lips.

The waitress reappeared and placed a bone china plate in front of Noah. Before having a chance to touch the salad he thought was his meal, he was feasting his eyes on the largest steak he had ever seen. Its juices puddled on and around the massive piece of meat. Beside it sat a baked potato, its fluffy white insides bursting forth from a crack in the middle. And heaped upon it were a large slab of butter, lots of grated cheese and a lump of sour cream. The butter melted and swirled in a marvelous trail into the juice of the steak. Noah's mouth watered so much he was afraid he would have to grab the cloth napkin in his lap to mop up his slobber. Instinctively, Noah cut his steak into five pieces. He was about to hand Mary Edith the largest cut when he noticed that she had her own. He couldn't help but think of his own family at home and what they would do if they saw this much food on one plate. The guilt soon gave way to guilty pleasure as he put the first succulent bite into his mouth. He had never tasted anything so wonderful. He loved Emma's cooking. But this was different. And that night, as he lay on a bed that felt like it was made of clouds, he had the worst stomach ache he had ever had in his life.

The dinnertime meal at the Franklin household was a little different than that of The Great Oaks. It was more than a little different. It was more like night and day. But one thing The Great Oaks couldn't offer was the care and love Emma poured into every meal she prepared, no matter how small.

Billy Ray was about to starve to death. He sat on the makeshift chairs in the Franklin kitchen. Emma sat down a steaming bowl of navy beans in the middle of the table and a plate of cornbread. Billy Ray waited for the rest. It never came. The clicking and scraping of frenzied spoons in the bowl made him somehow know that if he didn't get his quickly, there would be none left. A vision of his favorite meal at The Great Oaks played a cruel trick on his mind. And to make it worse, he knew Noah would be enjoying it right about now. He decided he wasn't that hungry after all. His spoon dipped with little enthusiasm into the mound of beans on his plate, and like a schoolteacher whacking the back of his hand with a ruler, Emma slapped his hand with her own spoon causing it to careen and clang loudly on his plate.

"Hey! What'd you do that for?" Billy Ray hollered as he scooted back in his chair and out of the way of his flying beans.

"Since when did you forget to thank the good Lord for his blessings!" Emma asked incredulously.

"Yeah! Good Lord knows you got a lot to be thankful for!" Billy Ray said sarcastically, while rubbing the red mark on his hand. "This ain't enough to keep a dog alive," he added.

"Noah Franklin! You should be ashamed a' yourself. You, of all people, have always been thankful. What's got into you, boy?" James demanded.

"Maybe I just ain't myself, okay?" Billy Ray pushed off from the table and ran out the front door, pushing it just hard enough for it to jump off its hinges.

Adam, then Moses, asked to be excused from the table. They followed Billy Ray. Emma and James looked at each other with concern.

"Maybe he's just tired," James tried to explain.

"Uh-huh. And maybe it's that school that's got him all eat up," Emma said sternly.

Outside, Adam grabbed the top of Billy Ray's dirty tee shirt and slammed his back up against the old elm tree in the front yard. Billy Ray pushed Adam harder. "Don't you touch me you dirty, no good ni...". Billy Ray stopped himself.

Adam grinned and wiped his face with the back of his hand. He held Billy Ray's tee shirt tight and leaned in close to where he was eye to eye. "Who is that in there, huh? Is that you, Noah?" Adam cocked his head and laughed slightly. "Who are you? Huh? Who are you?" He paused and let go of Billy Ray's tee shirt. "Go ahead and finish. What is it you were gonna call me? A dirty, no good nigga? Was that it? Go on. Say it. You're dyin' to ain't ya'?" Adam backed away. "Where's my brother? What 'chu done with him? And what the hell is goin' on here?"

Billy Ray realized the insanity. He slumped beside the tree and buried his face in his hands.

Adam squatted several feet away facing Billy Ray. "How does it feel now? Huh? Tell me, white boy. How does it feel?" Adam stood and looked down on Billy Ray. "You ain't no better than me. You just an angry white boy just like I'm an angry nigga'." Adam smiled, picked up a handful of dirt and flung it at Billy Ray, making him flinch.

"Leave him alone, Adam," Moses said, as he moved toward Billy Ray. "He ain't done nothin' to hurt you."

Billy Ray looked up at Moses. His eyes were moist but not tearing. Had he heard right? Someone of a different race coming to his defense?

"Shut up, little brother!" Adam demanded. "This is the same white boy that pert near killed our brother. You ain't got no business defendin' him."

"Leave him alone, Adam. Like I said. He ain't done nothin' to you."

Adam sneered at Moses, shook his head, then waved him away. Adam walked away from them both. "Ahhhh! I don't want nuthin' to do with it. This is insane."

Emma and James witnessed the commotion from inside but believed it best to let the brothers work it out on their own.

Moses knelt down closely to Billy Ray. "You alright?"

Billy Ray stared at Moses but said nothing.

Moses stared at Billy Ray a while longer, tilting his head trying to figure out what was going on. Embarrassed, Billy Ray tried to avoid eye contact.

"I don't like what you done to my brother. And I'm sure I'll forgive you one day. But it's not somethin' I can do right now. Still, I don't want to hurt you anymore than you're hurtin' already. If Noah was here, he'd be helpin' you. He wouldn't care what you'd done or anything. That's just the way he is. Maybe you don't feel the same way about him or us but, they don't come no better than Noah. The thing is, I can't help you if you don't tell me what it is that's goin' on with you and my brother."

Billy Ray covered his face with his hands then rested them on top of his head. "Don't need your help. Ain't nobody can help me. I'll figure it out myself."

Moses stood up and stuffed his hands inside his overalls pockets. "Suit yourself." Moses started walking toward the house.

"Wait!" Billy Ray called out.

Moses stopped.

"Why do you want to help *me*?"

Moses thought. "Cause I'm not like you. If someone needs

help, that's just what you do. It don't matter what color they are. And when I see you, I see Noah and I'd like to have him back." Moses turned to face Billy Ray. "You gonna let me help you?"

Billy Ray stared at Moses but did not answer.

Moses turned. "You know where I am."

~ 6 ~

A large red and black rooster sat atop the fence post not five feet from the bedroom window of Billy Ray's new bedroom. As the sun began to spread streaks of red and orange across the eastern sky, the rooster trumpeted its morning cry. Billy Ray bolted upright in his bed. "Damn bird" he said, just barely audible. He was accustomed to his mother's cheerful but slightly irritating sing- song way of waking him every morning. He had slept unusually soundly, and had all but forgotten his trauma of the last forty-eight hours. Reality raised its ugly head he looked around at the small, cramped quarters he shared with his two new brothers sleeping close by on old mattresses with shaky, squeaky frames. He fell back onto the long ago worn out feather pillow then pulled the sheet over his head. He hoped for the slightest possibility that if he pulled the covers back again, he'd be in his own bedroom at the Sawyer mansion.

"I see you've met Henry," Moses said.

Billy Ray pulled the sheet from his face. "Who?"

"Henry." Moses pointed to the rooster. "We can't afford no real alarm clock, so we got the next best thing."

Billy Ray sat up and slung his legs over the edge of his bed. He rubbed his eyes. "Where's the bathroom?" The night before he had gone into the woods to relieve himself after Emma sent him out to give some scraps to the dog, Woody.

Moses pointed toward the window.

"What? Where is it?"

Moses walked to the window and pointed toward a small outhouse.

"You're joking, right?"

"Welcome to my world," Moses smiled. "Might wanna put on a shirt. It gets a little chilly out this way in the mornin'."

Billy Ray sighed. "I ain't even believin' this." He put on his shirt and rubbed his eyes again.

Moses laughed while Adam snored.

"Does he do that all the time?" Billy Ray asked Moses.

"You'll get used to it."

"I ain't gonna be here that long. Ain't gotta get used to nuthin'."

"Whatever you say, man."

Billy Ray walked toward the bedroom door.

"Don't forget to flush!" Moses laughed.

"Real funny. See how hard I'm laughing?"

Billy Ray opened the door to the outhouse and was immediately struck by the pungent odor. "Oh God! Geez! You gotta be kiddin' me. No way!" He shut the door and stepped back.

Emma watched from the kitchen.

Billy Ray dry heaved several times at the thought of the smell. He opened the door again. Same odor. Same result. He slammed the door and fell to his knees and puked.

"What in tarnation is wrong with that boy?" Emma muttered to herself.

One more time, Billy Ray stood up and opened the outhouse

door. He held his nose and stepped in but when he tried to prepare himself to urinate, he let go of his nose and the gag reflex revisited once more. Billy Ray bolted from the outhouse, hit the ground and threw up the yellow lining of his stomach. When he was through, he looked around for a sizable tree. He found one not too far from the outhouse and commenced to relieving himself the old fashioned way.

Emma watched from inside.

When he was through, Billy Ray leaned against the tree and composed himself for a few minutes. After he got his senses back, he stepped inside the house where the rest of the family was sitting at the table ready for breakfast. Emma stared at Billy Ray for a spell.

"What?" Billy Ray asked.

"Nothin'. Just wonderin' if you was alright. That's all." Emma answered.

"I'm fine. Just got some things on my mind. It's nothin'."

"Well, take your seat and eat somethin' before you go to school," Emma ordered.

Adam gave Billy Ray a dirty glance. Moses nodded at him, almost smiling. Moses wanted badly to help. Billy Ray didn't want it.

Billy Ray traded glances with Adam.   "You want somethin'?"

Adam threw his hands in the air in a defensive motion.

James leaned forward over his plate of scrambled eggs. "Boy! What in tarnation's eatin' you! There somethin' you wanna share with us or you just gonna stay in a bad mood the rest of your life?"

Billy Ray bolted from his seat and stormed outside before anyone could stop him.

"Noah!" Emma shouted, rising from her chair.

"Let him go, woman. Let him work out whatever it is he needs to work out."

Moses and Adam looked at each other. Adam shook his head while scarfing down what was left on his plate. Then he ate Billy Ray's.

"Momma!" Noah cried out when Emma came through the kitchen door at the Sawyer mansion. He gave her a big hug which she accepted stiffly.

"Billy Ray? You feelin' alright? I don't spec your momma would appreciate you callin' me that."

Noah pulled away quickly. "Oh, yea, sorry." What he wanted to say was, "Momma! It's me, Noah! You *are* my momma and I miss you so much!" It tore at his heart not to tell her the truth.

"Billy Ray, sugar? Are you all ready for school? Emma, fix him some eggs, quickly. You know he'll be late if you don't hurry. Billy Ray honey, how late will you be this afternoon?" Mary Edith inquired.

"Ma'am?" Noah wasn't sure what she was talking about.

"Football practice, darlin'. Is it a long or a short practice today?"

Noah froze and panic ensued. Billy Ray was the star quarterback of the team. Noah had never even held a football.

"I can't practice. Wrist's hurt, and I couldn't throw anything." The second part of the statement was true.

"My poor baby!" Turning to Emma, she snapped impatiently, "Those eggs ready yet?"

Emma put a plate of runny scrambled eggs in front of a disgusted Noah. "Barely cooked, just like you like them, Billy Ray." Even though he was used to eating one egg, and there were six in front of him, Emma had always cooked them well done for her own family.

"Gosh, mom, I'm not that hungry this mornin'. I'd better get to school."

Noah walked out the side door to the wraparound porch. Mary Edith followed him.

"Billy Ray? What were you talkin' to Emma about?"

"Nothin'. Why?"

"Well, I don't pay Emma to visit. I pay her to work."

"She was just bein' nice."

"Well, I don't pay her to be nice either. She may just find her pay cut if that kind of behavior continues."

Noah swept past Mary Edith and back into the kitchen.

"Mrs. Franklin? Are you happy, doin' what you do?"

Confused, Emma answered, "Why yes, Billy Ray. Why do you ask?"

"I don't know. Just wonderin' I guess."

"It helps put food on our table. In a perfect world, we'd all pick up after ourselves and there wouldn't be no one better than anyone else."

"Yes, ma'am, that would be nice."

Emma wiped her hands with a red gingham dish towel, looking puzzled.

"Billy Ray, what's goin' on? You ain't said this many words

to me at one time since I started here almost two years ago. And if you don't mind me sayin', you half acted like I wasn't here, 'ceptin if you wanted something. What's changed you?" Emma wasn't sure she should be so frank. She could lose her job by being so candid.

"You wouldn't believe me if I told you."

"I might." Emma smiled. "Have you met my boy, Noah, yet? That would be so nice if you and he would become friends."

"I've met him. Don't think we'll be friends, though."

Emma chuckled softly, and shook her head. "What am I thinkin' a white boy and a colored boy bein' friends."

Noah walked the halls of Webber High, keeping his eyes out for Coach Mabry. He had heard that Billy Ray was the quarterback, but had not thought of the predicament caused by the past days' events. He knew he could not fake the wrist injury for very long. He felt a twinge of guilt that it would be himself putting on the football uniform and being cheered on by the crowd, not Billy Ray. And he felt a rise of panic, that it would be evident immediately that "Billy Ray" had lost his magic.

Lunch was more than awkward for Noah. He couldn't, no he wouldn't sit with Billy Ray's obnoxious friends. He wouldn't be accepted by his old friends. So Noah just picked a table at the far end of the cafeteria to sit by himself. He couldn't help but feel the stares and hear the murmurings he knew were aimed at him. Across the room Billy Ray was sitting, also alone. Both had friends who tried to sit with them and both had indicated that they wanted to be alone.

Suddenly Noah felt the bench bend a bit beside him. He knew without looking up that it was the head football coach.

"How's my best player? And what're you doing off here by yourself?"

Noah didn't know what to answer. He had never talked to the man in his life.

"Well, don't matter. You be at practice today?"

"No, sir. I hurt my wrist yesterday. Don't think I can throw."

"Wrist? I thought you hurt your ankle?" Noah didn't realize Billy Ray had already visited the coach with his own story. "I'll expect you this afternoon."

"Coach?"

"Yeah, son?"

"What do you think about the colored boys comin' out and playin' for us?"

"Billy Ray, I'm proud of you. Shocked, but proud. The assistant coach and I were discussing it. We could always stand to beef up our team. Not sure how the home crowd'll take to it, though."

"They'll come around. I think it's a good idea."

"I think it may be worth a try. See ya at practice, then."

Noah wasn't sure why he'd suggested that to the coach, but he was glad he did. There were a lot of athletic boys that deserved a chance to play for their school. And, in a way, he was doing it for Billy Ray. Now if he could just get the coach to make Billy Ray the new black quarterback.

~ 7 ~

Word spread like wild fire around the school and then to town that Coach Mabry was going to let "the coloreds" play ball for Webber High. Emotions ran from shock to outrage. There were threats, and more than one call to the administration to get Coach Mabry fired. But Coach Mabry was a legend in his own right, and in the end, it was more important to keep him coaching than to make the town happy. The townspeople figured it would be a failed experiment, and that the new players would be a curiosity only, staying on the bench.

Billy Ray went out for the team. He couldn't have stood by and watched Noah claim his glory. His body was tall and lean. Noah's was heavier by about twenty-five pounds. He was a natural for any position on the field, and Coach Mabry took advantage of it immediately. Billy Ray worked harder than he ever had before in practice, and Coach Mabry took notice. He slapped him hard on the shoulder and praised him repeatedly. Billy Ray was impressed. This man didn't seem to look at the color of his skin, only at his abilities and work ethic.

Noah struggled at the position of quarterback, but he improved with the daily practices. Coach Mabry was concerned, and couldn't figure out what was wrong with Billy Ray. Perhaps his wrist was hurt. He was sure by the first game that he'd be back on target once again.

Although they practiced together, the white students and the black students refused to mingle. Some were cordial, but most were cold and stared hatefully at each other. Noah tried to catch Billy Ray's eyes, but Billy Ray avoided any acknowledgment. He had one thing to live for now, and the endless hitting and September heat just moved him ahead in his quest. He hated Noah, and felt in his heart that somehow Noah had caused all this. Noah wanted to take his place, to be the hero of the team. He wasn't going to let that happen.

At the Sawyer's, Noah was forced to endure the tirades by Mayor Sawyer about the inclusion of the black students to the football team. Sawyer was one of the more outspoken members of the community, but even at his high political status, Coach Mabry remained the coach, and the players remained integrated.

~ 8 ~

The smell of football permeated the air. It was finally Friday night... not just any Friday, but the first game of the season. A crisp breeze cut through the usually muggy night, making it the perfect night for a game. Excitement buzzed in the air and the crowd noise mixed with the clink of the metal bleachers as men, women, and children climbed the steep steps into their chosen seats.

Football was the focal point of fall in Webber, Alabama. The Crimson Tide was, of course, the city's favorite college team. The Webber High Warriors were held in even higher esteem in this hometown. They had been the state champs more years than not in the fifty years the high school had been in existence, and this year the school was expected to retain its title. With Billy Ray Sawyer as its star quarterback, there was no question.

The Jonestown Jaguars, the visiting team, ran into the end zone amid their visiting fans' cheers, and a few courteous claps from the Webber folks. Then the Webber Warriors broke through the large paper banner and the crowd erupted with whoops, hollers, cheers, and stomping. They were the heroes of the moment, the youth of tomorrow with the promise of everything good and exciting and hopeful.

From the other end of the field Billy Ray, Noah, and their Warrior teammates stormed to the twenty-five yard line, bunched all together, and proceeded to jump up and down chanting, hollering and banging helmets. After releasing their pent up testosterone, the blue and gold clad players raced quickly to their pre-destined warm up area. For this moment, the color of their skin did not matter. For this moment, they were Warriors, preparing for battle.

Noah was nervous. It was his first game ever, and he was expected to be the quarterback, the leader of the team. Billy Ray was pumped up for the game, the only familiar thing that had happened to him since the "event". The excitement, however, was mixed with resentment, as *he* should be the one standing where Noah now stood. *He* should be the one the players were looking to. *He* is the one with talent, not Noah. And now Noah could possibly end up with his scholarship offers.

Twenty rows up and straddling the 50 yard line, Mayor Sawyer and Mary Edith proudly waited the start of the new season. In the back of both their minds, they knew that scholarship offers would flood in later in the Fall. The University of Alabama would be the only one considered, but it was a gratifying feeling to see the letters arrive. Mayor Sawyer scanned the left half of the field until he spied the three quarterbacks warming up. Mary Edith smiled and patted Joshua on the leg when she too, spied number two.

The officials called the opposing head coaches and their head captains to the dead center of the field to give both teams the final rules and instructions before kickoff. Coach Mabry shouted to Billy Ray front and center. Billy Ray bolted upright from his stretching position and started running full steam ahead to the middle of the field. From the corner of his eye he saw Noah running fast to catch up. Embarrassed, Billy Ray slowed his pace and pretended that he was warming up. He shot Noah a hateful look and quickly bolted back the other way. Luckily for Billy Ray, all the players were so into the first game of the season that none even noticed what he had done. He finished his stretching and warm-ups and grew angrier by the minute.

They stood side by side on the sideline. Both held their helmet to their side with their left forearm while their right hand covered their heart during the singing of the Star Spangled Banner by a terribly off key senior choir member. Billy Ray leaned slowly into Noah's shoulder. "You gonna' be runnin' for your life tonight. I hope you got the legs."

From the stands Mayor Sawyer saw the big muscular black kid whispering to his son. He didn't like it one bit. "They're gettin' too close, Mary Edith. I don't like it at all."

"Shhhhh," Mary Edith pushed her index finger over his mouth. "The National Anthem, honey," she whispered.

Mayor Sawyer stood straight and slapped his hand to his heart. He shook his head and mumbled something to himself.

"You hear me boy?" Billy Ray turned his head slightly toward Noah.

"You're only hurtin' yourself," Noah answered.

The singer of the National Anthem hit the final note and the crowd roared its approval despite her lack of talent.

Billy Ray put his helmet on and went face to face with Noah. "You think I care? You really think I care? The only thing I care about right now is seeing your coon ass spread all over this turf. And if I can have a part in that, then all is well and good."

Noah put his helmet on and tightened his chin strap. He figured it might be a good idea. He wasn't as nervous as he thought he would be. He'd learned all the plays, the formations, the blocking schemes and the audibles. But he still had never played a single down of football, so the jitters were there.

"Sawyer!" Coach Mabry yelled loud over the cheers of the crowd. "Get over here!"

Billy Ray eyed Noah. "Go on, boy. Coach is calling you. Don't matter what he tells you though. Your fifteen minutes of fame is over tonight. Enjoy it." Billy Ray was seething. This was supposed to be his night. His senior year. Captain. Quarterback. Scholarship offers. The Bear himself calling him on a weekly basis. All around stud. And now this nigga was taking it all away.

Coach Mabry laid his hands on both sides of Noah's helmet. "This is it, Billy Ray. This is what you've worked your entire life for. It's your night. Your time. All those two-a-days. All those suicide drills. The puking until your gut wrenched. The weights, the running, the yelling, the crying. The cheers from the crowd. This is it. It is your moment, son. Go make it happen!" The coach slapped Noah's helmet and shouted for the whole team to gather around right as the head referee blew his whistle to line up.

Noah was stunned. Suddenly he knew exactly what Billy Ray meant. As hard as Noah may have had it in life, Billy Ray had worked his tail off to get to this moment and now it could all be taken away. Noah wished he didn't feel empathy for this boy that had been nothing but hateful to him. But being a

Christian meant sucking his thoughts up and doing the right thing. He wanted to tell the Coach and let the real Billy Ray move to quarterback, but Coach would never believe it. The best way was to play as best as he could and try not to make mistakes. Noah was confident he could play well because he had worked hard at practice and gotten praise from all the coaches. If he played well, it would bode well for Billy Ray and at the end of the day, it was the right thing to do.

The players gathered around the Coach with their hands held high in the air. Coach Mabry reminded them of the sacrifice that each and every one of them had made during the hot summer practices and that this was their chance to show the state of Alabama that the Warriors continue to dominate the State.

"Warrior Pride!" was shouted in unison as they broke the huddle.

The referee held his left hand high in the air as he blew the whistle that signified another start of a football season in Webber, Alabama. It's what the town lived for and, thank God, it was September again!

The Warrior return man had a good return. He took the ball at the five yard line and returned it to the 24 before he took a pretty solid wallop from a kid about half his size.

Noah jogged two steps onto the field before Coach Mabry grabbed the back of his jersey and pulled him back to the sidelines. "Don't try to do too much, Billy Ray. Let the game come to you. Let it come to you. Now get out there and make this town proud."

"More pressure. Yeah, that's just what I needed," Noah

mumbled to himself as he trotted to the huddle.   The first person he locked eyes with as he leaned down in the huddle was Billy Ray, who just looked up and grinned.   "Eagle left T ninety-three on one!"

"Don't you mean right, Billy Ray?"   a voice in the huddle asked.

Noah shook his head.   "Yeah, yeah.   Right.   Right.   Eagle right T ninety-three on two!"

"Two or one genius?"   Billy Ray chided.   "You said one then two.   Which is it?"

Nine heads swiveled toward Billy Ray.   They could not believe that this new black kid, who was lucky to even be playing, would have the nerve to smart off to this All-State, All-American quarterback.

"Two.   On two!"

Billy Ray smiled.   He felt a strange sort of power over Noah.

The huddle clapped its hands together and broke.

"Just calm down BR," the center said, holding back before breaking to the line.   "First night jitters.   We all got 'em."

Noah stepped to the line and looked over the defensive scheme before moving up close under his center.   He began barking the signals.   "Blue Forty-two! Blue Forty-two! Set! Hut! Hut!"

Noah felt the ball seated firmly in hands but had no sooner looked up when he found himself flat on his back looking skyward, the ball somewhere between his third and fourth rib and approximately 650 pounds of beef resting on top of him.

The whistle sounded and the defenders extricated themselves from Noah's torso.   The first sight he saw was Billy

Ray towering above him with a satisfied smile on his face. Noah extended his hand toward him for help up but Billy Ray just shook his head and walked away. Two other linemen quickly assisted Noah to his feet. "Dang, Billy Ray! What happened?"

"My fault man," Noah answered. "Didn't get a good handle on the ball."

They huddled again as the official spotted the ball at the 20 yard line, four yards back from where it was. "Calm down, Billy Ray," a voice from the huddle called out. "We're fine. Just gotta take our time."

"Call the next play, hot shot," Billy Ray demanded.

Nine helmets turned in unison toward Billy Ray. "Man, what the hell is your problem, Noah? You think you could do any better?"

"Yeah. As a matter of fact I know I could."

Some in the huddle snickered nervously, some just stared.

"Just call the next play," Billy Ray snapped. "Maybe you can stay on your feet longer than a second this time."

"Maybe if you blocked your man I could."

"That's right. Blame me for your shortcomings."

The players could not believe what they were hearing. This colored kid had a lot of nerve teasing and criticizing the Hero-In-Residence.

"Call the play! Call the play!" Coach Mabry screamed from the sideline.

At the same instant a whistle blew and a yellow flag came flying across the field. "Delay of game, offense," the official said crossing his arms in front of his chest. "Five yard penalty from the previous spot."

"See what 'cha did now, all star? Keep this up and we'll be runnin' our offense from the end zone."

The official moved the ball back and spotted it at the 15 yard line. He held up two fingers and shouted out that it was second down.

"Huddle up! Huddle up!" Noah commanded, trying to take control. The team gathered around him. "Come on, guys. Let's put our gripes aside for the night and win this game." Noah aimed his words and gaze at Billy Ray. "Forty-one flare on three! Forty-one flare on three!"

The team members slapped their hands in unison and shot toward the line. Billy Ray was lined up as the fullback, a quarterback's last protector. Noah looked the defense over and assumed his position behind center. "Green twenty-eight! Green twenty-eight!" He called out the signals with authority. "Hut! Hut! Hut!" The ball was planted firmly into Noah's hands. He took two steps backward and set his cleats firmly in the turf to make a quick flare pass to the tight end. With one eye on his target and the other on Billy Ray, he watched as Billy Ray fell flat on his belly without even attempting to block his defender. And with that, Noah was brought down before he could even cock his arm to throw, resulting in a seven yard loss.

Billy Ray got up quickly and raced over to Noah who was still on his back. "Lemme' get this right. We're supposed to be moving the ball forward, right? I just wanna make sure 'cause I don't think we're doin' that."

Noah stared at Billy Ray but said nothing while two of his teammates helped him to his feet.

The official spotted the ball at the eight yard line. It was now third and 26 yards to go for a first down.

Billy Ray walked up to within inches of Noah's face.

"You got something to say to me?"

"Time! Time!" Coach Mabry shouted from the sideline. He ran half-speed to his offense and right up into Noah's face. "What the hell is goin' on out here? My God! I've been coachin' for nearly twenty years and I swear I don't think I ever used a time out two plays into the game. Does somebody mind telling me what the hell is going on? Somebody? Sawyer?"

The team was silent.

"Sawyer?"

Noah shook his head and lifted his arms. "I don't know. Nerves. First game jitters maybe."

"Nerves? Jitters?" Coach Mabry shouted. "What are you, Sawyer, a freshman? For cryin' out loud, you're a senior! You've been leadin' this offense for three years now! What the hell do you mean nerves? You think that's an excuse?" Mabry asked rhetorically. "Listen up every last one ya'. If you can't get your act together I've got eleven second stringers sitting on that sideline that would love to come in here and take the place of every one of ya. Do I make myself clear?"

"Yes sir," they said collectively but quietly.

"What?"

"Yes sir!" the starters shouted.

"Then do it!" Mabry turned and ran half-speed from the field. He could be heard mumbling "For the love of ..." as he stomped back to the sideline. Mabry signaled in the next play to Noah.

"Alright. Huddle up! Huddle up! You heard Coach. We're embarrassing ourselves right now. Let's don't let this team come in here on our home turf and whip us!" Noah glanced at Billy Ray, whose expression was cold and indifferent.

"Call the play, stud," Billy Ray continued his bullying.

"Knock it off, Noah. Man, you're lucky to even be playing. You don't have to like Billy Ray to block for him". Mike Boswell lowered his voice and came in close to Billy Ray's helmet. "I know what he did to ya, but cut him some slack, will ya'?"

"Just call the play," Billy Ray said.

"You're an idiot, Noah," Mike continued. "Makes me wonder if I shoulda left you out in the woods that night. Thought you were different. You're no better than Billy Ray."

"What the hell are you talkin' about, Boswell?" Billy Ray shot Mike a baffled look

"Post right thirty-four angle on two! Post right thirty-four angle on two!"

The offense clapped its hands and got into position. Noah took notice that Billy Ray's assigned man to block on this play was the defensive end wearing jersey number 48. "Blue fourteen! Blue fourteen! Hut! Hut!" Noah barked the signals and dropped back, rolling right to pass. No more than three seconds had elapsed when Number 48 wrapped Noah from behind in a giant bear hug and slung him to the ground, slamming his right shoulder into the turf.

As quickly as a frog's tongue snags a fly, Mayor Sawyer jumped from his seat and pointed to the field. "Did you see that? Did you see that? Somebody tell me they saw that? That nigga' just gave that kid a free shot at my boy!"

Noah pulled himself to his knees but came up holding his shoulder.

"Way to go, Franklin! You just got our quarterback hurt," snapped receiver Ryan Mitchell.

"He got himself hurt," Billy Ray answered. "Maybe if he could run a little faster we'd be on the forty instead of our own two."

By now Mayor Sawyer was halfway down the bleachers and yelling at Coach Mabry. "Get that nigga' out of the game, Mabry. He shouldn't be playin' anyway." He found the gate to the sideline but had trouble opening it.

In obvious pain and holding his injured arm and shoulder close to his chest, Noah approached Billy Ray. "You happy now? Is this what you wanted?"

"I don't give a damn about you, boy, or for this team for that matter." Billy Ray said, edging closer to Noah.

Noah almost laughed. "Don't you get it, man? You don't get it, do ya'? I was trying my best to do good man. For you." Noah stepped a few inches closer to Billy Ray. "I was only trying to help you. Don't cha' see? If I do good. It's you that does good. It's you that gets the glory." Noah shook his head. "You're so blinded by hate that you can't see it. I feel sorry for you. I really do." Noah turned, still holding his arm and shoulder so the pain would not radiate so badly, and jogged off the field.

Billy Ray stood silent and motionless and watched Noah run from the field in obvious pain.

By now Mayor Sawyer had managed to open the clasp of the gate and marched valiantly over to Coach Mabry. "I know you saw that. You had to have seen it. That ni'..."

"I saw it Joshua. I saw it." Mabry turned to the second string fullback. "Woods!" he shouted. "Get in there for Franklin. Fromke, you're in for Sawyer."

Noah made it to the sideline bench with the help of the trainers and the second team quarterback made his way onto the field. Mayor Sawyer sat down beside Noah. "That boy's gonna' pay for that I can promise you!"

"No!" Noah shouted, wincing in obvious pain as the trainer cut his jersey to assess the damage. "It was my fault. I didn't get off the ball quick enough."

Mayor Sawyer looked at Noah as if he'd lost his mind. "You what? Son, that boy clearly did not block his man. He let him through on purpose. I watched the whole thing."

"No! It was my fault. I'm tellin' you I could have avoided the tackle. It was my fault."

Mayor Sawyer sat stoned face. He couldn't believe what he was hearing. "Billy Ray. What are you doing son? You takin' up for that nigga'?" Mayor Sawyer looked around. "Do you realize if your shoulder is shot, the season is over and so is your scholarship? It's all that nigga's fault!"

Billy Ray clanked down on the same bleacher only twenty feet away. Mayor Sawyer saw him and made the twenty foot distance in less than three seconds and before anyone could stop him. "Who the *hell* do you think you are?" Mayor Sawyer smacked Billy Ray hard across the side of his helmet. "Do you realize what you've done, you pathetic excuse for a human being?" Sawyer smacked the other side of his helmet and then grabbed the face mask, jerking Billy Ray's head to face him.

"You did that on purpose! You got no business out here. Your stupid laws and your stupid politicians have ruined everything!"

Noah ran and held Mayor Sawyer's arm before he could hit Billy Ray again. "Stop it!" he shouted. "You don't know what you're doing! Stop it!"

Startled by the action, two assistant coaches arrived just after Noah and pulled Mayor Sawyer away.

"You haven't seen the last of me, boy! You understand? You'll regret this. You'll regret the day you ever came here!"

Several Webber County Sheriff's deputies were on the scene by now and managed to calm things down. One deputy pulled Mayor Sawyer further away. "Please don't make me do anything I don't want to do, Mayor."

"What're you gonna' do? Arrest me for protecting my son?"

"You weren't protecting Billy Ray, Mayor. Now I don't wanna' have to take you in but I saw you attack that boy. You better hope he don't wanna press charges cause if he does I got no choice."

Mayor Sawyer read the name embroidered on the deputy's shirt. "Phillips? Deputy Phillips?"

"Yes sir?"

"Do you know what the chain of command is, son?"

"Yes sir, I do."

"And do you understand where I am in your chain of command?"

"Yes sir, I do. But that don't make no never mind to me, sir. I saw what happened. Now if'n you wanna fire me for doing my job then you best do it. If not, I suggest you apologize to that boy and best hope he is the forgivin' sort."

"You suggestin' I apologize to a *nigga'*?"

"Yes sir, I am."

Mayor Sawyer wiped his hands against each other. "Well, that is not going to happen, Deputy Phillips. I can assure you of that. Now if you are going to arrest me and make a fool out of yourself, I suggest you do so." He put his wrists out dramatically, ready to accept handcuffs.

Deputy Phillips pulled his radio from his belt. "Does the boy want to press charges?"

Mayor Sawyer watched Billy Ray as the second deputy spoke with him. Billy Ray stood and glared at his father for several seconds before shaking his head no.

"That's a negative," the voice on the radio crackled.

Deputy Phillips carefully placed his radio back into his belt. "Your lucky night, Mayor. I suggest you go back to your seat and enjoy the rest of the game."

Mayor Sawyer straightened up his jacket and his fedora. "What's there to enjoy? My boy is out of the game. We might as well forfeit. And it's all that..that..nigga's fault," he said, motioning toward Billy Ray.

The game continued but without Billy Ray or Noah. The team Doctor quickly determined that Noah's injury was not a separated shoulder but just a deep bruise. He would be as good as new with a couple days of ice treatment. News wasn't as good for the team. The Warriors lost 21-0. Without their star quarterback, the team gave up before halftime.

~ 9 ~

The Henley Bridge connected Webber County with neighboring Knox County. The thirty year old bridge had been painted blue on some strange whim of a county executive, and now boasted bright red rust spots popping through the peeling blue paint. Billy Ray stood on the edge, looking down at the churning brown water racing below. He held carefully to the railing, and then climbed over, looking over his shoulder to make sure no one saw.

He sat down, his legs dangling over the side of the bridge. He thought for a moment what people would say. "What could possess the star quarterback, bound for college glory, and the mayor's son, to end his life this way?" "It must have been an accident," some would say. "He must have had demons in his life no one knew about," others would comment. The old cliché "Just goes to show, money doesn't buy happiness," would be repeated over and over again. Then he tossed his head back and laughed mournfully. "Oh, yeah, they won't be saying that, cause, they don't know who I am. I'm that colored boy in town, Noah Franklin," Billy said out loud to himself. And then it struck him. No one he knew would care. To them it would be just another colored boy, a nobody. "Good riddance," some would dare to say, including his father. Billy Ray felt nauseous when he realized that only a few weeks ago, he would have been one of those people.

The most intense feeling of loneliness overcame Billy Ray. His father hated him, or this Noah, he didn't know which. His mom would hate him if she knew what he was like now. He had no friends, and if they knew the truth they would be embarrassed by him. His only source of pride was his football fame, and that was being ripped from him. He had no home, no family. And Billy Ray didn't understand why this crazy thing had happened, and if it would ever be reversed.

"I can't take one more second of living in this black skin!" Billy Ray shouted to the silence. He sat there, for over an hour, looking out at the lights of the city. His mind was blank, like it was shutting down under all the stress. He watched as the stadium lights at his high school were shut off, just as his life was about to be shut off as well.

"I'm going to die and no one is going to know or even care. Billy Ray Sawyer... came, went and nobody gave a..."

Suddenly, two large hands grabbed him by the shoulders of his jersey and hoisted him over the rail. He was pitched unceremoniously onto the bridge surface, causing reverberating pain through his elbow where he landed.

"Don't you even think about what I think you're thinkin' about. You mess up that body and I ain't never gettin' it back. And I sure as heck ain't livin' the rest of my life as *you*!"

Billy Ray squinted to try and make out the large figure that had pitched him to the ground. Of course he recognized his old face as the bits of city lights reflected on Noah's face, and the number two jersey. If he hadn't been so surprised, he would have attacked the smug face.

Noah grabbed his shoulder and winced, realizing he shouldn't have lifted the 185 pound athlete with his newly hurt shoulder. "And another thing," Noah began. "What do you mean, lettin' all those guys get to me tonight? You know I didn't know what I was doin', anyway. A little, just a little bit of protection would have been nice."

"That's *my* position!" Billy Ray cried out, stabbing his finger into his own chest. "Mine! You can't just come in and take away the only thing I have in the world that I'm proud of!" The emotions of the week and the struggles of the night built up in Billy Ray until he couldn't hold them in any longer. Embarrassed, he wiped the tear that trailed down his dirty face.

"Like I had any choice! You got to face it, Billy Ray, we're stuck like this for God knows how long. And we got to make the best of it. My momma always said that God has a reason for everything. She made us memorize, 'For I know the plans I have for you, plans for good and not evil. To give you a hope and a future.' Like I said that day out at the lake, I think this is all part of God's plan. And it's for good, not evil. We got to believe that, Billy Ray. And you can't go around takin' things into your own stupid hands. I hated you tonight, starting after the first play when I had a half ton of linebackers on top of me."

Billy Ray allowed a slight smirk to appear on his lips recalling the scene.

"But you know, I prayed. I prayed that God would take that hate from me, and he did. And I prayed that somehow, someday we'd actually be friends. I feel pretty lonely right now, too. I can't be with my family or my friends. And even though you got a really nice house and you eat good, I would give *anything* to be back home. So while you're here feeling all sad and sorry for yourself, I'm feelin' pretty much the same way. We've got to get through this together, Billy Ray, like it or not. But I really think we will be better and stronger for it."

Billy Ray wanted to say something really hateful back, or maybe just hit him, but he was drained, and tired. And actually, Noah made sense in a crazy way. What would come of his taking his own life? Nothing, as no one would really know what happened, or who it happened to. Something warmed in him towards his nemesis, but he was not going to admit it just yet.

"I'm leavin'," was all he could muster.

Noah wondered if he had chipped just a little into Billy Ray's hard heart. And as he walked along silently with him, he never let on that the sight of himself sitting on the edge of the Henley Bridge had put a terror in his heart he had never felt before. The gravel crunched beneath their feet as the cool September wind whipped up the hill and wrapped around them. Noah looked up into the clear sky and was awed by the majesty of the stars above. He felt the greatness of God and a certain peace that reminded him that God was still in control.

~ **10** ~

Noah walked through the front door of his "new" home. It was almost midnight and no lights had been left on like they usually were. He shut the door quietly behind him careful not to wake the Sawyers. When he turned to make his way up the winding staircase, there, sitting in the early 1800's rocker that legend claimed Jefferson Davis once owned, was Joshua, stone faced and still red with anger. Shocked, Noah jumped back just slightly.

"Whoa! I didn't see you there."

"Didn't mean to startle you, son," Joshua said with an eerie calm voice.

"No, that's alright. I'm alright." Noah took one step up the staircase.

"Are you?"

Noah stopped. "Am I what?"

"Okay?"

"I'm fine, Pop. Really. Thanks for asking though." Noah took two more steps up the stairway.

Joshua never looked Noah in the eye. He deadpanned straight ahead toward the front door. "Somethin's gotta be done, son."

Noah took one step down. "Whattaya' mean?"

"You know exactly what I mean."

Noah stepped down the stairs and moved directly in front of Joshua. "No, I don't."

"I'm not just gonna stand by and watch the niggas' take over our town. If we let 'em, next it'll be the state, then the whole damn country."

"Pop. If you're upset about the shoulder, it's just a bruise. Doc said with ice it'll be good by next Friday."

"It ain't the shoulder, Billy Ray. That's just a small part of the problem. That's just an example of what them people are capable of doing. They think we're a bunch of racists and hate mongers, but what that boy did to you tonight is every bit as bad if not worse. Inexcusable is putting it lightly."

"It ain't that big a deal, Pop. Like I said, I'm good to go next Friday."

"You're missin' the point, Billy Ray. Somethin's gotta be done. We got to kill it before it grows."

Noah's stomach turned as he sat down on the bottom step. "You're just speakin' out of anger right now. You're mad because of what happened. You'll think different tomorrow."

Joshua shook his head quickly from side to side as if he had awakened from a bad dream. "Feel different tomorrow? What! What the hell has gotten into you lately? I don't like this radical hippy social conscience attitude that you all of a sudden seem to have gotten. Who the hell you been hangin' out with? I taught you better than that. I taught you the way things are supposed to be. It's time, son. It's time."

Noah stood and walked directly in front of him. "Time for what?"

Joshua stood and placed both hands on Noah's shoulders.

"Time for things to return to the way they were." Joshua half raced up the staircase and around the oval shaped landing that encompassed the entire second floor of the mansion. Noah watched as Joshua disappeared into his "secret" office at the end of the landing. An office that neither Billy Ray or Mary Edith had ever been allowed to enter. An office that only the highest political figures in Alabama had ever seen the light of. The only thing visible to Noah was the faint yellow light that glowed from the bottom of the doorway. The only thing audible was the low mumble of Joshua talking with someone on the other end of the phone.

The creaky screen door screeched as it shut and slapped twice against the wooden frame. Billy Ray slung himself down on the twenty year old couch whose cushions had been sewn up more times than anyone could count. He covered his face with his hands and rubbed his eyes.

"Get up," Adam demanded.

Billy Ray removed his hands from his face and saw Adam standing at the end of the couch. "Where the hell'd you come from? Why aren't you in bed?"

"You heard me. Get up!"

Billy Ray rolled over on his side. "Go away. I'm tired. Can't a white boy get any peace?"

With all his strength, Adam grabbed Billy Ray by the front of his shirt and jerked him up. He pulled him to within inches of his face.

Billy Ray tried to pull away but was unsuccessful. "Man, what the hell is your problem? Let go of me!"

Adam had no problem pulling a strongly resisting Billy Ray across the wood floor and down the tiny hallway that led to their bedroom.

"I said let me go you stupid ni..!"

Adam practically threw Billy Ray into their bedroom. Trying to regain his balance from Adam's forceful push, Billy Ray stopped himself from saying anything else when he saw Emma and James hovering over a bloody and battered Moses. Emma gently dabbed a wet rag on the deep cuts on Moses' head. Billy Ray looked back at Adam and then again at Moses, Emma and James. He stared in stunned silence. He edged an inch or two closer. He didn't know what to feel but in all that had happened, Moses was the one that seemed to care most about him. Moses was the only one that genuinely wanted to help him.

"What happened?" Billy Ray finally summoned the courage to ask.

"This is your doin'." Adam said.

Confused, Billy Ray looked back at Adam. "What?"

"This is your fault," Adam answered.

Billy Ray seemed even more confused. "I have no idea what you're talkin' about."

"Moses went to see his big brother play football. He was real proud of you. His big brother was gonna be the first colored starter in the history of the school. So proud that he bragged to everybody around that his big brother was the startin' fullback."

Billy Ray closed his eyes and rolled his neck back. A hard knot formed in his throat. He knew exactly what happened.

Adam continued. "Guess there were some white kids there that didn't take too kindly to his brother purposely missin' a few blocks and their all-star quarterback gettin' hurt."

Billy Ray grasped his hands together and rested them on top of his head.

Adam motioned toward Moses. "And they took out their frustrations on Moses."

James shot a quick look towards Adam. "Come on, Adam. This was Noah's first game. He was just confused, not sure what to do. You can't blame this on him."

"No Daddy, he knew exactly what he was doin'. You were there, you saw. It was obvious to everyone. He *let* those guys get to the quarterback. He wanted him hurt," Adam said, his eyes in a steely lock with Billy Ray's.

"Is it true, Noah?" Emma asked. "Tell me it ain't true. That's not like my Noah."

"You're right, Momma. Not a thing like *our* Noah," Adam replied, his eyes narrowing with disgust. Billy Ray said nothing and could not look any of them in the eye.

"You don't gotta say nothin'. You just told me everything," James said.

"How could you, Noah?" Emma asked not expecting an answer. "I don't care what kind of hate Billy Ray or any other white kid is showin' you right now. You gotta' show 'em back love. You gotta let it go and give back love no matter what." Emma stood and walked to Billy Ray. "I'm ashamed of you, Noah. Truly *ashamed*. I raised you better than that."

Billy Ray was silent. He looked at Adam and back at Emma.

"Don't you have anything to say?" Emma asked, staring

into his eyes.

In his heart he believed he was sorry, but he couldn't bring himself to say it.

"Then you're no better than the ones that's been mistreatin' you. I am ashamed of you, Noah."

Billy Ray sat down on his bed and hung his head. Emma returned to Moses' side. Adam shook his head and walked out of the room.

Emma hummed an old religious tune as she continued to dab the wet rag on Moses' cuts. James sat patiently by Moses' bedside rubbing his hand. Billy Ray had a strange feeling as he witnessed the love being poured out for this boy. A different love than he had been shown in his seventeen years.

There was an awkward silence and after several minutes Billy Ray summoned up the courage to speak. "He needs to go to the hospital. He needs stitches. He could have internal injuries."

"Whatta' you care," Adam shouted from another room.

"Enough!" Emma shouted loud enough for Adam to hear.

"He needs a doctor. He needs to go to the hospital." Billy Ray got up from the bed and leaned over Moses. "He ain't sleepin'. He's unconscious. We really should get him to the hospital."

Emma stroked Moses' head and wiped droplets of blood from his cheek.

"You know we ain't got no insurance, son," James said. "Can't afford no doctor bill."

"No, no. You don't understand," Billy Ray attempted to explain. "If we take him to the ER, they have to treat him and it won't cost a thing. They got to. You know they got to," Billy Ray tried to find the words for "indigent" but he didn't want to offend them.

"I know what you're trying to say, Noah. They gotta give us poor folk free medical treatment causin' we can't afford to pay for it," James interrupted. "But I ain't never took it and don't intend on startin' now. Moses'll be fine. He'll be fine in the mornin'."

"And if he ain't?" Billy Ray asked.

"Maybe Noah's right, James," Emma added. "Maybe it's time we swallowed our pride and did what's right by Moses."

"No! I will not be a burden to the county or the state! Our family is not a charity case!" James said, his voice cracking. "The boy's bruised up a bit and the scars'll be there a while, but he'll be fine. That's final. Discussion is closed. We'll take care of him here."

"But." Billy Ray tried to make his case.

"No!" James cut him off.

"You heard your father, Noah," Emma added.

Billy Ray leaned down and whispered into Moses ear. "If you can hear me, I'm sorry. I really am." Billy Ray rose and looked at both Emma and James before leaving the room and the house. Billy Ray perched himself on the warped boards of the front porch to think.

Billy Ray woke himself swatting a mosquito that was taking a bite from his forehead. He had fallen fast asleep on the porch with the chirping crickets serenading him. It was still dark. He rubbed his eyes and contemplated spending the rest of the night outside, not only because of his foolish actions the night before, but because the slight breeze that filtered through was cooler than the stagnant air inside. He smacked another mosquito or two from his face and decided the stagnant air inside his bedroom was better than being eaten alive by the Alabama insects. Billy Ray pulled himself to his feet and quietly opened the creaky screen door, remembering to catch it before it slammed shut. Halfway down the hallway he could hear the incessant snoring of Adam. Once in the bedroom the three boys shared, he observed James asleep in a chair. Emma was fast asleep, halfway on the floor and halfway on the bed beside Moses. Billy Ray stared and wondered if his own mother had ever cared for him like that. He was sure she had but couldn't help but wonder. Like a stalking cat, he walked slowly and quietly over to Moses and lowered his ear to Moses' mouth and nose.

Billy Ray could barely sense any breath. He placed his fingers on Moses' neck and detected a light pulse. Billy Ray knew he had to get him to the hospital and wondered if he was bleeding internally and possibly to death. He started to wake Emma but knew if he did, she would not let him take Moses. Waking James was out of the question. He looked around like he needed some sort of justification. Slowly, he leaned in and gently removed Emma's hand from Moses' chest and placed them by her resting head. Defying all authority, he slipped his arms underneath Moses' shoulders and legs and lifted him up and over Emma and then carefully outside, carefully inserting his foot between the screen door and the door jamb to muffle the creak.

The Franklins did not own a vehicle. The money just wasn't

there.   Not even for an old, beat up pickup truck James attempted to buy a couple years earlier. He couldn't come up with enough for a down payment and the bank refused the loan. So everybody was forced to walk anywhere they went whether it was school, work or church. The hospital was a little more than a mile away. Moses was smaller than Billy Ray, but not by much. The dead weight would make the walk even harder. But Billy Ray knew what he had to do and so he did. He had caused this. Black or white did not matter. This was his doing. He hoisted Moses slightly to get a better grip and then took off into the night.

Billy Ray had been through two-a-days in 100 plus degree heat in full pads for three straight seasons. He'd lifted more weights than he cared to remember. He fought off 275 pound linemen. He'd been hit so hard in practice and games it seemed hours before he regained his breath or his senses. But this had to be the toughest ordeal he had ever encountered. Every hundred yards or so he would stop to rest. His heart pounded so hard he could feel it beat in his temples. In the distance he could see the lights of the hospital. His body ached, but he kept going. By now Moses was draped around Billy Ray's neck and over his shoulders, the only way he knew he could finish. What seemed like an hour's long journey was in reality a little over twenty minutes, a testament to his physical condition.

Billy Ray stepped on the black rubber entrance that controlled the electronic doors and stepped inside. He was so drenched in sweat he looked like he'd been swimming. His face shimmered because of the perspiration covering it.   The emergency room was open but empty. No one was at the desk when Billy Ray approached it, so he pounded on the desk. "Hey! Help! Is anybody here?"

"Calm down, calm down," the nurse on duty said, obviously awakening from a nap. She looked more like a child's nightmare than a caregiver. Five feet tall at best with frizzy red hair and cat eye glasses and about a hundred pounds more than her poor body should have had to endure. Her voice was rough, almost like a man, the result of years spent smoking cigarettes. "What seems to be the problem?"

"Moses Franklin. He's hurt pretty bad. He needs to see a doctor."

She took her time looking for a pen. "I know it was here before. Where'd it go?"

"Ma'am. I don't mean to rush you but he really needs a doctor right now."

The nurse looked at Billy Ray with a scary stare then returned to her search. "Where'd that pen go. I just had it." She ducked behind her counter and out of sight of Billy Ray who rolled his eyes.

"I saw that," she said. "There it is. Must've fallen on the floor while I was asleep...uhhh...looking at some charts."

"Right. Ma'am. Can he please see a doctor?"

The nurse licked the tip of her pen. "Name?"

"Mine or his?"

"His."

"Moses Franklin."

"Age?"

"Age? I..I..don't know."

She put her pen on the desk. "This is your brother?"

"Yes."

"And you don't know how old he is?"

"Yeah. Yeah. He's about 14."

She looked at Billy Ray.

"About?

"He's 14. 14."

All the while the nurse questioned Billy Ray, blood dripped from Moses' face to the floor below.

"Ma'am. I don't mean to irritate you or nothin' like that, but my brother really needs to see a doctor right now. Can't I answer all these questions later?"

The Nurse looked over her glasses at Billy Ray and answered him with silence. "Address?"

"You gotta be kidding me!"

"Sir. I don't have to take that tone."

Billy Ray rolled his eyes. "I don't know the address."

"You don't know your own address?"

Billy Ray looked down, sweat dripping from his face to the counter. "It's in the bottoms. That's all I know."

She rolled her eyes. "Insurance card."

Billy Ray paused. "Uhhhhh. They don't have insurance."

"Figures," she said condescendingly.

"Excuse me?" Billy Ray said, shifting his legs to avoid the crushing weight Moses was putting on his body. "What did you say?"

"Put the patient over there," she said pointing to a stretcher in the hallway. "When a room is available we'll move him in there."

Billy Ray looked around and saw nobody. "Ma'am. We are

the only ones here. There's gotta be a room available and a doctor on duty."

"I said when a room is available we will move him. Now put him on that stretcher."

Billy Ray glared at her, but was glad to have a place to lay him. He placed him carefully on the nearby stretcher. He then walked past her into the examining room. "Here's an empty room!"

"Excuse me! That room is being cleaned. Now, wait in the waiting room, please," she snapped.

"No! I will not!" he shouted and pounded his fist on the counter.

The nurse jumped back. "Boy, I will call the police if I have to."

"Go ahead and call 'em. What're you gonna tell 'em? That you caused my brother to die because he was colored or because he didn't have insurance. Which one?"

"Well, I never!"

"I'm sure you haven't," Billy Ray said. Being completely ignored, he sat down on one of the orange plastic vinyl chairs. He looked up at a black cat clock whose eyes looked back and forth with the wagging of its tail.

A young white mother entered into the waiting room with her young daughter in tow. The child's finger was bandaged with what appeared to be toilet paper. She approached the front desk, and after a short discussion, mother and child disappeared into the examining room. Twenty minutes later the pair reappeared, the little girl smiling with a new bandage on one hand and a lollipop in the other. An elderly doctor, a friend of Mayor Sawyer's, came from the examining room behind them.

"Doctor! Doctor Sanders! There's someone... uh... my brother... he's hurt real bad. If you would just look..." Billy Ray rambled, grabbing the doctor by the coat sleeve.

Dr. Sanders jerked his sleeve from Billy Ray's grasp, clearly annoyed. "I'm terribly sorry. I've got to get home." He looked at his watch as if to emphasize how late it was.

"But, you don't understand. I think he could die. He's been unconscious quite a while, now."

Billy Ray had always liked Dr. Sanders, his father's friend and hunting partner. But now he realized what kind of man he really was. With a hand raised, the doctor walked past him and out the door.

Frustrated, Billy Ray went back to the front desk. He leaned over the desk with both hands firmly placed on it. "I want to see a doctor, and I want to see one NOW!!"

A young dark haired doctor appeared from a treatment room in the hallway and addressed the nurse. "Miss Darling?"

"Darling? Your name is Darling? Wow." Billy Ray smirked.

She put her hands on her hips. "And what's that supposed to mean?"

"Is there a problem up here?" the young doctor asked.

"Yes sir. This. This boy is violent and being very disrespectful."

The doctor approached the stretcher Moses was laying on. "Looks like he was on the losing end of a fight."

"Yes, sir. He was."

"I'm Doctor Hill," he introduced himself and extended his hand to Billy Ray. Billy Ray did likewise.

"Bil...Noah Franklin."   He would never get used to this. "That's Moses, my brother."

Dr. Hill pressed on Moses' belly and chest. "Let's get him back here to a treatment room."

"I thought they were all being used," Billy Ray said facetiously as he glanced at the nurse.

"Doctor. You should know they have no insurance."

Doctor Hill stopped and turned to face her. "Uh-huh. And are there any other reasons you think I should have for not treating this young man?"

"Uhhhh. No, doctor."

Doctor Hill was an averaged sized young doctor in his early thirties. He had jet black hair that had begun to recede on both sides. His gold-framed wire-rimmed glasses gave him an air of distinction. Nurse Darling stared at him coldly as he signed the form she had been filling out. As they rolled Moses back to an examining room, Billy Ray turned and gave a slight wink to her, horrifying her.

Doctor Hill poked and prodded the unconscious Moses. "Who beat him up, Noah?"

"Don't know."

He used both palms of his hands and placed them on either side of Moses' neck and rubbed back and forth. "Has this happened before?"

"I don't know. No," Billy Ray answered. "I don't think so."

"Yes or no?"

Billy Ray lifted his shoulders. "No."

Doctor Hill pulled a small flashlight from his white doctor's jacket and lifted Moses' eyelids to shine the light. "Why didn't your parents bring him in?"

"What're you gettin' at, Doc?"

He looked up at the clock on the wall. "I'm just wondering what two young men your age are doing out at 3:20 in the morning. Nothing good can come from that."

Billy Ray paused. "We ain't got insurance. My father wouldn't bring him in 'cause he says we ain't a charity case. I had to wait till they were asleep."

"Well, your father's wrong. You may've saved his life. Stitches are simple. But I think he's got some internal bleeding. Won't know how bad 'til we get some x-rays, but if you hadn't brought him in, I don't know what might've happened." Doctor Hill patted Billy Ray's shoulder and smiled. "Moses can be glad you're his brother."

Billy Ray followed Doctor Hill out of the examination room. At the nurses' station, the doctor ordered some x-rays and other tests. When he was through with official business he added a personal note.

"Miss Darling, I know that you know as well as every employee in this hospital knows that the county has funds set aside for incidents like this one. If this ever happens again while I am on duty you can start submitting your applications elsewhere. I trust I've made myself clear." He looked at her sternly while he delivered the lecture.

"Yes, sir," she answered, her face red and her ears burning.

"Excellent. Noah, you go on home and get some sleep. I will call you and your parents as soon as I know something."

"I think I'll just stay here if you don't mind, Doc. Besides. We ain't got a phone anyway, and I'd kinda like to stay with him until mornin'."

"That's fine. You're a good brother, Noah. I'm sure your parents are very proud."

Proud? Yes, his parents had been proud of his popularity and his prowess on the football field. But proud because he did something for someone else? That was new. It felt good. Despite the blood, sweat and tears, he felt really good.

Doctor Hill approached Billy Ray and whispered. "By the way, I apologize for Nurse Darling. Not everybody is like her."

Billy Ray nodded. Only hours earlier, he had been...just like her.

The little bit of sunshine that broke through the blinds was just enough to wake Billy Ray. He had fallen asleep in a stiff, dingy, awful green and very uncomfortable chair that all hospitals all have. His poor body ached from the night. He stretched and scratched the back of his neck. Moses was sound asleep but looked much better. His cuts had been stitched and bandaged and his body had lost most of its swelling. He was breathing easy and regular. Moses was still hooked up to a machine or two and there was a bag of some kind of liquid hanging above him that dripped slowly into a needle stuck in his arm. Every fifteen seconds or so a beep would sound from one of the machines that monitored his pulse.

Billy Ray noticed a Bible on the table next to Moses' bed. He picked it up and opened it randomly. Like a two by four across the back of his head, he had opened it to the scripture about the Pharisees and all the rich people of their day who thought they had it all. "Man, that hits home," he whispered to himself. He read a little further where Jesus loves the downtrodden, the outcasts, the ones pushed aside by the wealthy. He wondered silently what Jesus would think of what he'd done. Billy Ray had been raised a Christian and he went to church every Sunday, but only because he had to. For his parents, it was a place to see and be seen.

The door opened and there standing with Doctor Hill were Emma, James and Adam. "Morning, Noah."

Billy Ray stood, almost embarrassed to look at Emma and James, ready to receive their wrath.

"I sent a car to get your folks. I told them what you did."

Billy Ray said nothing. He waited, wondering if he was about to be yelled at, something he was used to from his own father.

Emma smiled at Noah and mouthed "I'm sorry," before going to Moses and stroking his face.

James walked over to Billy Ray and gave him a great big bear hug. "I knew we were wrong about you, son. I just knew it. Thank you for being there and for ignoring this old fool." James held Billy Ray for what seemed like hours and finally let go before going to the other side of Moses' bed opposite from Emma. Billy Ray took note that this was the first time he had not recoiled at a hug from a colored person.

Adam remained in the doorway staring at Billy Ray. Billy Ray stared back. Adam shook his head, sighed and left the room. Billy Ray chased after him.

"Wait!" Billy Ray called out.

Adam stopped in the middle of the hospital hallway but

didn't turn around.

Billy Ray stood a few feet behind Adam. "I think I understand you less than I understand myself. Whatta' you expect from me, man? I did what I thought was right."

Adam turned and faced Billy Ray. "Did ya'?"

Billy Ray stepped closer. "Your point?"

"Was it from your heart, or did you do it to make yourself look good?"

Billy Ray laughed incredulously and took one more step toward Adam. "Myself? Myself? Are you kidding me? Look at me, Adam. I'm black. I'm your brother Noah. Who am I making look good?" Billy Ray shook his head. "Maybe you should check *your* heart. Maybe see where *it* is." Billy Ray paused. "Look in the mirror.....*brother*," he said with emphasis. "See if you like what you see."

At that precise moment Noah rounded the corner of the hallway and bounded the length of it to where Billy Ray and Adam were standing in about three seconds. Not until he was racing by them did Noah notice the two standing there. He froze in his tracks. The three stared at each other.

"Well ain't this interesting," Adam joked.

"I..I..I.." Noah stuttered. "I heard your brother was in the hospital. I wanted to check and make sure he was alright."

"He knows, Noah. Adam and Moses both know."

Noah's shoulders relaxed, like a huge rock had been lifted.

Adam looked at the clothes Noah was wearing and had a good laugh.

Noah looked down at his crisp shirt, khakis and loafers. "Yeah Yeah Yeah."

"Moses is gonna be OK," Billy Ray said. "Just a few cuts and bruises. He's gonna be fine."

"Thanks to your best friend, here," Adam said, sarcasm still in his voice, as he motioned to Billy Ray.

"Yeah, that's what I heard," Noah said. "Thanks, Billy Ray."

Billy Ray nodded his head.

"You okay?" Noah asked, noticing Billy Ray's strange expression.

"Yeah, I'm fine. I'm fine."

"You sure? You don't look fine."

Billy Ray shook his head and started walking away. "I'm okay. Really. I'm fine. Just tired."

Noah ran after Billy Ray and grabbed his arm. "Billy Ray." Billy Ray pulled away

"Man, I thought I was startin' to understand you, but I guess I was wrong."

"Maybe you were."

Noah grabbed his arm again. Billy Ray tried to pull away again, but Noah refused to let go.

Adam watched from where he stood in the hallway.

"Nope. I ain't lettin' go this time till you tell me what's up. You did the right thing, man. You did what anybody with a heart and a conscience would a done." Noah eased his grip on Billy Ray's arm. "Now you gonna tell me what's goin' on?"

Billy Ray walked to the wall and leaned into it face first, his forehead resting on his arm. "I'm not supposed to feel this way man. It ain't how I was raised. I know it's right and all, but it ain't our way."

Noah put his hand on Billy Ray's shoulder. "Don't ya see?

What you just said. It's exactly why God made this happen."

Billy Ray looked back over his shoulder. His eyes were moist. "Don't matter what God did or didn't do. It ain't gonna change nothin'. It's still gonna be the same whether we change back or not."

"Maybe it will. But you'll be different." Noah patted the top of Billy Ray's head. "One heart at a time, Billy Ray. One heart at a time. That's God's way." Noah looked back and saw Adam shaking his head in disapproval. "See Adam over there?"

"What about him?"

"Hopefully he'll be next. Maybe he'll switch with your daddy."

Billy Ray couldn't help but laugh at the mental image. He wiped his eyes.

"Let's go see Moses." Noah wrapped his arm around Billy Ray's shoulder and neck and they walked side by side to the hospital room.

~ 11 ~

The football team went through their stretching exercises and all the hooting and hollering that most high school teams do prior to practice that following Monday. Billy Ray went through all the warm-up exercises with his fellow backs but stood alone, apart from the rest. The team had not forgiven him for what had happened on Friday night.

"Franklin!" Coach Mabry's voice could be heard clear from the other end of the practice field.

Billy Ray was in a seated position and stretching his hips but paid no attention. When he heard the name Noah or Franklin, he still did not comprehend he was being addressed.

"Franklin!" Mabry shouted even louder

Again, Billy Ray paid no attention.

"Hey, Noah," one of his teammates halfway shouted.

Again. No response from Billy Ray.

"Franklin!" the Coach shouted one more time.

"Franklin! Are you deaf, man? Coach is calling you," another teammate called out to Billy Ray, tossing his helmet toward him to get his attention.

Billy Ray swiveled his hips around toward Coach Mabry who was yelling his name again. Billy Ray popped up, grabbed his helmet from the turf and bounded toward the Coach. "Sorry, Coach. My mind was somewhere else."

Coach Mabry tossed Billy Ray a green practice jersey with the number ten in white letters.

"What's this?" Billy Ray asked.

"Billy Ray separated his shoulder Friday night. He's out for the season. God only knows why but he wants me to take a look at you. Says you got a pretty good arm. My number two guy is just too short and 100 pounds soaking wet. Lord knows I'm taking a huge chance here givin' a...a...well, you know...a shot at the most coveted position on the team. Hell, I might even get lynched. And I should be kickin' you off the team after what happened Friday night. I'm hopin' beyond hope it was just a rookie mistake. But if it works, it'd be worth it. Put the jersey on and come on down to the twenty. I wanna see if Sawyer knows what he's talking about."

"Yes, sir." Billy Ray struggled with his jersey but finally managed to get it on over his shoulder pads. When he pulled it over his head, Noah was standing in front of him, his shoulder all strapped up and bandaged.

"Hey," said Noah.

"Hey."

"Here's your shot man. Don't blow it."

Billy Ray looked at the contraption on Noah's shoulder. "I thought your shoulder was just bruised."

Noah lifted his shoulder higher than he would have been able to if it had really been hurt. He winced but was obviously faking.

Billy Ray looked at him, unconvinced.

"Shhhh," Noah pressed his finger to his lips.

"Why?"

Noah shrugged his shoulders. "'Cause I have no idea what I'm doin' out there. And my linemen won't protect me." Billy Ray winced. "This is your position, and you deserve to be the quarterback."

Billy Ray tugged on the bottom of his jersey to stretch it into place. He couldn't deny he was excited about moving back into the quarterback position. "I know what you're doin' and don't think I ain't grateful or nothin'. But you never think of the consequences do you?"

Noah cocked his head slightly. "Consequences?"

Billy Ray tucked in his jersey and moved even closer. "I ain't Billy Ray Sawyer, man. I'm Noah Franklin. I'm that nigga' that caused Billy Ray Sawyer's season ending injury. How's that gonna look? The nigga' that caused Billy Ray's injury takes his place on the depth chart. A nigga' quarterback. Just thinkin' out loud here, but I don't think that's gonna go over so well down here in these parts."

Noah was silent.

"Yeah. Like I said. It ain't that I ain't grateful, but you done opened a whole new can a' worms." Billy Ray stared back at Noah as he jogged back to Coach Mabry.

Noah stared back only now realizing what he'd done.

Coach Mabry flipped Billy Ray the football. "Ryan!" Mabry shouted to his starting wideout. "Get over here and run some routes for Franklin."

Ryan Mitchell, a lanky, tall and limber kid, followed the Coach's orders. He lined up wide left of Billy Ray. "What route ya' want me to run, Coach?"

"Just go out, Ryan. I'm not worried about routes right now."

"Aiight den."

"What if he runs Right Gator Zip?" Billy Ray asked.

Coach Mabry looked at Billy Ray like he had gone completely nuts.

Billy Ray knew immediately he spoke too quickly. "I...I...I...I...just been learnin' the plays in practice Coach. Kinda hard not to learn 'em when you're runnin' them over and over."

"Okay. Fine then." Coach Mabry was still not convinced that the new quarterback could jump right in and know a play to run. "Lemme' see what'cha got."

Billy Ray barked a signal and Ryan took off like a bolt of lightning down the left sideline. Billy Ray cocked his arm and the pigskin flew off his hand with precision timing. Ryan turned at the precise time and like clockwork, the ball was delivered just over his outside shoulder forty yards downfield. Ryan made the catch, slowed and turned back up field. "Dang!" he said, loud enough in his southern drawl for some of his teammates to laugh.

"Dang!" Coach Mabry chimed back.

Hoots, whoops and hollers rang from some of the players stretching.

"Was that good, Coach?" Billy Ray asked facetiously.

"Yeah, Franklin. That was good. Real good. Let's see if you can do it on the other side." Taylor Crockett, a four year receiver starter lined up for the next reception attempt.

He lined up on the right side of the ball close to the sideline. Billy Ray called the signal and Taylor sped off down the right sideline. At just the precise second, Billy Ray released the ball and it landed just over Crockett's outside shoulder right into his awaiting hands.

"Dang," Coach Mabry repeated.

"Sawyer, meet your replacement!" a distant voice from the other side of the field shouted.

"Was that alright, Coach?" Billy Ray knew it was alright. He knew he hadn't lost his touch. He just wanted to hear it.

"Yeah, Franklin. It's very alright." Coach Mabry had a pained expression.

Noah, who was watching and smiling from the sideline, stepped onto the field where Coach Mabry seemed shell-shocked. "Coach. You alright?"

"I'm fine, Sawyer. Just tryin' to figure out how in the Sam Hill I'm gonna explain this to your father. After that I'll figure out how to break it to the community." Mabry walked away and told his new quarterback to practice and make sure he knew all the plays and everybody's role before Friday night arrived.

"Yes sir, Coach," Billy Ray answered even though he already knew everything he needed to know.

"Are you back?" Noah asked Billy Ray.

"Oh, I'm back alright. But it's about to get very interesting." Billy Ray took off his helmet. "Son, you don't know it, but you've just stirred up a hornet's nest."

"Maybe not," Noah responded weakly.

"Trust me. I'll give it twenty-four hours and everybody in this God forsaken town will know. And then it'll start."

"What'll start?"

Billy Ray stared at Noah and blew out a deep breath. "Hate." Billy Ray glanced away and then around at all the players, many of whom were already resenting the change. He looked again at Noah. "Hate." Billy Ray adjusted his chinstrap and put his helmet back on. Jogging away to join the offense, he glanced back at Noah. It was too late now.

~ 12 ~

Noah pulled Billy Ray's pick-up truck into the Sawyer driveway about thirty minutes after practice ended. He whistled some unrecognizable tune as he struggled to retrieve his school books from the passenger seat with his one hand. Even though his shoulder was not hurt nearly as bad as everyone thought, he had to keep up the appearance now that he committed by telling Coach Mabry.

He was met immediately by Mary Edith as he entered the massive foyer. If looks could kill he'd been dead on arrival.

"What's wrong?"

Mary Edith motioned with her eyes but stood sternly, her arms crossed.

Noah looked around her and saw Mayor Sawyer in the parlor adjoining the foyer, pouring himself a shot of bourbon from a half-empty bottle of Jack Daniels. He looked again at Mary Edith. "What's wrong?"

"Billy Ray!" Mayor Sawyer shouted.

"Yes, sir?"

"Get your ass in here and get it in here now! Do you hear me?!" From the sound of his voice, the shots of bourbon had begun much earlier.

Noah looked at Mary Edith for help.

"I can't help you out of this one, Billy Ray," Mary Edith said as she opened the front door, walked outside and sat down on the porch swing. She pushed with her feet, making the swing creak with each forward movement, hoping the noise would drown out her husband's tirade.

Noah was nervous. He could feel his hands shaking. His palms were sweaty and his mouth suddenly was as dry as the Sahara. He had heard all about Mayor Sawyer's temper from his mother over the years but never witnessed it.

"Are you comin' or I am gonna have to come and drag your butt in here?" Sawyer screamed, his words now slurring from the liquor.

"I'm comin', sir." Noah started with baby steps, sure he was going to be the recipient of this man's inebriated wrath.

Mayor Sawyer threw back the shot glass and downed the current shot of bourbon in one swallow. Just to further his point, he slammed the glass down on the mahogany desk. He turned and saw Noah's pace. "Damn it, son! Get in here now! It's your shoulder that's hurt and not your leg for cryin' out loud!" Sawyer barked out his demand.

Noah picked up the pace and finally made it to the parlor.

"Shut the door," Sawyer ordered.

Noah complied.

"Sit down."

Noah sat.

Mayor Sawyer poured himself another shot of bourbon.

"Don't you think you've had enough, sir?"

Still standing, Sawyer faced Noah, glass in hand and looked down on him. He threw back the shot glass and in one gulp it was gone except for one drop that dribbled down the left side of his chin. Sawyer wiped it off with the cuff of his white sport coat. He looked down on Noah. "Don't you dare suggest what I can and cannot do in my own home," he snarled.

"I'm not sir! I'm not. I'm sorry."

"I made you what you are, boy! I brought you into this world and taught you everything you know. This is my house and I'll be damned if you're gonna come in here and belittle me. Do you understand me, boy?"

Noah pushed his back as far into the couch as he could. "I'm sorry. I didn't mean to upset you. I just don't want…"

"Don't… want…. what?" he snorted, pausing between each word. "Huh? Don't want what! Don't want me to drink? Don't want me to get drunk again like Friday night after what happened? Don't want me to speak my mind? Don't want me look out for my own kin, my own kind?"

"Why are you so upset? What happened?" Surely the news could not have come back to him so quickly.

Sawyer turned and picked up the Jack Daniels bottle and poured another shot. He then sat down on the couch next to Noah, but with two feet of separation. "Tell me it ain't so."

"What?" Noah asked. He realized it had.

Sawyer edged slightly closer to Noah. "Tell me it ain't so, Billy Ray."

"Tell you what ain't so? I don't know what you're talkin' about."

"That nigga'!" he shouted. "Did he take your place?"

Noah stared a thousand miles away.

Billy Ray predicted twenty-four hours and Mayor Sawyer probably knew it before practice was over.

"Well? Did he?" Sawyer leaned toward Noah, his breath wreaking of alcohol.

Noah searched for a way to answer but knew there was no other way. "It's not that big a' deal sir."

Mayor Sawyer fell back against the couch and stared at the wall.

"Sir?" Noah reached and nudged Mayor Sawyer's knee. "Are you alright?"

Sawyer closed his eyes then squeezed them tightly shut. He rubbed them profusely with the fingers of his right hand. Sawyer leaned over and rested his forehead in the palms of both of his hands. "I'm going to ask you one question Billy Ray and I want the truth."

"Yes sir."

Mayor Sawyer paused and rubbed his eyes harder. "Is this your doin'?"

Noah paused, searching hard for an answer. He swallowed, still battling his dry mouth. "You can't understand why."

Sawyer threw himself back against the couch. "Oh God. It is true." Sawyer took turns glancing at Noah and the wall. "Do you have any idea how humiliating, how embarrassing this is Billy Ray? Do you have any idea of how this town is going to react?"

"Maybe they won't react at all. Maybe they'll accept it."

Sawyer's eyes narrowed. "Are you kidding me Billy Ray?" Sawyer half shouted. "He's the reason you're hurt! He's the reason your season is over! He's the reason your scholarship is gone! And *now*, not only is that nigga' takin' your place, it was *your* idea! Are you insane? Do you have any idea how humiliating this is to me? Do you have any idea of what you've done?"

"I didn't mean no harm. I was just tryin' to do the right thing."

"The right thing?" Sawyer shook his head. "Why *him* Billy Ray? Huh? Why *him*? Are you trying to get back at something I did? Just tell me. Why *him*?"

Noah scooted up on the edge of the couch. "Cause like it or not, he was the only one ready to take over and like it or not, he's gonna be good."

"You don't get it, boy. You just don't get it. It don't make a hill a' beans if he's the next Johnny Unitas. This town ain't gonna tolerate it."

"You mean *you* ain't gonna tolerate it don't ya'?"

The words were barely out of his mouth when Sawyer backhanded Noah. "Don't you disrespect me, boy! Don't you evah' disrespect me. You understand me?"

Noah stood and rubbed his face. "Don't mean no disrespect and I'll forgive you for that 'cause that's the liquor talkin'. But sooner or later this town, and you, has gotta change." Noah turned and walked away.

"Boy! Get back here! Now! You're dead to me, boy! You leave now, don't bother comin' back! I am disgusted by you!" Sawyer shouted at the top of his lungs, spit exploding from his lips as he yelled and banged on the coffee table in front of him.

Noah did not turn or look back. He could hear Sawyer screaming even after he shut the front door behind him. To his right, Mary Edith swung herself on the porch swing while humming and staring stone-faced ahead.

"He's your father, Billy Ray."

Noah stopped at the edge of the porch but did not look back at her. "No, he's not. He's a drunken fool."

"He's still your father."

Noah looked up into the western sky that was a dark red hue. "No, he's not. I can't stay here. I gotta go for a while."

"No, sweetheart, it's gonna get better. He'll calm down, I know he will."

"I have to. I'll be fine. Don't worry. Maybe if he calms down some I can come back. Right now it's just not a good idea. I'll call ya'. I'll be around. Just won't be here."

Even as he got into his truck, Noah could hear Sawyer yelling about his turncoat son and how he wasn't fit to carry on his name.

~ 13 ~

Brown dust from the speeding wide tires kicked up, swirled around, and suspended momentarily in mid-air. Noah pulled hard and fast into the half-gravel, half-dirt driveway, his brakes squeaking as he threw the gear shift into park. He jumped quickly from the truck and slammed the door behind him. Noah rubbed his face, still stinging from Mayor Sawyer's backhand.

Inside, Billy Ray was finishing an early dinner of leftover chicken livers from the night before and the night before that. He heard the screeching brakes and knew right away it was his truck. He wiped his mouth from the napkin in his lap and stood up.

"What the hell does that boy want and what the hell is he doin' here?" James asked, looking out the window.

"Noah! You sit down right now and James...watch your mouth at my table," Emma ordered.

Billy Ray ignored her command.

"Noah!" she demanded slightly louder.

"Sorry, ma'am. Somethin's wrong. I gotta go talk to him."

Emma reached out to grab him as he walked by, but Billy Ray pulled away. "Noah!" she shouted. "I'm beggin' you to not go out there. I'm tellin' you that boy is trouble." She turned and pleaded to James. "James! Do somethin'!"

"Can't stop the boy, woman. If he's got it in his head to get involved with that trash, can't do nothin' about it."

"Adam! Moses!"

"He's stubborn Mama. Can't tell him nothin'," Moses said.

Emma watched from the kitchen window. The boy she knew as Billy Ray Sawyer was passionate about something. His arms were flailing and she could hear his muffled voice inside the house. "I'm tellin' you James, that boy is up to no good and he's gonna get our son caught right up in the middle of it and you're gonna sit there and do nuthin'!"

"Calm down, woman! Noah's got a good head on his shoulders. He ain't gonna do nuthin' that ain't right."

Billy Ray leaned against the driver's side door, his hands resting on top of his head. "I told you this was gonna happen. I told you. Didn't I? You just had to go and get all socially conscious all of a sudden. What the hell you gone and done?"

"I done what was right, and you know it."

"May a' been right. Don't make it smart."

"What're we gonna do?" Noah asked.

Billy Ray came off the car and leaned in toward Noah. "We? We? Whattaya' mean we? I don't recall gettin' all warm and fuzzy and makin' the groundbreakin' decision to get the races together and everybody livin' happily ever after." Billy Ray stomped away. "Hot dang man. What the hell were you thinkin'?"

"Like it or not, you're in this as much as I am."

Billy Ray turned quickly and moved face to face with Noah. "Like *hell* I am. You made the mess. You get yourself out of it."

Both Billy Ray and Noah turned toward the shack when

they heard the sound of the creaky front door slam against the frame. Adam ambled outside, hands tucked firmly into the pockets of his overalls. He sat down at an angle on the paint cracked railing running down the length of wood steps. A sheepish grin formed on his face. He chuckled slightly. "Uh-uh-uh. What chu boys gone and done now?"

"None a' your business. Go back inside where you belong," Billy Ray barked out his order.

Adam stood, walked down the steps and toward the truck. "Touchy, touchy, touchy. Did I touch a nerve?" As he approached Billy Ray and Noah, he noticed the red mark on Noah's face. Noah tried to turn away so Adam couldn't see it, but it didn't matter. Adam reached toward Noah's face. "Well, well. What a' we got here? You run into a door? A wall maybe? Fall down? Hit a rock?"

"It's nothing."

"Who hit you Noah?" Adam asked.

"Didn't nobody hit me."

"Mind your own business," Billy Ray demanded.

Adam looked at Billy Ray then at Noah and back at Billy Ray. He tilted his head slightly, like a dog does when he hears a high pitch whistle. "Oh. Oh. I get it. Uh-huh. Your poor excuse of a drunken whitey daddy no good pig done that, didn't he?"

Out of nowhere Billy Ray slugged Adam, catapulting him to the ground.

Adam rubbed his face and smiled. "Like father like son."

James rushed onto the front porch, shotgun resting across his forearm. He was calm but firm. "You best get on outta here son. You done caused more trouble than you know. Now you turned my sons 'gainst one another. I suggest you go before my temper has a chance to catch up to my emotions."

Noah started walking toward his father, forgetting for a moment who he was. It was time to explain.

James raised his shotgun and leveled at Noah. "I ain't gonna ask ya' twice."

Noah froze and held his hands in the air. "There's somethin' you need to know."

"Only thing I know is you a load a' trouble and you ain't wanted 'round here. You ain't worth wastin' a bullet on, but if I have to I will. Now I suggest you get yourself back into that fancy truck a' yourn and ride back to the safety of that pompous ass you call your father."

"James!" Emma shouted from the doorway.

"That's enough, woman. I don't wanna hear it. Our family been a doormat to this boy's family for longer than I care to think about. If you lose your job then so be it. But this family ain't gonna take it no more." James never took his eye off Noah.

Emma stepped inside and closed the door.

"Go on now," James motioned with his shotgun. "I ain't as young as I used to be and my trigger finger's a little shaky. You best not take any chances."

Noah peered back and forth from James to Billy Ray to Adam. He finally backed away slowly. James kept precise aim on him. He made it to the truck, hands still in the air. "I need a place to stay," he said to Billy Ray while staring at the shotgun aimed in on him.

"Well, as you can plainly see, you are more than welcome

here," Adam said sarcastically while rubbing his chin. "Would you like a feather or foam rubber pillow?"

"Knock it off, Adam," Billy Ray barked.

"We need to tell him the truth and we need to do it now," Noah said.

Adam laughed hard. "You talkin' about your daddy, boy. First, he won't believe a word of it. Second, if you take one step in that direction, you'll be dead before you hit the ground. You know his aim."

"I'm gonna count to ten," James shouted.

Noah put his hands down and climbed into the truck. "We need to talk Billy Ray. Meet me at the bridge in an hour."

"You forget. I ain't got wheels."

"I'll meet you at the end of the road in thirty minutes." Noah pointed at Adam. "Not a word to Daddy. I mean it. Not a word."

Adam raised his arms. "Don't worry, boys. This is your mess. Get yourselves out of it."

Noah peeled out of the dusty driveway, spewing tiny bits of gravel on Adam and Billy Ray.

James lowered his shotgun and leaned it beside the doorway, expecting to see more trouble before the night was over.

~ 14 ~

Billy Ray and Noah sat on the old wooden, one lane bridge with a wooden canopy, their feet dangling over the side. The bridge wasn't used much anymore by local traffic since a new state highway had been built to connect several counties a year or two earlier. They knew they'd be safe here. A moderately swift, but narrow river swirled thirty feet below.

"I kept thinkin' it would change back to the way it was," Noah said, staring down at the fast flowing water reflecting a half moon. "It's been over a month and I still don't know what God is doin'."

"Why do you just assume that God had anything to do with it? How do you know this ain't somethin' ole' Satan himself concocted up and we're just the pawns in his evil plan. Look. I've tried to find the good in this too, and so far I ain't seen nothin' but bad. I gotta sincerely question God's motives if this is His doin'."

"That's blasphemous talk, Billy Ray. Talkin' 'bout God like that."

"Look, Noah. I got nuthin' 'gainst God. I go to church every Sunday. I believe in God and Jesus and Mary and all that. I'd like to think God's got a sense of humor. But this ain't funny, and it's headin' south faster than I like."

"Whatta' you suggest we do?" Noah asked.

"I'm up for suggestions." Billy Ray answered. "You know, tellin' anybody ain't gonna do squat. Ain't nobody gonna believe us. We either gotta wait it out and hope for the best or just hunker down and get used to it."

Noah looked up at the half-moon. "You think we'll ever put a man up there?"

Billy Ray peered skyward. "Sometimes I think bein' up there would beat the heck outta bein' down here."

"I don't know 'bout that. As bad as it can be sometimes, seems there's always hope somewhere." Noah paused. "You a Christian, Billy Ray?"

Billy Ray looked at Noah then quickly looked back at the moon and smirked. "Where'd that come from? Just told 'ya I go to church every, well, nearly every Sunday."

"Just curious."

Billy Ray remained silent, his blue eyes locked on the half-moon.

"Well. Are you?" Noah inquired, not looking at Billy Ray.

"Hell, yeah! Why? Don't I look like one?"

"Not quite the response I was expectin'."

"Don't you think that's a private matter 'tween me and God?"

"Not particularly. Ain't nothin' 'bout bein' a Christian that should be private. Either you are or you ain't. Ain't no in between and you shouldn't be afraid to admit it."

"I ain't afraid, man!" Billy Ray said, becoming perturbed. "Like I told you. I go to church every Sunday and sometimes on Wednesdays."

"That don't make you a Christian."

"Man, get off my back! I go to church. I know the Lord's prayer almost by heart. Mama always makes me give ten percent of my allowance to the offering."

"Do ya'?"

"Do I what?"

"Give ten percent."

Billy Ray shook his head. "Look, that's not the point, and who the hell gave you the right to ask about my beliefs? Ain't none a' your damn business and I'd appreciate it if you'd just drop it."

"Fine."

"Fine."

"Consider it dropped."

"Good."

"It was just a simple question."

"Drop it, Noah."

"It's dropped."

"Good."

"Good."

"Fine."

"Fine."

"You should at least think about it."

"Think about what?"

"The real meaning of being a Christian."

"Ahhhhhhhh!" Billy Ray shrieked as he rose from his seat on the bridge. "Man, you don't give up do ya'? Look. Don't worry about me. Me and God get along fine. Well, I guess 'till lately. I ain't real happy 'bout what's 'goin right now, but I'll figure it out and get back to him about my future plans with his son who, quite frankly, if he were who he claims to be wouldn't have put us here."

"Don't say that Billy Ray! You know you don't mean it. God's got a purpose in all this and you know it. Don't give up hope yet. The cross may be all me and you got to lean on since everybody else seems to be against us."

Billy Ray looked down on Noah and shook his head. "Yeah. I'll remember that when I say my prayers tonight."

Noah tossed a handful of gravel into the stream below then stood up and dusted the dirt from the back of his pants.

Billy Ray started walking down the dirt road.

"Don't you want a ride back?" Noah shouted.

"Nah. I need the exercise. Oh, my window is always unlocked and there's a ladder behind the fence next to the pond. He'll still be sloshed and he won't hear you climbing on the roof. Just make sure you leave before he gets up in the morning. He'll check."

"Thanks."

"Don't mention it."

~ 15 ~

Billy Ray stepped off the school bus and slung his backpack over his shoulder for his walk into school. The school bus carrying the black kids always arrived thirty minutes before school started so there was always ample time to get that last minute studying done or eat one of the muffins Emma had cooked several days earlier that were supposed to last all week. As he bit into one of the very stale bran muffins, he noticed his truck tucked into the furthest corner of the school parking lot next to the edge of the woods. Odd, he thought. Since he had the truck to drive now, Noah never arrived more than five minutes before the first tardy bell rang. Billy Ray looked around and half-walked half-ran to his truck. Inside the bed of the truck was Noah sleeping soundly on a bed of pine needles. Billy Ray snickered to himself and waved his muffin under Noah's nose like a nurse awakening a patient with ammonia.

Noah smiled and rubbed his eyes before opening them and seeing the muffin and Billy Ray.

"I've got another one if you want it. I was gonna give it to the baseball team in case they needed another ball. But if you want it, it's yours."

Noah sat up. "Very funny. You're talkin' 'bout my mama's muffins you know."

"So you want it or not?"

Noah finished rubbing his eyes and shook his head no. "I'll pass. Mama's a great cook... she makes the best biscuits in Alabama. But I never really loved her muffins."

"You're just gettin' used to that fancy rich white food!"

"Maybe...but I still never liked Mama's muffins. Just didn't dare tell her. But the birds and squirrels sure loved 'em. 'Specially in the winter."

"I take it the window was locked."

"Locked, boarded and sealed. Your secret wasn't a secret. The ladder was nowhere to be found so I climbed up the tree and risked my life to cling to the lattice and finally to your room. Window was locked, but wouldn't have made no difference. He'd boarded it up from the inside."

"Don't know that I've ever known him to be this upset. He gets mad but gets over it in a couple of hours or after the liquor wears off. Give 'em another day or two and he'll get over it."

"Don't know, Billy Ray. I know I ain't been around him like you or know him like you, but I don't think this is somethin' he's gonna get over for a while."

"Look. You can't keep sleepin' in the back of my truck. Tell Red. He'll let you stay at his house until this blows over. His folks ain't crazy 'bout my daddy anyhow. They'll be glad to help."

Noah laughed.

"What's so damn funny?"

Noah smiled. "I was just thinkin'. If this thing ever ends and you and me switch back, maybe we shouldn't tell Red."

"That's probably a good idea."

Noah stood and brushed the pine needles from his clothes

and hair. He jumped over the side and onto the pavement and retrieved his books from the cab.

"Sure you don't want the extra muffin?"

"I'm sure."

"What would Emma say?"

"I guess we'll never know."

"Don't forget your shoulder's hurt. Might wanna play that up a little."

Billy Ray and Noah walked side by side toward Webber High School. A little closer, a little warmer, but still worlds apart.

~ 16 ~

The stadium lights shone down on the football field. It was another Friday night in Webber. Another glorious Friday night where businesses shut down and fans rush to the gates to get their tickets early, choosing the best seats possible. But this night was different than any other Friday night in Webber and maybe in the entire state of Alabama. Webber High was about to make history. Some fans and residents were overjoyed and secretly happy to see the uppity Sawyers put in their place. There were others, many others, who could not believe and still refused to believe this day ever arrived. A black kid not only was on the football team but was starting at quarterback. And on top of that, it was because of him a week before that Billy Ray Sawyer, the next All-American hopeful at the University of Alabama, would be standing on the sideline with a separated shoulder. Even the local newspaper played it up with the headline reading "NEW QB TO START" and then the sub line announcing "NEW STARTER BLAMED FOR SAWYER'S INJURY." Half the crowd would be there to cheer on their team no matter who played. The other half was there for nothing more than curiosity.

Billy Ray stretched at mid-field. He felt every eye watching him from both stands…and the other teams' members as well as his own. He swung his arms in 360 degree motion not only to relax his tight muscles but to calm his nerves. Billy Ray surveyed the stands that were filling up quickly. He didn't see his father and wondered if he would come.

"Franklin!" Coach Mabry shouted out over the team's grunts and groans of pre-game stretches and routines.

Still not quite used to his identity, it took the coach another shout to get Billy Ray's attention.

"Yes, sir," Billy Ray answered.

Coach Mabry sauntered up from behind. "How ya' feelin' son?"

"Fine, sir. I'm fine."

Coach snickered. "Uh-huh." He knew his new quarterback was lying. "It's okay to be nervous, Franklin." Coach Mabry looked into the stands. "I don't gotta tell you that everybody up there is judgin' you tonight. Not only on your quarterback skills, but on the color of your skin. If you pass the test, most won't give you credit. If you fail, you'll catch all the blame." The coach put his hand on Billy Ray's shoulder. "I'm here to tell you, only people you gotta concern yourself about tonight is yourself, your team, and me. I don't want you worryin' 'bout nobody else. You understand?"

"Easier said than done, Coach."

"I know. But you got talent, son. No matter what you hear comin' out of those stands tonight you gotta know it's ignorance. You go out there and play to the best of your ability and if there's folks up there that don't like it, then so be it. Life ain't fair son, and there's people in this world that wanna be in control of things they got no right to be in control of. You just gotta watch out for yourself and do what's right. If I did what a whole lotta people wanted me to do, you wouldn't be standin' right here much less on the sideline. But I decided a long time ago I wasn't gonna let wrong trump right. Maybe I'll get fired at the end of the season. Hell, who knows, I could get fired tonight. But if that's what it takes to do the right thing, then I'll take my lumps."

"I won't disappoint you, Coach. I promise."

"Be confident Franklin. Not cocky."

"Yes, sir," Billy Ray replied, with a look like he said the wrong thing.

"Ease up, son. Just kidding. I like a little cockiness in my quarterback. Sawyer had it. I want you to have it too."

Billy Ray smiled. "Yes, sir."

Noah, his arm and shoulder all strapped up for no reason, watched Billy Ray and the Coach from the sideline. The brace caused discomfort and he would have just as soon not have to wear it but he had to play the part. He looked over his shoulder and saw Mary Edith moving down her row to her seat on the 50 yard line. Mayor Sawyer was not with her. At the extreme left side of the stands he noticed his mom and dad coming to watch with pride for the boy they thought was their son. It made him sad they were being deceived. He looked back around and saw Billy Ray by himself at midfield practicing his drop back. Noah headed in his direction.

"Hey."

"Hey," Billy Ray reciprocated.

"You ready?"

"I reckon I better be."

"I got a feelin' you're gonna light it up tonight, man."

"You mean *you* gonna light it up don't 'cha'?"

Noah couldn't respond because he had nothing.

"Cat got your tongue?"

"No. Just don't know what to say...so I guess the cat does have my tongue."

Billy Ray continued his drop back practices. "You gotta know this is a no win situation for me, right?"

"Whattaya' want me to do, man? I thought I was doin' you a favor. You belong back there, not me."

"I may belong back here, but look at all those people up there," Billy Ray said motioning with his head toward the stands. "Every one of them people wants me to fail. Every last one of 'em, Noah. You know how that feels?"

Noah stared at Billy Ray. "Yeah. I do. I know exactly how it feels."

Billy Ray stared back, rolled his eyes and shook his head. "Don't start that nonsense with me. All the bellyachin' in the world ain't gonna change nothin' and you know it."

"Maybe you can start the change tonight, Billy Ray."

Billy Ray stopped the drop backs and went face to face with Noah. "Look man! Don't you get it? This is a fluke. I could throw five touchdown passes tonight and run for three more and it ain't gonna matter. None of this matters. Everybody is against me. Everybody is hoping I fall apart out here."

"Who's bellyachin' now? Don't give them the satisfaction Billy Ray. Don't give them the satisfaction that they're right."

Billy Ray turned his head toward the stands and there he was, taking his seat by Mary Edith. "Oh geez!"

"What?"

"He's here."

Noah turned and saw Mayor Sawyer taking up more than the one seat he was allowed.

"I was really hopin' he wouldn't show. This ain't good. Hell. I can smell the bourbon from here."

Noah turned to sniff.

"It's a joke, man."

"I knew that."

"Look. Whatever you hear tonight comin' out of his mouth. Just try to ignore it, alright?"

"Franklin!" Coach Mabry shouted from the twenty yard line. "Let's go! Time to run some plays."

Billy Ray ran backwards while facing Noah. "Like water off a duck's back!"

"You just take care of business out there like you should and let's see what happens." Noah meandered back to the sidelines and watched as Mayor Sawyer slipped the pint bottle of bourbon from his vest pocket. He poured some into a white Styrofoam coffee cup before slipping the bottle back into the same pocket.

David Scott, offensive lineman, and one of Billy Ray's oldest buddies, slid up next to Noah as the National Anthem was starting. "We've been talkin', Billy Ray. We're gonna give Franklin a taste of his own medicine. We're not blockin' for him. Before the quarter's over, he'll be out with more than a separated shoulder." He grinned and looked to Noah for approval.

"No way, Scott, no way! It was a stupid move Franklin pulled last week, but he goes down, the team goes down. It's not about me, or him, or you. It's the Warriors. As much as I'd like to see him flat on his face, I think he's good. I think we can win with him. And I want to make State. Maybe I'll be back by then. I want to make State. I mean it, pass it on. He's gotta have protection, understand?"

David looked confused, but it made sense. "All right, if you say so. I guess you're right. We can take care of him another time."

"Sure, another time." Noah felt like he'd dodged another bullet.

Webber won the toss and elected to receive. Those familiar butterflies that Billy Ray always got before the game had returned with a full vengeance. The kickoff returner made it to the 25 yard line. Billy Ray huddled with his offense just off the sideline as Coach Mabry called the first play. The eleven players bolted onto the field and went directly to the ball and lined up. No huddle. Billy Ray barked the signal but did not get a solid grip on the ball from the center. His first play from scrimmage resulted in a fumbled snap and a turnover to the opposing team.

The center stood face to face with Billy Ray. "C'mon Franklin. I can't snap it any better than that. Calm yourself down and think."

Billy Ray knew his teammate was right. It was a perfect snap. He just handled it wrong.

Coach Mabry bent over and grabbed his knees as the cat calls started from the home stands. The opposing fans just laughed.

Mayor Sawyer poured another shot of bourbon into his cup

but said nothing. He didn't need to. Enough Webber fans were already saying it for him. He was confident this farce was about to end.

"What happened?" Coach Mabry asked the center and Billy Ray.

"I handled it bad. It's my fault. It was a good snap."

"Don't make a fool of me, Franklin. I took a huge chance on you. Don't make me regret this the rest of my life."

"I won't, Coach." Dejected, Billy Ray walked to the bench with the other offensive starters and sat down beside them. Four players, two on either side of Billy Ray, got up and moved to another seat leaving Billy Ray by himself.

"Sorry," he said, with no one left to hear. Billy Ray was leaning over with his elbows on his knees and his head in his hands when he felt a solid thud beside him. He looked up and saw Noah, who then planted his arm firmly around Billy Ray's shoulder. "I don't need no more lectures."

"No lectures here. Just support." Noah patted Billy Ray on his head. "The game starts the next series. Forget about what happened. Just go out and do what you do best, man."

The players could not believe what they were seeing. Billy Ray Sawyer was encouraging Noah, the same guy who had gotten him injured, taken his position and ruined any chances of a scholarship.

Mayor Sawyer observed the same thing from the 25th row on the 50 yard line. He, too, could not believe his eyes. He began to seethe. His face grew redder with each second. His only cure was to have another drink of bourbon or to vent his anger through words. He chose the bourbon because five or six rednecks leaning over the fence continued to shout racial epithets toward Billy Ray and pretty much the same thing toward Noah.

Noah looked back at the rednecks hanging over the fence smoking their filterless cigarettes and all but one wearing sleeveless tee shirts. The remaining one was shirtless. Noah smiled, waved and called out, "Ya'll havin' fun?"

One redneck flipped his cigarette toward Billy Ray and started in with the racial epithets. They believed they all should go back to where they came from and that Coach Mabry would surely go to hell.

Another redneck worked up a mouthful of saliva and spit it six or so feet where it landed on Billy Ray's neck. The players watched. They didn't know what to do. On one hand they felt they needed to protect him especially since Billy Ray had. On the other, what would their parents, their friends think?

Noah watched as the players turned a blind eye. He pulled a handkerchief from his back pocket and handed it to Billy Ray.

"Thanks," Billy Ray said, rubbing the handkerchief over the thick blob on his neck.

Noah stood up, handkerchief in hand, and ambled over to the redneck who had spat on Billy Ray. "Hey."

"What the hell you doin' takin' up for that darkie, Billy Ray? Your daddy taught you better than that. What's gotten into you lately?"

Noah motioned for the redneck to come a little closer. Noah grabbed him with his arm and shoulder that was taped and with one firm tug, pulled him over the fence and onto the sideline where the players stood. The boy tried to get up, but

Noah pushed him back down, again with his supposedly injured arm.   With his other hand, Noah shoved the handkerchief into the redneck's mouth. "I think you lost this." With both arms, Noah picked him up by the back of his sleeveless tee shirt, hoisted him high and threw him back over the fence.

The play on the field continued, but the home crowd watched Billy Ray manhandle the spitter.   The team wasn't watching the action on the gridiron, they were watching the same show the home crowd was.   One of the players asked him about his shoulder.

"Yeah.   Adrenalin.   Still very sore."   Noah slung it around in a circle, pretending it hurt.

"Dang, imagine how far he can throw it when it heals up," one of the players observed.

Noah approached the other rednecks.   "C'mon guys.   Let us play some football."

They quickly dispersed.   The one redneck Noah manhandled told him his father would hear about this.

"I'm pretty sure he already knows."   Noah plunked himself down by Billy Ray again.

In the stands, Mayor Sawyer drank another shot.

"If I didn't know better I'd say you're beginning to like this," Billy Ray said, using a stray sock he'd found to continue wiping away spit from his neck that was no longer there.

"I could get used to it."

A roar sounded from the opposing fans.   Their team scored off Billy Ray's turnover.

Noah picked up Billy Ray's helmet from the ground and

handed it to him. "Go make somethin' happen. No excuses."
Noah walked to the ten other offensive starters. "Guys, this is
his team, now. Get behind him."

"You heard him guys!" the center shouted. "Let's do it this
time!"

After the fumbled snap, Billy Ray could do no wrong. He
led the offense with perfection and the team never looked back.
Billy Ray passed the opposition silly with five touchdown
passes, the longest a ninety-seven yard strike to Tyler Morgan.
He ran for two touchdowns himself, one a fifty yard run and the
other for seventy-five yards. He was on the mark for twenty-
three passes on twenty-seven attempts for 395 yards. The final
score was 56-7. Some jokesters in the crowd swore it was Billy
Ray posing as a colored. He ran like Billy Ray, passed like Billy
Ray. If only they knew. When the horn sounded, Billy Ray was
carried off the field on the shoulders of his teammates.

On the 25th row on the 50 yard line, Mayor Sawyer was
drunk. Not falling down drunk, but drunk enough. He
watched the celebration taking place on the field below. He
could bear it no more. Mary Edith had left earlier as the putrid
smell of bourbon made her sick to her stomach. Mayor Sawyer
staggered his way down the bleachers, shoving people out of
his way. He made it to the fence but was too drunk and too
chubby to pull himself over, though he tried hard. All night
long other fans did his talking for him. Now no one was saying
a word.

"Get that nigga' down from there! Get 'em down now! He
don't deserve what he's got. Get 'em down now!" Mayor
Sawyer shouted at the top of his lungs, turning his head around

searching for anyone who would listen and agree with him.

The team stopped at the sideline. They could hear his tirade.

"Who do you think you are?" he shouted even louder, slurring his speech. "This is all your fault. 'Cause a' you my boy is finished. Do you hear me, you no good nigga'? You're dead! You hear me boy? You're dead!"

Two deputy sheriffs, close buddies to the Mayor, tried to calm him down. Sawyer pushed them both away and cursed them. "Don't you see what's happenin' here? Don't you see it?" he shouted. "Are you all blind?"

The deputies tried again. Each gently grabbed an arm and tried to lead him away telling him he could take care of it later, but Mayor Sawyer wanted nothing to do with that. He jerked his arms violently away from their grasp and ran back to the fence cursing, shouting and pointing his chubby finger at the boy he had no idea was his son. The crowd behind him knew of the Mayor's feelings and opinions and many agreed with him, but they never imagined his anger boiling over to this degree.

Billy Ray still sat atop his shocked teammates shoulders. Noah was right in the midst of them. "Lemme' down guys. Lemme' down." His teammates gently placed Billy Ray on the ground. Billy Ray had seen his father angry many times in his young life but never like this. He began walking toward him.

"That's right you miserable, no good nigga'. C'mon over here where I can show you your rightful place."

Coach Mabry stretched his arm in front of Billy Ray to stop him from going any further as the deputies moved in once again to try and calm the Mayor.

"That's right, you coward. Just like the whole lot a' ya.

Always lettin' somebody else do your talkin' and fightin' for ya'."

Coach Mabry tried to keep his distance, but Mayor Sawyer edged closer. "Mayor. Ain't no reason for all this. I don't think that's you talkin."

"Now you callin' me a drunk, you pitiful no good excuse for a coach? How dare you let this happen here tonight! What gives you the right?" he continued to scream, saliva spewing from the corner of his mouth every time he opened it. "You're done here, Mabry. It's over. You've coached your last game. Don't bother showin' up for work Monday morning. Did you forget who I am? Did you forget who signs your paycheck? Did you forget everything, Mabry? Do you realize what you done tonight? We're the laughing stock of Alabama...of the South...hell, of the whole damn country!"

Suddenly, he caught the eye of Noah. "And *you*! *You're* the worst of the lot. My own son turned against me!" Noah took one step toward Mayor Sawyer, but Sawyer put his hand up.

"No! Stop, dammit! I don't know you no more. I got no idea who you are or what you've become but you ain't my son. I never knew you. You're dead to me! You hear me, boy? You are *dead* to me!"

"You don't mean that," Noah said, his heart aching for Billy Ray.

"I mean it with every ounce a' my soul and with every fiber of my being. You're dead to me, Billy Ray. You might as well be six feet in the ground 'cause ain't nothin' you can do to change what's happened." Sawyer straightened his jacket and turned to the deputies. "Gentlemen, your presence is not needed here any longer. I am leaving now. I'll leave it to you to handle these nigga' lovin' renegades."

The deputies followed Sawyer toward the exit to drive him home and to try to talk some sense into him. It would do no good. Sawyer did not want to hear any of it. In his mind, he was right and there was nothing anybody could say or do to change it.

The players remained frozen in place. Noah turned to face Billy Ray, whose stare was a thousand miles away.

"What do we do now, Coach?" a player asked from the center of the mass.

Coach Mabry thought for a minute. "I tell you what you do. Enjoy tonight. Celebrate the win like you would any other and come back Monday afternoon ready for practice. This was a good effort, men, and I'm not going to let it be spoiled. You deserve this night. Don't let ignorance take it away."

The team moved in mass toward the locker room, all except Billy Ray and Noah. Coach Mabry moved with the team but noticed Billy Ray and Noah standing together, alone. "Sawyer. You alright son?"

"I'm fine Coach. I'll be fine," Noah said.

"If you need a place to stay, you know where I live. Doesn't matter what time it is. Alright?"

"Yes sir. Thanks, Coach."

Mabry started to turn but couldn't help but notice the blank stare across the face of his new quarterback. "Franklin. You alright, son?"

Billy Ray did not respond.

"Franklin. Is everything okay"

Noah nudged Billy Ray with his elbow.

Billy Ray looked at Noah. Everything the coach said went in one ear and out the other. "Yeah."

"Coach was talkin' to ya'."

"Oh sorry, Coach."

"Just makin' sure you're alright. This should be a happy night for you. You look like you lost your last friend." Mabry put his arm around Billy Ray. "You can't let what he said bring you down. Words hurt. They hurt awful bad. But in the end, they can make you a better person." The coach faced Billy Ray and put both his hands on his shoulder pads. "You ever heard that expression, whatever doesn't kill you only makes you stronger?"

"Yes sir."

"You got an opportunity son, to grow stronger and make things better. You got a unique gift of athleticism from God. A unique gift indeed. Scares me to think it could've been overlooked just because of your skin color. Take it. Grow it. Make it mean something. Let it do your talking for you. And let it make you stronger. Don't you dare let what happened here take you down one notch. You understand?"

Billy Ray heard him. What his father had said only moments earlier shattered him. His blank stare remained. "Yes, sir. I do."

"Okay. You boys go celebrate this win. With your talent and Billy Ray's help, I got a few more plays I've drawn up in my head I'd like to go over on Monday." Coach Mabry ran quickly to join the team filtering into the locker room underneath the stadium.

Billy Ray sauntered over to the bench and threw himself onto it. Noah followed four or five steps behind but remained standing.

"You okay?" Noah asked.

"No. I'm not okay."

"I know what he said hurt. I know it hurt, Billy Ray. But you gotta know it was the alcohol talkin' and not him."

"That's where you're wrong, Noah. That ain't the alcohol talkin'. That's him talkin'. One hundred percent. The only thing the alcohol does is embolden him. He means every word he says. The sooner you understand that the better. I can never go home no matter if this craziness ends or not and you best not go home either. I've seen what he's capable of. I know what he can do."

"I think his bark is worse than his bite."

Billy Ray glared at Noah. "This ain't a joke, man. You've known him for a month, maybe a month and a half. I've known him all my life. You don't want to go up against him, Noah. He don't like losin'. He'll win every time and he'll do whatever he has to win and he don't care who he steps on along the way." Billy Ray stood and picked up his helmet from the grass. "You best be on your guard, Noah. Trust me on this one. We both best be on our guard." He put on his helmet just in case any angry fans remained that wanted to pelt him with ice and then headed toward the locker room.

Noah took a seat on the bench and wondered silently, if maybe this wasn't God's doing at all. Maybe it had nothing to do with God. He felt bad for thinking this way. His mother had always told him God had a hand in everything. But he tried to make sense of this and what possible purpose there was for something so hurtful. But one thing kept ringing inside his head. Maybe Billy Ray had it right. No God of his, no God of peace would ever bring this upon him.

~ 17 ~

Billy Ray's body bumped in rhythm with the school bus as its worn out shocks felt every divot in the road. He had ridden it enough times now to anticipate every bounce as it duplicated each morning's ride down the dirt roads of his neighborhood to the thinly wearing pavement of the county highways. He laughed to himself that if he ever got out of this predicament, he would bring the matter of failing roads up to his father. He wondered if being a community organizer was in his future because a future in football sure seemed to be questionable at this point. Sure, he'd had a great game three nights ago, but as far as he knew and the last time he paid attention, no colleges were recruiting black quarterbacks. And if this situation ever changed back to the way it was, he wasn't the one having a great season. The phone calls and letters from coaches to Billy Ray had dried up, and he didn't expect it to pick up any time soon.

The bus pulled up to the curb in front of the main building to let the black students out. From the corner of his eye, Billy Ray saw Noah leaning against his pickup truck with his arms folded. He couldn't tell, but it appeared Noah was waiting on him. Billy Ray jumped from the second stair of the bus door to the curb and crossed back in front of the bus and half ran, half walked to the parking lot where Noah stood.

Billy Ray got to within ten or fifteen feet of Noah and stopped. "Everything alright?"

"Yeah. Why?"

"You just kinda looked funny," Billy Ray said, edging a little closer. "You look well rested. You sure everything's alright?"

"I took Coach up on his offer. Mattress is kinda hard, and I hate to tell you this. But Coach's wife is a better cook than my mama. Don't tell her I said so."

"That's not what you stood out here to tell me is it?"

"No." Noah flashed a sheepish grin.

"Un-uh. Un-uh," Billy Ray mumbled while shaking his head from side to side. "Whatever it is just get it outta your head right now. Right now you're battin' zero, and you got two strikes against ya'."

"You don't even know what I'm gonna say," Noah said, uncrossing his arms.

"Don't care," Billy Ray responded quickly. "Whatever it is, it ain't gonna work, it ain't no good and will probably just get me in more trouble. So whatever it is you're thinkin', just stop."

"Don't 'cha even wanna hear?"

"No. To be honest with you, I don't." Billy Ray turned and started to walk back toward the school.

Noah rushed to catch up and grabbed Billy Ray's shoulder. "Too bad. You're gonna hear it anyway."

Billy Ray stopped immediately and jerked his shoulder away from Noah's grip. "Look. You don't get it, do ya? You think this is all a big joke. You're up there livin' all high and mighty, drivin' my truck, wearin' my clothes and up until a few days ago livin' in my house, sleepin' in my bed and eatin' my food. You're livin' the high life while I'm sharin' one bowlful of fried potatoes with five people and sleepin' on a worn out mattress that should have been thrown out years ago. You're out there runnin' around like this is some...some...some big joke and enjoying every minute of it. You've taken my identity and made it your own personal playground of social conscience."

Noah backed away. "Is having a social conscience wrong?"

"It's wrong cause your doin' it with my skin and not your own."

"Nobody would listen if I did it," Noah said almost apologetically.

"Maybe I don't want 'em to listen. That's the point, Noah! Don't you understand it? Like it or not, we come from different sides of the track and it don't matter what you think, say or do. Things ain't gonna change."

"Maybe we can start it."

"No!" Billy Ray shouted loud enough for the students milling outside the main school building to hear. Billy Ray and Noah looked at the students and half waved to let them know they were alright. "We? We? Whoever said I wanted anything to do with it? Whoever said I wanted anything to do with your change? You think just because this happened that I think different than I did before? Is that what you're thinkin'? Is it? I don't care what it is you're thinkin' or whatever stupid plan you have up your sleeve. It ain't gonna work and the sooner you learn that the better off you...and me'll be. You gotta leave it alone, Noah. Just leave it alone, man. We'll all be better off in the long run."

"I think you do think different. You just ain't realized it yet. But, hey, I didn't mean to upset you, man."

"That's another thing. You come off actin' like you got a social conscience and it's all a black thing...that...that only your people are affected. You got no idea, man!" Billy Ray emphasized his point by pushing his finger into Noah's chest. "You got no idea that there's poor whites strugglin' just as much." Billy Ray straightened the backpack now falling at an odd angle down his back. He turned to leave then turned back to Noah. "Look, I'll be the first to admit I've had a good life. I've never wanted for nuthin'. I'm one of the lucky ones. But it's not all about you, Noah. This ain't a black thing and it ain't a white thing. You come talk to me about change when you're willin' to admit that it ain't just your people that suffer." Billy Ray turned and started walking away.

"I know about your uncle, Billy Ray."

Billy Ray stopped dead in his tracks.

"I know what your daddy done to 'em. I know what happened. What your daddy did."

Billy Ray turned to Noah.

"I know your uncle's dead 'cause a' your father, Billy Ray."

"They never proved that."

"Might not a proved it but everybody knows what happened. Your daddy was just able to wash his hands of it. And you know that's the God's honest truth."

"Why would you even bring somethin' up like that?"

"Cause I know what it did to your aunt and cousin over in Rock County. I know that's who you're talkin' 'bout Billy Ray. I know they're the ones you're talkin' about sufferin'."

Eight years earlier, Joshua's brother Daniel tried to change the world for the better. Daniel involved himself deeply in cases of social injustice whether it was against minorities, religion or any other social cause. Mayor Sawyer tried many times to convince his brother that his efforts were worthless and that he was wasting his time and turning his son into a radical zealot. Neither did it help Mayor Sawyer's chances for re-election or his reputation for being a hard-liner in the old Alabama ways.

Joshua tolerated his brother's views for a time until he started speaking to newspapers, preachers, the FBI and anybody that would listen about all of the goings-on in Webber County. This didn't sit well with Joshua. One dreadful night, Daniel appeared at a Klan rally screaming and yelling about how their evil deeds would send them straight to hell. That was the last night anyone saw Daniel alive. His decomposed body was found several weeks later in a landfill two counties away. Nobody was ever charged or arrested. No trial ever held. The local Sheriff conducted an investigation which was laughable if anyone ever took time to read the file. The FBI investigated for a civil rights violation but when nobody talked, no evidence was found to substantiate anything. The investigation was closed.

Honest people speculated about what they thought happened and how Joshua Sawyer killed or had his own brother killed. But there was no proof. Over time the story faded and it was never mentioned again. Billy Ray's aunt had no skills and his cousin was only eleven years old at the time. Joshua did not have one ounce of sympathy. His brother had brought this on himself and his family. Out of spite, Joshua forced the bank to foreclose on the house. His sister-in-law had to go and live in Rock County with her widowed sister who was dirt poor and lived in a dilapidated shack smaller than Noah's. Billy Ray would have liked to have known his cousin better as they were about the same age. They had actually been the best of friends when they were little. But Joshua would have none of it. He kept them apart and refused to have anything to do with his brother's family. Joshua strictly forbade any contact. The last time Billy Ray saw or spoke to his cousin was a couple of days before his uncle was killed. The only thing Billy Ray knew was his father would not allow them to be friends, much less family. Whenever he would ask about his cousin, Mayor Sawyer always changed the subject.

Billy Ray stood silent.

"Your Aunt Bess and your cousin Jake. I'm sure they're good people, Billy Ray. They ain't deservin' of what happened. Just like my family ain't deservin' of our lot." Noah slowly approached his awkward friend. "You can stand there and say nuthin'. Just keep your mouth shut. Or you can do somethin' about it. Choice is yours, man. You want me to back off, I will. Your call."

Billy Ray stared at Noah and for once in his life had nothing to say. He crept slowly to his truck, leaned on it and buried his face into his cupped hands. Noah could hear him crying.

Noah watched for a moment, unsure of what to say or do. This is one emotion he didn't know Billy Ray possessed. Noah turned and saw many of the students, black and white alike, staring at them from a distance. He slowly approached Billy

Ray and softly placed his hand on his shoulder. "Didn't mean no harm, Billy Ray."

The startled students couldn't believe their eyes. Billy Ray Sawyer, the white kid who had bullied so many black kids since school began, was now giving comfort to the same boy he tried to kill only weeks earlier.

Billy Ray straightened himself and wiped his eyes with the back of his hand. "No, man. It's not you." Billy Ray leaned back against his truck and wiped his tears again. "I gotta ask you a question."

Noah nodded.

"I know you may not think it, but I do believe in God. My daddy may've taught me a lot of bad things, but he did teach me about God. Least ways my momma did."

"I believe you."

Billy Ray clinched his eyes as tightly closed as he could.

"What is it, Billy Ray?"

Billy Ray sighed and looked toward the sky. He placed his intertwined fingers atop his head. He then stared boldly into Noah's eyes. "Do you think it's a sin to know somebody done wrong and not say somethin' about it? Does God forgive ya' for somethin' like that?"

"I've always been taught that He will, if you ask."

Billy Ray turned to face his truck. He rested his forehead in his cupped hands.

"Did you do somethin', Billy Ray?"

"I guess I done plenty a' stuff I ain't proud of, but I ain't talkin' about me."

"Is this about your daddy?"

Billy Ray nodded his head.

"What'd he do, Billy Ray?"

Billy Ray breathed hard and thought long. "I was there the night he killed my uncle. I reckon with all the stuff he's drilled into my heart and soul over the years I 'bout forgot about it. But that don't change the fact a' what he done." Billy Ray turned to face Noah. "I watched as he shot his own brother point blank in the head and then stuffed him in somebody's trunk. I was nine, maybe ten years old, and tried my best to forget. But now it seems like yesterday," Billy Ray quietly explained, his eyes staring off in the distance. "He shot him like a pig, Noah. I can see it plain as day. His own brother. Shot him like an animal." Billy Ray shook his head and looked skyward. "I can still remember what he said that night." Billy Ray paused and had a faraway look. "He looked me right in the eye and laughed. He *laughed*! Can you believe that? Murdered his own brother and laughed about it. Then he leaned over to where he was eye to eye with me. I'll never forget that look in his eye. He stared right into my eyes and said, 'Sometimes we got to take out the trash, Billy Ray. Sometimes we got to take out the trash'".

Noah leaned his back against the truck next to Billy Ray. "Wow."

"You think God can forgive me for what I done?"

"You didn't do nothin' wrong, Billy Ray. You were just a little kid."

"I coulda' said somethin'."

"You were just a kid, Billy Ray. And it was your father. Probably scared outta your mind. I don't think God would condemn nobody under those circumstances."

"I don't think God'll ever forgive me. I coulda' said somethin'. I coulda' done what was right and I didn't. I stayed quiet and over time started feelin' the same way he did. Having the same thoughts."

"It ain't too late, Billy Ray. You can make things right with yourself. You can make it right with God."

"I can't turn him in. As bad as some of the things he's done, he's my daddy. I couldn't ever do that."

"Nobody can tell you what to do, Billy Ray. Your daddy done cast his lot with the Almighty. One way or the other, he'll pay for what he done."

"Whattaya' mean?"

"If'n the law don't ever get 'em, he'll have to account for what he done to God."

"So you think God understands if I didn't say nuthin'?"

"I ain't speakin' for God, Billy Ray. What you do or don't do is between you and him. I ain't got no say-so one way or the other. You gotta search your own heart and know what's right."

Billy Ray leaned on the truck, peered skyward and angrily shouted. "Whattaya' want me to do, God? You want me to betray my own father?"

"He ain't gonna give you the answer you wanna hear. You shouldn't try and justify what your daddy done by tryin' to make God the guilty one."

"Ain't tryin' to make God guilty. I know what's right and I shoulda' done somethin' about it the night it happened. But I can't turn on my own flesh and blood. God may send me straight to hell for what I done, but I just can't betray my own father."

"That's tween you and God, Billy Ray. You gotta live with whatever choice you make."

Billy Ray slid his back down his truck and squatted beside the back wheel, his face buried in his hands. "Look. I know I'm wrong. You don't gotta go and make it worse." He removed his hands from his eyes. "What would you do if it was your father?"

"Don't matter what I'd do."

"That's not an answer, Noah. I wanna know what you'd do."

Noah stared at Billy Ray then joined him by squatting beside him. "I don't know, Billy Ray. Honest to God, I don't know what I'd do. But whatever choice I made, I reckon I'd have to ask for forgiveness."

A barely noticeable smile formed across Billy Ray's face.

Noah smiled back. "That way you're covered!"

Billy Ray went from squatting to sitting. Noah followed suit.

"Look, Billy Ray. I don't know what you plan to do. Like I said, that's your business and I ain't gonna get involved in it."

Billy Ray glanced at Noah and gave him a puzzled look. "You're not?"

"Starting right now! Starting right now, I ain't gonna say another word about it. It's your call. Only you know what you should do. But I think there's something you and me and anybody else brave enough to join in can do that is the right thing and if nothin' else, it might help you ease your mind of what happened that night."

Billy Ray smiled and shook his head. "Oh man, here we go. I don't know what you're about to get me involved in but I got a feelin' it ain't gonna put me, or you, on good footin' with my daddy." Billy Ray leaned forward and wiped his eyes one last time as the school bell rang from a distance signifying first period started in ten minutes.

"You okay, Billy Ray?"

"I'm fine, Noah. I'll be fine. You just worry 'bout yourself and don't get me killed in the process." Both stood, shifted their backpacks and ambled toward the school building.

"My eyes red?" Billy Ray asked.

"You're good."

In the lobby, Billy Ray was mobbed by the throng of students that couldn't wait to congratulate him on his outstanding play in Friday night's football game. Even though he knew it was Noah they were heaping their praise upon, it still felt great. It was the same warm feeling he'd felt so many Monday mornings past. He soaked it all in and basked in the glory while Noah stood back to let him enjoy the moment. And what made it even better for his fellow students was to see the two of them, Billy Ray and Noah, together, smiling, friends. Even Billy Ray's chums were slapping him on the back. Maybe some change had come after all.

Red and Davy Lee saw the commotion and made their way around the crowd to Noah. "You okay with this, Billy Ray?" Red asked.

Noah smiled and put his arm around Red's shoulder. "Yeah, Red. I'm okay with it. Everything's good."

~ 18 ~

Noah grabbed a sandwich and chips from the cafeteria and raced outside to find Billy Ray by himself at his usual place under a huge oak tree that had lost most of its amber leaves from the rapidly fading autumn. Soon after the change had occurred, Billy Ray found this place, a sort of respite, to get away from everything that was happening.

"Thought I'd find you here." Noah said, sitting down, opening his chips.

"Didn't have to look very far, did you?"

Noah laughed. "Yeah. You've become very predictable."

Billy Ray brought out a piece of Emma's cornbread. "Piece of cornbread?" Noah loved his momma's cornbread, and took a piece. He offered Billy Ray half of his sandwich, which he gladly took. "So out with it. What you got up that sleeve of yours that's gonna get us both arrested or killed?"

"Neither, man. You gotta think positive. Even your daddy can't get upset at this."

"Oh, trust me. It don't matter what you got cooked up. He'll find a way to be upset."

"It's all about community, Billy Ray. We gotta unite the community. Both sides. Black and white, rich and poor."

Billy Ray forced a chuckle. "Are you serious? Are you forgetting it's 1965? It ain't gonna work, Noah." Billy Ray pitched a piece of cornbread to a patiently waiting sparrow. "I know you got good intentions and all but you're livin' in a dream. There is absolutely nuthin' you can do that's gonna unite anybody in this town or anywhere in this state."

"Oh ye of little faith," Noah smiled. "Nobody said we're gonna convince everybody everywhere. But we start small, man. We start small and go from there."

"Look. I ain't promisin' nuthin'. I gotta be perfectly honest. I don't think anythin' you got planned is gonna work. People just ain't ready for it. Hell, I don't know if I am ready for it, and you're talkin' 'bout a whole community."

"I've already got most of the student body on board. Even Red and Davy Lee ."

"Well hell fire! Red and Davy Lee? It's a sure fire success right there," Billy Ray reacted facetiously. "Fine. Let's hear it."

"I think you're gonna like it, Billy Ray, I really do. Tell me what you think of this. We've picked two homes to paint, do some routine maintenance and some minor repairs. So far we got about sixty or so students, split pretty much down the middle black and white, that are gonna help out. We chose homes in pretty much the poorest of the poor areas to do the work."

"Okay so far. Definitely good for the community I guess. Maybe it could work," Billy Ray said slightly pessimistic. "Whose homes you gonna do?"

Noah looked away and rubbed the back of his head. He glanced at Billy Ray with a sheepish smile then looked away again.

Billy Ray paused and laughed. "Oh, I get it. Well ain't that just convenient as hell. Organize this little kumbaya and get your home all re-done in the process. I gotta say man, nicely done. Nicely done. But not exactly what I'd call community spirit."

"It wasn't my call, and it ain't what you think. Billy Ray, you gotta understand. This ain't about me. I was against fixin' my folk's house because of what it would look like, but every student involved refused to join unless it was one of the homes we did. You've lived there. You know how bad it is."

"I reckon. Who's the lucky contestant for the second makeover. Hey! I got a great idea. Let's do my folk's mansion. We can make it a clean sweep! No one will suspect a thing!"

"Your aunt and cousin over in Rock County."

Billy Ray lost his smile and his sarcasm.

"Cat got your tongue?"

"I..I..I reckon I don't know quite what to say."

"That's a first. You don't gotta say nuthin'. Just join us." Noah patted Billy Ray's knee. "It's like you said, man. It ain't a black and white thing. It's a people thing, Billy Ray. It's takin' care of people no matter who they are. So. You in?"

Billy Ray nodded. "Yeah. Count me in."

Noah stood to leave. "I'm gonna start passin' the word."

"How you plan on payin' for all this?" Billy Ray asked.

Noah placed his hands on his hips and looked away. "Yeah. Uhhh. I've kinda been meanin' to talk with you about that. Inasmuch as I've been you for the last little while, I took the liberty of opening up your bank statement that came in the mail last week. Man, must be nice to have your own personal bank account."

"Wait a minute. You opened up my bank statement? That's

illegal man. It's a federal crime! You know you can't open up mail that don't belong to you!"

"With all due respect Billy Ray, until the Good Lord says different, I am you. And from what I saw in your statement, you can afford to buy paint, paint brushes and all the equipment we need to make this work and hardly make a dent in your account."

"Still don't make it right."

"So you want me to call everything off 'cause you got your feelins' hurt?"

"No. Just feelin' a little violated. That's all. I'll get over it. What else you know about me? Let's get it all out in the open."

"That's all man. I swear. You've gotten a couple a letters that are pretty obviously from girls. There's even one from Miss Becky Lay! Got perfume sprayed on it. I left 'em alone. Thought that was best. Also thought it best not to give 'em to you in your present state and all."

"Yeah. Well I appreciate you decidin' what's best for me."

"Don't mind at all."

"That was sarcasm, Noah. Bring me the letters. 'Specially the one from Becky."

"You'll have 'em tomorrow." Noah started to walk away.

"Hey, Noah."

"Yeah," Noah answered without turning around.

"I think it's a good thing you're doin'."

Noah turned to Billy Ray. "We, Billy Ray. It's a good thing we're doin'."

Billy Ray nodded. "I reckon."

~ 19 ~

Sixty-five teenagers assembled in the school parking lot on a chilly Saturday morning in late autumn. Those that didn't have a ride were cheerfully picked up by someone who did. Noah was the last to drive up in Billy Ray's pickup truck that was loaded full with paint and enough supplies to paint a small neighborhood. The sky was clear and the weather report promised it would warm up. Noah took charge passing out scrapers, buckets, rags, brushes and cans of paint. Noah would be in charge of the team going to his home and Billy Ray was in charge of the team going to his aunt's home.

"Before we break away, lemme' just say a couple a' things," Noah said, jumping into the now empty bed of Billy Ray's truck. "You guys didn't have to come today. You did this on your own. That says a lot about your character, your grit and your spirit. We may not change one mind or one person by what we're doin' but our actions will be heard by many. And that does mean somethin'. Be proud of what we're doin' today and don't let nobody tell you different."

Noah and his team piled into a handful of cars and trucks and Billy Ray and his team did likewise. Both teams headed in opposite directions but with the same goal.

Emma stood at her kitchen window washing the dishes when she noticed the dust from the road rising high into the air several hundred feet away. She called James in and both wondered aloud what was happening. Dust in the air usually meant the police were after somebody. James and Emma watched from the kitchen window as at least ten cars or trucks drove into their dirt and gravel covered driveway. Over thirty teenagers, black and white, poured quickly out.

"Oh my," Emma said, backing away slightly from the window, not sure of what was happening.

In one bound, Noah bolted over the creaky steps and onto the time worn porch.

"It's the Sawyer boy," James said. "This ain't good. This ain't good at all."

Adam and Moses were awakened by the commotion and stumbled into the kitchen.

"What's goin' on out there," Moses asked.

"Don't rightly know son, but go get my shotgun right now."

Adam rubbed his eyes and saw Billy Ray approaching the door. He knew it was Noah. "You ain't gonna need your shotgun daddy. Everything's okay."

Noah knocked on the door.

"Whatchu' talkin' bout everything's okay. That boy ain't nuthin' but trouble and that's all he's ever been. Get my gun."

"No!" Adam shouted. "Trust me, daddy. You ain't gonna need your gun."

"Pray tell why?"

Noah knocked louder. "Mrs. Franklin. Mr. Franklin. I don't mean you no harm," Noah announced from outside the door, resisting the desire to throw his arms around the two of them. "As you can probably see, we came to help out." Noah motioned to his classmates pulling paint and all the other supplies from the truck. "We wanna' make things better. We thought this was a good place to start. I promise we're here to help. You can open the door."

James glanced at Emma who was unsure of all of this. James looked out the kitchen window at the sky. "I don't see no pigs up there."

Moses looked at his father like he was crazy. "What?" Moses looked skyward. "What?"

"Nothing son," James said. "I'll explain some other time."

Noah knocked one more time. This time Emma answered.

"Hey, Mrs. Franklin."

"Billy Ray." Emma nodded, still unsure.

"With your permission, me and some of my classmates would like to give your house a fresh coat of paint and maybe do some minor repairs that Mr. Franklin hasn't gotten around to quite yet."

Emma turned to James and smiled.

James rolled his eyes. "I'm a busy man."

"No disrespect, sir."

James stared at Noah but saw Billy Ray.

"James," Emma prodded.

"None taken, son. None taken."

"Some of us from school kinda got together and decided this was maybe something we could do to bring change, maybe spark some thought. You should know that Noah is on his way to another house to do the same."

"I knew that boy was up earlier than normal for a Saturday," James added.

"So it's okay if we get started?" Noah asked.

Emma looked at James for his approval, not that it mattered. Emma was going to let these kids fix up her house whether James liked it or not. James nodded. Emma turned back to Noah, with a hand pressed against her chest. "You kids go right ahead. We are very grateful."

"Yes, ma'am." Noah noticed Adam and Moses in the background. "Hey, Adam, Moses."

Adam and Moses nodded then stuttered. "Hey...Billy...Ray, how's it goin'?" in anything but unison.

Puzzled, James and Emma looked at both boys. Moses and Adam looked at each other, both waiting for the other to say something. "He's...changed," Adam said before he could think of anything better to say. "I'm gonna...go back to bed."

"I think maybe you both should get your paintin' clothes on and help. No children of mine will laze away the day in bed while others do work for you. Get on out there!" James stated emphatically.

"I guess we'll get to workin'." Noah started down the steps.

"Billy Ray?" Emma stopped him

Noah turned. "Yes, ma'am?"

Emma walked out onto the porch and hugged him. "Thank you. Thank you so much. You have no idea what this means to me." Noah returned the hug and hoped she wouldn't notice that he didn't let go right away. How he missed her hugs! Emma released her grip on Noah and addressed the rest of the students. "Thank you all so much. God will bless each and every one of you for what you're doing."

A county away, Billy Ray knocked on the front door of his aunt's home that was in far worse condition than Emma and James' home. He was nervous, and guilt-ridden about seeing his aunt and cousin after all these years. The other students, both black and white, unloaded their supplies.

A tired and ragged woman, who looked to be in her late sixties but in reality was in her forties, answered the door.

"Aunt Bess?" Billy Ray said, forgetting he now looked like Noah Franklin.

"'Scuse me? Do I know you?" Aunt Bess scoured the yard, or what yard there was, and wondered aloud what was going on.

"I'm sorry. I'm a friend of your nephew Billy Ray's. He's talked so much about you and Jake I feel I know you. And these are a few of my friends from school. We wanted to come by and put a fresh coat of paint on the house and maybe do some minor repairs."

Bewildered, Aunt Bess stared at Billy Ray. "Scuse me? Go back. You said you were a friend of Billy Ray's?"

"Yes, ma'am."

"Billy Ray Sawyer?"

"Yes, ma'am."

"Billy Ray Sawyer. Son of Joshua Sawyer?"

"Yes, ma'am."

"Mayor Sawyer?"

"Yes, ma'am."

"But you're a negro."

It was a hard thing for Billy Ray to say, but he managed a "Yes, ma'am. I am that."

"And you're a friend of Billy Ray's?"

"Yes, ma'am."

Aunt Bess shook her head. "I've either died and gone to heaven or the Good Lord has worked a miracle."

"Well, you ain't dead." Billy Ray smiled.

"That I'm not." Aunt Bess looked out at the busy kids preparing to work. "What is it again you kids are up to?"

"We're just trying to do some good, you know. Show the community we can come together, work together for good."

"You boys and girls would make Jake's daddy very proud."

"If it's alright, we'll get started."

"You kids are alright. God bless you. You let me know if you need anything."

"There is one thing," Noah said. "Is Jake here? I'd like to meet him. I feel kinda like he's my cousin, too."

"Oh honey. I guess you didn't know. I reckon Joshua kept them apart so Billy Ray may not have known either. Reckon it's goin' on seven, eight years now. Jake disappeared the same night Jake's dad did. Jake went with his father that night. Neither one of 'em come back. I know what happened to my husband, and I try not to think about what may've happened to Jake. The Christian in me wants to believe somebody took him, but I know deep down that probably didn't happen. I just don't wanna believe that even the most evil person in the world is capable of doing to a child what they did to my husband. He was just an innocent little boy, that's all. The FBI looked for him, but he never turned up. I pray for him every night to come back, but I know he won't."

Billy Ray stood in stunned silence. The pit in his belly made him nauseous. He never saw Jake at the Klan rally that night, but knew it didn't mean he wasn't there. Billy Ray searched for the right words but he couldn't think of any. "I'm very sorry, ma'am. I didn't know and I'm sure Billy Ray didn't know either."

"That's okay, young man," Aunt Bess touched Billy Ray's shoulder. "What is your name?"

"Noah, ma'am. Noah Franklin."

"Well, Noah, I'm just so happy Billy Ray has a friend like you. He's a good boy. Had the sweetest heart when he was a little boy. And I'm so happy he hasn't followed in his father's footsteps. I forgave Billy Ray's father a long time ago for what he did. It's the only way. If we can't forgive, we're no better than the ones needin' the forgivin'."

"Yes, ma'am." Billy Ray thought about what his aunt said. She eased his guilt just a bit. "You're right, you know? I reckon I've been on both sides, the needin' forgivin' side more than the other."

"You seem like a nice boy, Noah. We all need forgivin' every now and then. Some more than others, but I'm sure you seen plenty a' bad in this old world that it's hard to forgive others for."

"Maybe. I reckon."

"Listen to me goin' off like that. I'm keepin' you and your friends from your mission. You kids are a ray of sunshine to this old lady! Thank you so much for doing this."

"Yes, ma'am." Billy Ray walked slowly down the old, worn out steps. He couldn't stop thinking about Jake and what probably happened on that fateful night.

The kids at both places went to work scraping old peeling paint from the worn out siding, porches and window framing. The flying bits of paint closely resembled an early snowfall. Workers' voices mixed with those of residents who gathered in the dusty streets wondering what was going on. Within an hour at both sites, neighbors were offering lemonade and cookies to the teenage work force who eagerly accepted the offers. When noon rolled around, Emma and Aunt Bess brought out sandwiches to the tired but resilient workers. More luncheon supplies were brought by neighbors and some of the students' parents who wanted to do their part. In a scene reminiscent of the loaves and fishes story in the Bible, the food just kept coming until everyone had their fill.

By early afternoon the wood was prepared and the paint was pulled out and ready to be slapped on both houses. Both Emma and Aunt Bess felt like teenagers themselves when they saw the gallons of paint ready for the exterior of their respective homes.

The kids worked harder than they had in their entire lives. The satisfaction was more than they could have dreamed possible. The kids were transforming dull lifeless houses into shining beacons. They were transforming, at least for a day, depressed lives into hopeful ones.

Less than an hour after the painting started, someone noticed a cloud of dust in the distance. As the car got closer, Noah knew who it was. Noah had laughed inside every time he watched Mayor Sawyer squeeze his chubby body into the small driver's seat. But Noah wasn't laughing this time. Everyone stopped their painting and prepared for the worst as they watched the red Mustang approach.

Mayor Sawyer slammed on his brakes and fishtailed into the dirt and gravel driveway. James, Emma, Moses and Adam stepped out on the porch. Noah stood frozen by the decrepit steps leading from the porch.

"Billy Ray," Emma started.

Noah motioned for her to stop. "It's alright. Everything's fine. He's probably just lookin' for me."

Mayor Sawyer flung open the door and tried to get out of the car quickly to show authority, but his large posterior made it difficult. A few students snickered but hushed quickly when they realized how angry he was. The Mayor's face was beet red and he was in no mood for frivolity. He finally extricated himself from the car seat and slammed the door behind him. He looked around at all the activity then for Billy Ray.

"Billy Ray!" he screamed at the top of his lungs. "I know you're here, boy! Get out here now and don't make me come find you!"

"Ain't no call for this, Mayor," James started.

"You stay out of this, Franklin. This got nuthin' to do with you. This is between me and that pathetic excuse for a son I have."

"That boy you call a pathetic excuse is doin' the Lord's work, Mayor. It's a bad thing to call him out like that," Emma chimed in.

"With all due respect, Emma, I don't need you to tell me anything about my boy when yours is the one causin' all the problems we're havin' right now."

Emma took a step toward the stairs, but James grabbed her arm before she could go any further. "Not a good move, woman," James said quietly.

Mayor Sawyer chuckled and halfway sat down on the hood of his car. "You're smarter than I gave you credit for Franklin. Keep that woman under control or she..."

"Or she what?" Noah stepped into the open where Mayor Sawyer could see him.

Mayor Sawyer looked around to where Noah was standing. "Who you hidin' behind this time, son?"

"Ain't hidin' behind nobody. What is it you want?"

"Get over here, Billy Ray!" the Mayor shouted.

Noah stood his ground.

"Get over here now, or I'll have everyone in this...this...so called mission arrested, includin' your adopted family there." Mayor Sawyer motioned toward the Franklins still standing on the front porch.

"Arrested! For what? We ain't done nuthin' wrong. You can't arrest us," Noah argued, his arms flailing.

"Mayor, all the kids was doin' was paintin' the house, and this is my property," said James.

"Allow me to correct you on that Franklin. Unless I'm sadly mistaken, you don't own this property. You don't own it at all. But by all means, tell me if I'm wrong."

"Well, sir, we rent this property from the county. But it's ours all the same."

"Ahhh. Stop. Let me stop you right there." Mayor Sawyer came off the car and started walking toward the front porch. "That's where you're dead wrong, if I heard you correctly, and I did hear you correctly. You rent this property from the county and might I add at quite a bargain price. That means you do not own it and therefore have no right whatsoever to make any renovations. Therefore, you and all these students here are in violation of county codes and ordinances and I have every right to haul every last one of ya' in. But I certainly don't want to have to do that." Mayor Sawyer stopped and was nose to nose with Noah. "You want me to call the Sheriff out here, Billy Ray? Huh? You want me to call the Sheriff and have him arrest all your friends...and you of course. You'll get to go along with 'em too. Wouldn't be fair for all your friends to spend the night in the pokey while you stayed free now would it?"

"Don't do it, Billy Ray. He can't arrest us and he knows it." Red climbed down off the ladder from where he was painting.

Mayor Sawyer laughed, shook his head and rubbed his eyebrows. "Red, Red, Red. Don't you test me, boy. If every red hair on that boney head a' yours had a smart gene, your IQ would still be the lowest in Webber County. This ain't somethin' you wanna be pokin' your nose into. By the way, does your daddy know you're here? Maybe I should call him."

Red glanced at Noah.

"Don't worry about it, Red. I can handle this," Noah assured him.

"Handle it?" Mayor Sawyer smirked. "Lemme' tell you how you're gonna handle it, Billy Ray. You're gonna drop the paintbrush and all the touchy feely cry me a river emotions with all these radical, zealot troublemakers you call friends. Everybody's gonna disperse like good little indians. Then you're gonna get in that car and we're gonna drive over to Rock County and do it all over again."

"And if we don't?"

Mayor Sawyer chuckled and looked over his shoulder. "There's ten patrol cars sittin' at the end of the road down yonder just waitin' on my call."

"I ain't the smartest tool in the shed, but I don't believe you can arrest us on somethin' as simple as a code or ordinance violation," Noah said.

"You tell 'em, Billy Ray!" shouted a voice from somewhere within the crowd.

Mayor Sawyer shook his head. "You know, son? You might be right about that. But seein' as how I don't know what other violations might have occurred here today, I don't wanna take any chances on anyone goin' free if some criminal violation has occurred on county property that I am not aware of. Like I always say. It's better to be safe than sorry. I'm sure it won't take the Sheriff more than forty-eight hours to figure out what violations may or may not have occurred. Question is, are you willing to sacrifice all your friends' freedom for your bonehead decision. So the choice is simple. Drop your paint brushes and leave here free. Or buck my authority and go to jail. Either way, what you're doin' here is over."

Noah observed his classmates defiant expressions. None wanted to leave.

Noah looked directly into Sawyer's eyes. "Go on and call 'em." Noah called his bluff, hoping he was right and Mayor Sawyer would have accomplished nothing but embarrassing himself.

Sawyer glared at Noah. "Fine. Have it your way." He turned and walked back to his car, reached in and pulled out a two way radio. "This is Sawyer. Come get 'em."

In the distance, the screeching of tires in the gravel was audible and the cloud of dust painfully clear. Noah had called his bluff and lost.

"Wait!" Noah shouted. "Wait!"

"Hold on," Sawyer radioed to the posse, hoping for a mass arrest. "Am I safe in assumin' you've had a change a' mind, Billy Ray?"

"You win. I'll go." Noah conceded and addressed his friends. "That's alright guys. It ain't worth it. It ain't worth the hassle. There'll be another day."

"That's where you're wrong, Billy Ray. There ain't gonna be another day. It won't be tolerated. You hear me? This time you got a warnin'. That goes for all a' ya'. Ya' hear?" Sawyer shouted to all the students. "Next time there will be no warnin'. Now all of ya' just go on home, and we'll pretend like this never happened."

Noah turned to James and Emma. "I'm really sorry, Mrs. Franklin. I sure didn't mean for none a' this to happen."

Emma stepped gingerly down the creaky steps and up to Noah. She caressed his face with her hands and gently pulled his head down, kissing him on his forehead. "Don't you worry about a thing, Billy Ray. The Lord knows what you done here today and He will bless you for it."

Mayor Sawyer kicked one of the open paint cans over, its thick creamy color making a river in the dirt. He turned and got back into the Mustang. Noah opened the passenger door and got in. Noah was crushed that the plan had failed. All he could think about now was how bad the beating he was going to get would be.

The drive to Rock County wouldn't take very long. It was just the next county over. But it only took a matter of seconds for Mayor Sawyer to start in on Noah. "What the hell do you think you're doin'! My God, Billy Ray! Are you trying to embarrass me? Ruin me? Both?" His anger rose the more he spoke. "Do you have any idea how this makes me look? Do you have an inkling," he banged hard on the steering wheel, "the slightest notion of the damage you've done?"

"All we were doing.." Noah started.

Mayor Sawyer threw his hand up. "Stop! I don't wanna even hear your voice right now. The mere sound of it nauseates me. Did you really think I wouldn't hear about it?" Again, Sawyer extended his hand toward Noah. "That's not a question. I want nothing but silence from you."

Noah folded his hands neatly on his lap and stayed quiet.

"Sometimes I wonder if you are my son. I don't know what's gotten into you, boy, but it ain't good and I ain't gonna stand for it. And I can assure you this. You will not win, boy. You will not win. As God is my witness. You will not win."

It took about fifteen minutes to drive to Rock County. After lecturing who he thought was Billy Ray for five solid minutes, the remainder of the ride was silent. As soon as Mayor Sawyer turned onto the road leading to Aunt Bess' home, Noah could see five or six county patrol cars with blue lights turning. He rubbed his face and shook his head.

"What's wrong, Billy Ray? Do you think I'm stupid? Huh? Did you really think I wouldn't figure this whole thing out? Again. Not a question. Your best option is to keep your mouth shut." Sawyer drove slowly through the patrol cars which were all manned by his cronies from the next county over. All were standing outside their patrol cars waiting for him to arrive. Two others stood on the front porch. They had already stopped the painting and forced the kids to sit and wait.

Noah witnessed all the dejected faces and felt totally responsible. Billy Ray sat on the front porch beside his Aunt with deputies standing guard on both sides. Noah turned to Mayor Sawyer. "Is this what makes you feel powerful? Run off a bunch of kids trying to do something nice?"

"You shut the hell up, boy!" Sawyer screamed at Noah leaning toward him and shaking his finger in his face. "I don't need it. Don't want it and didn't ask for it! You got no idea what you done! You got no idea the damage you done I gotta go undo! Not another word! You understand me? Not another word!" Mayor Sawyer was so mad his voice screeched. His face turned deep red as sweat poured down it. He jammed the gear shift hard into park and opened his door.

"Stay here, Billy Ray. Don't need any more of your help today." Sawyer used the roof of the car like a pull up bar to get himself out of his seat. He slammed the door as hard as he could and stormed toward Billy Ray and Aunt Bess where they sat on the front porch. Ignoring his demand, Noah got out of the car and followed eight to ten steps behind. Mayor Sawyer bounded the creaky wood steps to the porch as quickly as his stubby legs would let him. Billy Ray rose from his seat beside his aunt, and within second was nose to nose with his father.

"You got a death wish boy? Huh? Are you wanting to die?"

"With all due respect, sir, you don't own Rock County like you do Webber. You can't tell us what we can or can't do over here," Billy Ray stated, refusing to back off.

"Oh, is that right? Well I suggest you maybe should look around boy. What do you see? Huh? What do you see out there? I got connections in every county in this state, boy. If I want somethin' done, I just say the word and there ain't a damn thing you or anybody else can do about it. Now I'm gonna give you the same opportunity I gave that no-good son of mine." Sawyer motioned back to the car where he thought Billy Ray was still sitting. "I thought I told you to stay in the car!" he half-way screamed at Noah who by now was at the bottom of the stairs.

Noah bounded up the steps. "I ain't gonna let you tell me what to do no more."

"Go back to the car, Billy Ray!"

"I ain't goin' nowhere. You want me back in the car, then you gonna have to put me there."

Mayor Sawyer grabbed Noah and tried to pull him down the steps. Billy Ray intervened by pulling his father's arms away from Noah. "Leave him alone!" Billy Ray shouted.

Mayor Sawyer was stunned. Never in his life had anyone, much less a member of a minority, ever laid hands on him. He looked up at Billy Ray and backhanded him across the face. "How dare you! How dare you even look at me, boy! You gonna live to regret this day ever happened. You hear me?"

Billy Ray reacted quickly before thinking about the consequences. But he knew he was right. He knew in an instant that everything his father had done and everything he stood for was wrong. He wiped away the blood oozing from his bottom lip. "You're nothing but a bully. You hide behind your office and your cronies, but you're nuthin' but a fat dried up old slob that's so poisoned by your beliefs you can't see right and wrong."

"Billy Ray, stop," Noah said, trying to stop his friend before he said much more. Billy Ray rubbed his face, still stinging from his father's backhand, with his forearm.

Mayor Sawyer narrowed his eyes then looked back at Noah. "What'd you call him?"

Noah realized his mistake. His throat tightened and stomach turned. "Didn't call him nuthin'."

"No. You called him Billy Ray. I heard you call him Billy Ray."

"No, I didn't. I didn't call him nuthin'. Just tryin' to get him to calm down a bit. That's all."

Mayor Sawyer turned back to Billy Ray and cocked his head slightly. Like daggers, he stared deeply into his son's eyes. "I don't know what you two derelicts are up to but I can promise you this, you ain't gonna outsmart me. I'm smarter than the two a' you put together. Understand that and understand it good. Now I'm gonna give you and all your hoodlum friends three minutes to clear outta here before these officers arrest every last one of 'em."

"Arrest 'em for what?" Billy Ray shouted, his arms outstretched. "They ain't done nothin' wrong!"

Mayor Sawyer rubbed his brow. "I really don't feel like going through this all over again and I sure as hell ain't gonna explain nuthin' to you, boy," he said, jamming his finger into Billy Ray's chest. "Take my word for it, boy. Ask your buddy here if it's in your best interest to defy my orders?"

Billy Ray looked at Noah who shook his head no.

"That's the best advice you gonna get in a lifetime boy. Now, are you gonna tell 'em, or should I?"

Billy Ray stared at the blue skies above and let out a sigh. "Go home, everybody. We gave it our best shot. Just go home."

"Smart move, boy. You don't wanna cross me. You don't wanna evah cross me."

"You haven't changed a bit, Joshua. Not one bit. You still bullying folk around like you always did ceptin' now you're pickin' on teenagers. Guess it must make you feel pretty powerful," Aunt Bess said, as she rose from the top step to face her long-time nemesis.

Joshua took his hat off and rubbed his brow with his sleeve. He chuckled slightly. "Bess, Bess, Bess. I mighta' figured you'd be smack dab in the middle of this...this...spectacle. You always seem to be right at the forefront of some boneheaded cause."

"Yeah. Guess your brother kinda rubbed off on me some. Seein' as how he ain't round no more, I gotta help carry on."

"Yeah. That's a real shame the way he run off like he did. Leavin' you and the boy and all. A real shame I'd say. A real shame. Man didn't have an ounce of responsibility in his bones. No good brother a' mine run off and got himself killed. Probably runnin' round with some two-bit hooker that done him in."

"The man didn't run off and you know it!" Billy Ray snapped before he thought.

Joshua turned to Billy Ray and edged closer to him. "What'd you say, boy?"

Billy Ray looked at Noah then at Bess. It was too late. His

mouth spoke before his brain stopped him. He decided to go on. "You heard me. You may have gotten away with it then, but the past has a way of catchin' up to us all."

Joshua moved face to face with Billy Ray and whispered. "Lemme tell you somethin', you little no good piece a' garbage. I don't gotta explain nuthin' to you or nobody else." Joshua shook his head and took one step back. "Why am I even talkin' to you? You are worthless to me. You and that no good son a' mine and everybody here. You are all garbage. Not worth the ground you're standin' on."

Billy Ray stepped toward his father, erasing the distance Joshua had just created. Again, face to face, Billy Ray leaned in and whispered in his father's ear. "So you gonna take out the trash like you did your brother?"

Joshua took two steps back and stared at Billy Ray. His face was pale white. For once in his life he was speechless.

Noah looked at Billy Ray and didn't even have to ask what had been said. Noah exhaled deeply and shook his head in disbelief.

Billy Ray inched closer to his father and leaned in once more. "Why Jake? Huh? Why did you have to kill Jake, too?"

Joshua shoved Billy Ray away. His face was still pale white. Joshua looked at Noah. "What kinda lies you been tellin' this nigga', Billy Ray? Huh? What kinda lies you spreadin' out there? You tryin' to destroy your own daddy? Is that what you're tryin' to do? Destroy me? For God's sake, Billy Ray. You might hate me, but don't go destroyin' me by spreadin' lies."

By now Billy Ray and Noah stood side by side facing Joshua.

Noah looked squarely at the side of Billy Ray's face as Billy Ray stared boldly into his father's eyes.

"You can't undo what you already done," Billy Ray said. "You can only hope God forgives you for it."

Noah shook his head, not believing his ears.

Joshua looked around at all the faces of the kids who had heard most everything. He looked back at Noah. "This is all your doin', Billy Ray. By lettin' this no good nigga' in your life you ruined everything. He took your scholarship away not to mention your dignity. Now he's done managed to turn you into a filthy liar." Joshua turned to all the kids. "You hear that? Your friend here, your mentor, is nothin' but a no good, nigga' lovin' liar. I'm happy for all a' ya'. This is the friend you've chosen." Joshua edged toward Billy Ray and lowered his voice. "As for you. You ever heard the sound of a shotgun bein' racked? Keep your ears and eyes open boy. It could sneak up on ya' in a hurry." He backed away and brushed off his sleeves with his hands even though there was nothing to brush off. He placed his hat back on his head. "Three minutes!" he shouted. "Three minutes to clear outta here before I have these fine officers arrest every last one of ya'."

Billy Ray watched hopelessly as his father and Noah walked back to the car. Billy Ray knew from experience that Noah was about to experience a beating worse than he ever had. Noah glanced at Billy Ray as he was getting in the car. He nodded his head slightly. Billy Ray nodded back.

~ 20 ~

Billy Ray sat on the bridge, his legs dangling precariously over the side. He grabbed a handful of pebbles and tossed them one by one into the slowly creeping stream below. Patiently, he waited for Noah, wondering if he would show up.

Billy Ray had been the recipient of a number of beatings as he grew up. He lost count of how many a long time ago. The severity of the beatings depended on the severity of the offense. Billy Ray suffered countless bruises and a few broken bones along the way. They were always explained to the doctor as sports related. Even though the doctor knew better, he never said anything. Mayor Sawyer was a very powerful man and one did not cross him. At most, the doctor would tell Billy Ray to call him if he needed anything. But Billy Ray never did. It would have just resulted in another beating.

In the distance, Billy Ray could hear the sound of tires crunching gravel down the country road. Billy Ray stood as Noah pulled up beside him and exited Billy Ray's truck. One eye was totally shut and the other partially. His nose was swollen and had remnants of dried blood on the side. His left wrist was wrapped with an ace bandage. The back of his right hand was bound with gauze and a square plug of white tape. He also had a noticeable limp when he came around the truck to greet his friend.

"Damn!" Billy Ray said. "You look like death warmed over."

Noah tried to smile, but it hurt and he grimaced. He gingerly sat down on the bridge. "For a chubby little man your father packs a mean punch."

Billy Ray sat down beside him. "You get any licks in?"

"Didn't know I was supposed to 'til he told me to fight back like a man."

"Yeah," Billy Ray said. "Probably shoulda' told you he wants you to fight back. Makes him feel more powerful, more like a man I guess. Like it don't count as a beatin' if you're fightin' back."

Noah lifted his right hand and peeled back the white tape to show Billy Ray the scar. "This was the one decent shot I got in. Just made him madder."

"Was it a good shot?"

"Oh yeah," Noah smiled then grimaced. He placed his clinched fist between Billy Ray's eyes. "Got him squarely right there. Knocked him over a table and down a stair or two. Then he just got up and came at me again. I pretty much just gave in. Wasn't gonna do no good to keep fightin' back. Seemed the more I fought, the madder and stronger he got. It took me a while to figure once I was on the ground and didn't come back up, he stopped. So that's what I did. Just stayed down."

"Then he gets all nice and wants to take care of ya'."

"You know him like a book don't cha'?"

"Lived with him seventeen plus years now." Billy Ray threw a handful of pebbles in the stream. "Took you to Doc Taylor then, right?"

Noah smiled and confirmed by nodding his head.

"Got hurt in football?"

"What?" Noah asked.

"He told Doc Taylor you got hurt in football, right?"

Noah laughed, grabbed his ribs and grimaced again. "Yeah."

"That's his style and nobody ever questions it."

Noah dabbed at his eye that was completely shut and winced. "Man, that hurts."

"Yeah, it will for a while. Usually he'll apologize over and over until the next time you do somethin' he don't like. Then it'll happen all over again. Don't think he'll apologize this time, though." Billy Ray paused. "Still like the change?" he rhetorically asked Noah. "All the fine dining, silk sheets and endless greenbacks ain't so great anymore, are they?"

Noah laughed, grabbed his ribs and grimaced again.

"He killed 'em, Noah. He killed my uncle and cousin. I got so wrapped up in his way of thinkin' that I put it clean outta' my mind. But now I remember. I was there and didn't do nuthin'. Didn't say nuthin'. Hell, I'm as bad as he is."

"We talked about this, Billy Ray. You were young and scared. There's nuthin' you coulda' done to stop what he did. Nuthin'."

"I gotta make it right, Noah. Somehow I gotta make it right."

"Look, Billy Ray. Your heart's in the right place. We tried and failed. We gave it our best shot and I gotta be honest with ya, I really ain't in the mood for another beatin' just yet."

"If it happens again, I'll make sure you don't take any blame."

"Easier said than done. Look. I know I've been harpin' on ya that we gotta do somethin' that makes a difference. But it ain't worth it no more, Billy Ray. It ain't worth the beatins', and it ain't worth ruining any chance at a relationship you might have with your father when this is all over and done."

Billy Ray turned to Noah. "Like I want a relationship now. You're the one that wanted change and now it's me talkin' bout it. Don't you want change no more?"

"Not at this cost, Billy Ray. We tried. We gave it everything we had and lost. I don't think there's nothin' else we can do. Least wise nuthin' more that won't get us in a heap a trouble."

"So you giving up?" Billy Ray asked. "Huh? Just giving up?"

"Whattaya want me to say Billy Ray? You want me to say okay it's time to move on to plan B and then if that don't work we'll move to plan C and then plan D and so on and so on? I don't know what else you want me to do. Let's just cut our losses and move on."

"Cut our losses?" Billy Ray said sarcastically. "Cut our losses? You been goin' on and on about this Reverend King that's been makin' some noise recently. Whattaya think he would say if you told him he should just cut his losses?"

Noah peered toward the creek below. He scooped up some pebbles and threw them in. "You seen what happened to him this past March when he marched on Selma?"

Billy Ray nodded. "Yeah. I seen it. So?"

"So!" Noah was almost angry. "So you seen what happened. I don't gotta remind you a' what they done to him and everybody that crossed that bridge."

"Yeah. Your point?"

"My point? My point?" Noah wasn't sure of his point.

"Yeah. Your point."

"You want what happened to them to happen to you? To me?"

Billy Ray scooped up a handful of pebbles and tossed them into the creek one by one. "Yeah. I guess you're right. We should just cut our losses. Forget change. Forget hope. I'm sure that's what your Reverend King would tell us to do. That's probably what he's gonna do, too. Had a bad day at the Edmund Pettus bridge down there in Selma, so let's just throw in the towel. It ain't worth it. It ain't worth the beatins'. It ain't worth the relationships. Let's just cut our losses and move on." Billy Ray paused, threw the last couple of pebbles into the creek and rubbed his hands together to rid them of the pebble residue. "Yeah. I reckon you're right, Noah. Just ain't worth it."

Noah stared at the creek. He had heard every cutting word Billy Ray spoke and it was as if he were talking to himself. He had become complacent while Billy Ray had changed. "After I wallow around a little longer in my self-pity maybe you can tell me what plan B is."

Billy Ray smiled, extended his arm toward Noah and helped him up. Noah winced and grabbed his ribs. "Do I gotta teach you how to protect yourself in a fight, too? Dang man. You gotta cover. You gotta cover." Billy Ray danced around in a boxer type motion covering his ribs and face while punching at the air.

~ 21 ~

Noah had never been inside the Webber County Courthouse before. It wasn't that he was not allowed in because of his color. He just had never had a reason to go in, although he had always wondered what it looked like inside. Outside the grand structure, he stood below five magnificent columns rising three floors. The building dated to the 1830's and was majestic. Built mostly of marble and granite, and probably by some of Noah's ancestors, it stood at the forefront of every historic event that ever occurred in the county. Its huge oak doors were even larger than they appeared. Inside, the marble walls were covered with twelve foot murals chronicling the state's history. Stone spiral staircases mirrored each other on both sides of the building. When people spoke, a distinct echo resounded off the walls and throughout the foyer that extended all three levels.

Noah was unsure of plan B, but he was more than willing to do his part. If Billy Ray was willing to risk everything then so should he. Billy Ray had explained to Noah where he could find the proper form in his father's office and that he was the only one that could pull it off. Noah waited outside until he saw Mayor Sawyer leave and a window of opportunity could present itself.

Noah bounded up one set of the curvy stair steps hanging on to the gold plated railing and to the second level where

Mayor Sawyer's office sat at the center overlooking the foyer. He walked ten or so steps to two oversized solid cherry doors bearing a gold sign engraved with "The Honorable Mayor Joshua Sawyer." Noah pulled the large gold handle and walked into a large receptionist area with plush green carpeting with the mayor's symbol sewed squarely in the center. The solid oak furniture sat grandly around the circular office and portraits of previous mayors hung stoically on the walls. One lone receptionist with stiffly sprayed black hair that flipped up at her shoulders sat at her solid mahogany desk gabbing on the phone in an obviously personal conversation. A Confederate flag hung on the wall directly behind her with an Alabama state flag next to it. Nervous as a cat, Noah crept slowly toward her desk and wooden name plate sitting on the front edge, indicating her name was Doris Sweeney. Doris held the phone tightly to her ear and gave Noah a three fingered wiggly wave without skipping a beat to whoever she was talking to. Noah smiled and waved back. He saw Mayor Sawyer's name emblazoned on the door just to Doris' right and edged toward the door that was slightly cracked open.

"Hold on," Doris said to whoever she was talking to.

Noah froze. His heart pounded. The jig was up. He knew he'd been had.

"Your daddy's not here, Billy Ray. Is there anything I can help you with?"

Noah, his back toward Doris, thought hard. "No. That's okay. He forgot somethin' and I'm just gonna get it for him."

"What'd he forget? Maybe I can help you find it."

"Umm. That's alright. It's just his briefcase. He forgot his briefcase. I'm sure it's right beside his desk."

"Are you sure? He just left, and I know he had it cause I had to remind him. He's always forgetting it."

Noah thought quick and turned to face Doris. "Not his briefcase. Somethin' he meant to put in his briefcase, and he forgot it. I can find it. Don't worry about it. You go on and finish talking." Noah turned and pushed the door to Mayor Sawyer's office open just slightly.

Doris stood up, phone still attached to her ear. "Billy Ray."

Noah froze. "Yes, ma'am."

"You sure you're supposed to be here? I know your daddy's been pretty upset with you here recently." She noticed the bruises on his face and didn't believe they were from Friday night's game.

Noah swallowed hard. "Yes, ma'am. I know. We've had a few differences lately, but everything's alright. Gettin' back to normal. That's why I'm here. Tryin' to get back on his good side, if you know what I mean."

Doris paused and narrowed her eyes. "Alright. If you say so. Sure you don't need some help?"

"No ma'am. You go on back to talkin'."

Doris sat back down and resumed her conversation.

Noah opened the door then closed it behind him. The plush green carpeting covered the floor of Mayor Sawyer's office. Embedded into the carpet in front of Mayor Sawyer's executive sized cherry desk was a gold circular emblem of the state seal. Noah did a 360 degree turn and was dumbfounded at the artifacts hanging from the oak paneled walls. Two Civil War sabers enclosed in a glass case were inscribed with claims of one time ownership by Robert E. Lee. A tattered Confederate flag with too many bullet holes to count was carefully encased in a large locked glass frame. On the wall opposite the sabers were several small pistols also enclosed in protective locked glass containers. The inscriptions indicated they once belonged to Stonewall Jackson. On the wall behind Mayor Sawyer's desk were authentic photographs of Confederate officers taken by Matthew Brady, photos of actual battles and Civil War letters from his great-grandfather who fought in many battles.

Noah edged closer to Mayor Sawyer's desk, which was exquisitely carved with intricate designs. Made of solid cherry, it had not one scratch, nick or piece of dust that marred the shine. It was neatly peppered with various papers and documents and a large blotter calendar. On the front edge was Mayor Sawyer's name plate engraved in fourteen carat gold. Directly above the name plate was a fancy gold plated lamp that was more for show than actual use. But probably the most valued possessions on his desk were two photographs in silver plated frames. One of Mayor Sawyer shaking hands with the two state senators and an even larger frame containing a color photograph of Governor George Wallace with his arm draped around a proud Mayor Sawyer, grinning ear to ear. Noah gently picked up the photograph, shook his head slightly, then set it back down.

Noah could still hear Doris gabbing nonstop on the phone. He laughed silently at the thought of whether a spider or other insect had ever burrowed its way into her bouffant hairstyle. He would have liked to look around more but knew he couldn't take a chance. Noah inched slowly toward the working side of

Mayor Sawyer's desk. He ran his hand across the soft, fine, genuine leather of the high backed executive chair. He couldn't resist sitting down just to see how far he would sink into the cushy seat and was surprised at how really uncomfortable the chair was. He chuckled slightly at what Mayor Sawyer would think if he knew a black man was sitting in his chair.

'Permits' he thought to himself. The reason he was there almost escaped him. Noah sprung from his chair, trying to remember everything Billy Ray had told him. Other than Doris talking on the phone it was relatively quiet. So quiet in fact, Noah could hear his heart beat in his ear. As luck would have it, now he couldn't remember which drawer Billy Ray said the form would be in. All he remembered was to make sure he got the right form, the one allowing a free assembly or the right to gather. It would probably say something like that or at least something close to it. Noah opened the middle drawer, the one that would be directly above Mayor Sawyer's lap if he were sitting down. He scanned his hand over some pencils, pens, paper clips and about two dollars-worth of loose change. Quietly, he closed the drawer and thought for a couple of seconds. "Top drawer, top drawer...top right drawer." Suddenly he could hear Billy Ray's voice in his head. He reached for the brass handle that was carved with intricate designs of small fruit. He pulled the drawer back ever so slowly, causing it to squeak each inch it moved. Noah stopped and listened to assure Doris was still on the phone. Noah pulled the drawer out the rest of the way and saw several different forms neatly placed inside. Lowering and cocking his head slightly, Noah wanted to make sure he got the right one.

"Oh great," he muttered to himself. The forms were there and probably the right ones. Only the forms had numbers. There was ASF 100156, ASF 287650, ASF 34234, ASF 56543 and ASF 67509. Noah deduced ASF stood for Alabama State Form. But there was nothing on any of the forms identifying what the form was for. He did the only thing he could think of and grabbed every form and stuffed them in his pockets. As the drawer closed it squeaked again.

The drawer halfway closed, he stopped suddenly when he heard two voices entering the receptionist area. One voice sounded vaguely familiar, but the other was definitely that of Mayor Sawyer. Noah spun around quickly hoping to spy an exit or even a closet to hide in. As the voices grew stronger, the only viable place he could find was underneath the desk. He pulled his legs tightly to his chest.

"Honest to God I don't know what's gotten into him. Just don't understand it. Don't understand it all," Mayor Sawyer said, opening the door and then entering his office. Sawyer froze for a second, hand still on the doorknob. He looked down toward the doorknob. "Could'a sworn I left that cracked." He shook his head. "Maybe not. Come on in." Sawyer closed the door behind him.

Noah pressed his back hard against the inside of the desk. His heart pounded violently in his chest and he felt heat flooding into his face.

"Like I said before. You gotta remember he's just a boy. Feelin' his oats as they say. Sometime you gotta let 'em speak their minds. You know. Get it out of his system so to speak."

"The problem is it's not *his* mind he's speakin'. I taught the boy better than that," Sawyer said, as he walked around his desk and shuffled some papers on top of his desk. "Where is that thing? I know I left it here somewhere."

"Whattaya mean?" the familiar voice asked.

Noah began to sweat profusely from his forehead. He wiped it with the back of his ace bandaged hand as slowly as he could, careful to make no sudden movements or noises.

"'Bout what?" asked Mayor Sawyer, still shuffling through the loose papers on his desk. His stubby legs straddled the opening where Noah hid.

"You said it's not *his* mind he's speakin'. Whose mind is he speakin'?" The man with Mayor Sawyer laughed.

"You go ahead and laugh. It ain't no laughin' matter to me. Not at all. And if it keeps up you won't be laughin' neither. So you just go on and laugh all you want. It'll only be a matter a' time."

"Oh come on, Joshua. Ease up a little. He's just a teenager. He'll grow out of it. Whatever seems to go against the grain is what they're gonna do. He'll grow out of it."

"Where in the hell did I put that?" Sawyer said, as he opened and shut the drawers on the left side of his desk. "That's easy for you to say. Your two are grown and I emphasize the word grown 'cause your two were raised when this civil rights crap wasn't an issue.

"Well maybe you're right but I think you gotta give him some time. You raised him well. You raised him right, what is and what ain't. He'll come around in no time. You'll see."

Sawyer stood up straight and placed his hands squarely on his hips. "What did I do with that? I gotta find it you know."

"It'll turn up," the man with the familiar voice said.

Sawyer gazed down and saw the half open top right drawer. He cocked his head to one side. "Somebody's been in here."

Noah shut his eyes as tight as he could. Visions of another beating danced in his mind.

"What?"

"I said somebody's been in here."

"Now you're going crazy Joshua. That boy a' yours has got you all worked up. Maybe you need to take some time off. Go fishin' or somethin'. Take the family to Miami Beach."

"I'm tellin' you, somebody's been in here."

"Fine. Somebody's been in here. And how do you know that?"

"The drawer."

"What about the drawer?"

"I always close my drawers. Call it a nervous tick, a personal habit. But I always close my drawers."

Noah clinched his teeth and silently cussed himself.

"Doris!" Sawyer shouted.

Doris continued her phone conversation and did not hear Mayor Sawyer calling.

"Doris!"

"Just a minute," she said to the person she was talking to. She opened the door to Sawyer's office and stuck her head in. "I'm right here. You don't gotta yell."

Sawyer's friend snickered.

"You been in here in the last fifteen minutes or so?"

"No. Haven't been in there all day. Anything else?"

"No. Yes!"

"Make up your mind."

"Has anybody been in here in the last fifteen minutes?"

"No."

Noah relaxed.

"Ceptin' for Billy Ray," Doris added.

Noah's body tightened and was overcome again with a burning sensation.

"He must've slipped out without me noticin'," Doris added.

"How long ago was he in here?" Mayor Sawyer inquired.

Doris looked at her watch. "Don't know. Nine, ten minutes, maybe. Surprised you didn't cross one another comin' and goin'."

Mayor Sawyer looked into the half open drawer, opened it all the way and noticed forms were missing. "They're gonna try and do a march."

"A march?" Sawyer's friend asked.

"Yeah. A march."

"How you figure?"

Sawyer slammed the drawer, causing Noah to jerk. "'Cause he took all the forms and the only one that's relevant to anything they might plan is the permit for lawful assembly. Bumblin' son a' mine didn't know which form was the right one so he just took em' all." Sawyer laughed.

"What's so funny?"

"Billy Ray and that nigga friend a' his don't realize it, but I'm the only one that can sign the permit allowin' em' to do it."

"What're you gonna do, Joshua?"

"Have 'em all arrested like I shoulda' done a couple weeks ago."

"Yeah. And you'll just end up makin' 'em all heroes. There's other ways a' dealin' with troublemakers you know. I don't gotta tell you that."

"Don't wanna talk about it right now," Sawyer shot back. "I just wanna find that list."

"How many names were on it, three?" Sawyer's friend asked.

"For now," Sawyer answered. "It may go to four and I need it before our next meeting."

Noah listened from underneath his hiding place.

"It'll turn up."

"Just don't want it to fall into the wrong hands. That's all. Can't believe I'd misplace that thing. Maybe I left it at home." Sawyer grabbed his garbage can from beside his desk and sifted through wadded up papers searching for his list. Not finding it, he placed the can back in its place and stepped to the side of his desk.

"Wait a minute," he muttered, dropping to one knee. With his shoulder and face planted firmly against the side of the desk, Sawyer reached as far as he could underneath the desk with his free arm. He grasped and felt all along the carpet coming to within an inch of Noah's pants. Noah pulled back as far as he could, holding his breath as if that would give him more room. Sawyer gave up and stood up. "Damn thing ain't here."

"It'll show up," Sawyer's friend assured him.

Noah breathed easier when he realized Mayor Sawyer and his friend were about to leave and he had not been caught. His body also relaxed ever so slightly, which caused his shoulder to bump the middle drawer. It squeaked and opened about an inch. Sawyer turned suddenly and walked back to the desk.

"What is it?" Sawyer's friend asked.

Noah's heart pounded hard inside his chest. He could hear it inside his head. He could see Mayor Sawyer's reflection coming back in the glass frame of the Confederate flag hanging on the wall behind the desk. Noah watched and waited to be caught. How bad would the beating be this time? Sawyer stopped abruptly directly behind his desk. Noah thought about reaching out and grabbing his legs, making him fall backwards. Then he could make his getaway. He would be caught, but at least he would forgo the beating for a while. But he thought better of the idea and instead shut his eyes tightly and awaited capture. Noah jolted at the slamming of the drawer he had just caused to open. Mayor Sawyer then walked away.

"Personal habit?" Sawyer's friend commented.

"Yeah," Sawyer answered. "Personal habit."

Noah stayed under the desk a while longer. He knew in time that Doris would be getting off work and the coast would be clear to make his escape.

~ 22 ~

Although all of the teachers were aware of the possibility of a demonstration, few took it too seriously. It was assumed by most that the vast majority of the student body would remain glued to their seats when the classroom clocks struck ten o'clock. And for insurance, it was announced that any student leaving the school without prior approval would be immediately suspended and possibly expelled.

Billy Ray eyed the clock. It was 9:55. With each minute that passed, virtually every teenage heart beat nervously along with the ticking second hand. Teachers tried in vain to continue their lessons, but were really only watching the clocks themselves.

At 9:58 the principal's voice cracked over the intercom giving one last warning to any students who planned on violating any school codes without mentioning the march. At 9:59 he moved to the doorway with a clear view of the hallway. Never in his many years of being in his position had he ever heard the school this quiet.

Billy Ray and Noah, in different classrooms, watched as the second hand swept. When it completed its round, every student in their classroom looked at them for leadership. They reciprocated then boldly rose from their seats. The teachers closed their books and did not try to stop them as each student followed suit.

One by one, students, black and white alike, defiantly left their classrooms and poured into the hallway in an orderly and disciplined fashion. The few that stayed behind were either too afraid or still unbelieving of the cause.

The principal, seeing Noah and Billy Ray approaching him near the main door, stepped in front of them to block their way. "Billy Ray," he said to Noah. "These kids look up to you. Always have. You've always been a strong leader. I urge you to be that leader now and go back to your classroom. If you do, the others will follow and we can put a stop to this now. We'll act like it never happened."

Noah gently grasped the principal's arm. "Mr. Lewis." Noah glanced behind him to see hundreds of students packed inside the hallway waiting to follow him and Billy Ray out the door. "All these people here believe in doing the right thing. We don't mean no disrespect sir, by doin' it this way. But the whole lot of us are speakin' with one voice and this is the best way we know to do it."

Principal Lewis raised his voice but not in anger. "Billy Ray. My God, son. Haven't you been around bigotry long enough to know you'll never win? There's nothing you or any of your classmates can do to make it go away. You'll just get taken down and take them with you," he said, motioning to the students in the hallway. "For God's sake son, think about it."

Noah smiled, turned and addressed the students. "Listen up everybody. Mr. Lewis is concerned about what we are about to participate in. If anybody wants to go back to class, nobody'll hold nothin' against ya'. It's gotta be your decision." Noah faced Mr. Lewis. "Will they be in any trouble if they stop now?"

"No! None. Not at all. It's all forgotten."

Noah turned back to the students. "Mr. Lewis assures me that anybody that wants to go back to their classroom right now will be in no trouble. So anybody that wants to go back, please go now. No one will think less of you."

Not one student moved.

Noah waited a few seconds, but every student remained stoic. He smiled at Mr. Lewis. "With all due respect and we do appreciate your concern, Mr. Lewis, I think we've spoken."

Mr. Lewis grabbed Billy Ray by his arm. "Noah. For the love of God. You gotta know what could happen if you go through with this. Can't you talk some sense into Billy Ray?"

"Don't get us wrong, Mr. Lewis. We appreciate you bein' all concerned and everything, but it's somethin' we gotta do."

Billy Ray and Noah pushed gently past Mr. Lewis and opened the large school double wooden doors as all the others followed.

"Billy Ray! Noah!" Mr. Lewis cried out. "For Christ's sake!" He paused just slightly. "You're upsetting some dangerous people! Do I have to spell it out for you?"

Billy Ray and Noah stopped, each still held one door open. "It's just a march Mr. Lewis. It's just a march."

~ 23 ~

Mayor Sawyer sat at his oversized desk pretending to write a speech he was to give later in the week to the Central Alabama Bass Association. Even though he grew up close to a lake, he'd never fished a day in his life but was good at the art of faking a passion for it. He'd been sitting with the same paper in front of him for an hour with the words 'My Fellow Bass Fishermen' at the top. His eyes had been going back and forth between the clock on his desk and the street below. He was sure this was nothing more than a prank and the street would remain clear. He was even more sure that Billy Ray would come to his senses and never take part in such a brash stunt.

It started as a muffled sound but grew stronger every second. Mayor Sawyer heard the shouts and chanting even before he looked out and saw the gathering crowd on the sidewalk. He was startled by the ringing phone.

"It's Judge Stevens!" Doris hollered from her desk.

Sawyer rolled his eyes. "I don't need this right now," he muttered to himself, returning to his desk and picking up the phone. "Hello, Harlan."

"Thought you told me there was nuthin' to worry 'bout. Thought you said you had your boy under control. Have you looked out the window?"

"I ain't blind. I can see."

"Then I reckon you can see who's leadin' the way."

Sawyer was silent.

"You there?"

"I'm here."

"Then do somethin' about it!" Stevens shouted. "Make it go away!"

"I will."

"Now!" Stevens shouted even louder.

Sawyer hung up the phone, leaned back in his fancy leather chair, and rubbed his eyes with both hands.

Outside the courthouse, a large crowd had gathered. Reporters from the local paper, as well as a few from neighboring cities, stood around with notebooks and pencils in hand. Merchants, shoppers and other citizens from Webber County stood wondering if the march would erupt in violence like the one in Selma had only months earlier. Some cheered the students on. Others booed and threw whatever they could get their hands on at the marchers.

This was a peaceful march. Led by Billy Ray and Noah, the two-hundred plus students marched in line, and stayed within the confines of the street. The marchers understood that to be effective, they had to stay calm and could not let onlookers antagonize them with cruel words or thrown fruit. Their signs were simple but to the point. Their chants were peaceful.

Five or six Sheriff's cruisers were now on the scene to dispel the rally. The deputies blocked the street on one side of the courthouse. The Sheriff and his five deputies positioned themselves in front of their cruisers and stood ready to stop the marchers as soon as they reached that point.

Billy Ray and Noah slowed as they approached the Sheriff and his deputies.

"Well, well, well. If it ain't the Mayor's boy," the Sheriff, leaning against the front of his cruiser, said to Noah, his arms crossed across his chest and held there by a fairly large beer gut. His jaw worked overtime on an over chewed piece of gum. A toothpick, half in and half out, protruded from the corner of his mouth. It worked its way up and down with every word.

Noah raised his arm to stop the marchers. "Yes, sir."

"You mind tellin' me what it is you and your...your...nigga' comrades are doin' out heah'?"

"We're marchin', sir," Noah answered.

The Sheriff laughed. Like playing Simon Says, the deputies laughed in unison. "I can see that. Do I look stupid?"

Noah wanted to answer but knew better.

"What is it you're marchin' about?"

"Equal rights," Noah answered.

"Equal rights?"

"You know what that is Sheriff?"   Billy Ray asked facetiously, unable to stop himself.

The Sheriff did not appreciate the comment. He leaned off the front of the car and moved face to face with Billy Ray. "Lemme tell you somethin', boy. If I wanna hear somethin' comin' outta that mouth a' yourn, then I'll ask for it. You got me?"

"Yes, sir," Billy Ray said, without hesitating.

The Sheriff moved and stood nose to nose with Noah. He pulled the toothpick from his mouth and pointed it at him. "And as for you. Does your daddy know you're down heah' marchin', protestin', demonstratin' or whatever the hell it is you's doin'?"

Noah was silent.

"That's what I figured. I 'spect if he did you wouldn't be here and your hind end would be about as red as that boy's hair back there for even thinkin' about it," the Sheriff said, pointing to Red who stood a few rows back. The Sheriff snickered and his deputies followed suit. "Although, I reckon it's safe to say he knows by now. His office is right up there, ain't it?" The Sheriff turned and pointed towards the courthouse second floor. "I'm sure your daddy must be real proud right about now." He turned to Billy Ray. "And what about you, boy? I know who you are, and I 'spect your mama and daddy would arrange it to where you couldn't sit down for a week if they knew you was out here brushin' up trouble."

The deputies snickered at their boss's comment as the numbers of curious onlookers continued to grow on each side of the street.

The Sheriff leaned back against his cruiser and folded his arms on top of his beer gut. "Now I want you boys to listen and listen good. I'm willin' to forget all this happened, but what you're gonna have to do is to turn this little parade around and go back to school. We'll just call it a...a...misunderstandin'. That's all. Just a big misunderstandin'. No harm, no foul as they say."

Noah reached into his back pocket and pulled out the folded piece of paper he and Billy Ray hoped they wouldn't have to use. He handed it to the Sheriff.

"What's this?"

"Permit," Noah answered.

"A permit? For what?"

"To march. To do what we're doin' right now," Noah said.

"Signed by the Mayor himself," Billy Ray added.

The Sheriff unfolded the paper and mumbled through it saying something audible every fifth or sixth word. He brought the permit close to his eyes to study the signature. "Danged if that ain't his signature." He folded the permit and pushed it into Noah's chest. "Can't believe you got 'em to sign it cause I'm sure he woulda' told me about it."

"You sure that's his signature Sheriff?" one of the deputies asked.

Noah and Billy Ray exchanged a stressed glance.

The Sheriff turned around to the deputy, shook his head and rolled his eyes. "That's why you're where you're at and I'm the Sheriff you big lug. I've seen that signature hundreds a' times. It's his."

"My daddy's pretty busy, Sheriff. I'm sure he just forgot to tell ya'. Probably just an oversight," Noah attempted to explain.

"Oversight? Ain't positively a hundred percent it was an oversight boy. But I reckon I ain't got a choice, now do I?" The Sheriff grinned and moved away from his cruiser and into Noah's face. "Lemme make somethin' perfectly clear. You...you...kids go on have your march, your protest or whatever it is you wanna call it. But I don't want no trouble from any of ya'. You got that?"

"Yes, sir," Billy Ray and Noah answered in unison.

"You stay within the confines of the street. I don't wanna hear any obscenities, gestures or any other unacceptable form of behavior."

"Yes, sir," they both answered.

"If anybody. I mean any one of you gets outta line, I'll haul the whole lot of you in. Is that understood?"

"Yes, sir. Perfectly," Noah said.

"Aight' den." The Sheriff motioned his deputies to move. "Boys, let's move it and let these troublemakers have their little march. But don't go far, cause I got a feelin' this ain't over by a long stretch." He then motioned to Billy Ray and Noah. "Aight' den. Go on. Have fun."

Noah called out to the students that the march would continue. Fists were raised and cheers filled the air. After another loop around the courthouse was completed, Noah climbed to the balcony of a local bakery which overlooked the courtyard lawn. National news reporters, already in Alabama covering another story, heard how two teenage high school students, one black and one white, had organized the march. They arrived just in time to hear Noah's speech. The cameras whirred and clicked as they recorded Noah's retelling of what the march was all about. When they heard it was the Mayor's son who was talking, their attention was even greater.

Across the street, Mayor Sawyer had hoped the Sheriff would dispel the march and he wouldn't have to involve himself. Unfortunately for him that did not happen. He finally worked up the courage to come out. It wasn't fear that stopped him at first but embarrassment. How could he face the townsfolk, many who sided with him, and try to explain his son's actions.

"You lookin' for your boy, Mayor?" chuckled the Sheriff,

standing and watching on the courthouse lawn. The Sheriff pointed toward the balcony. "Think that's him up there. But then again, I could be mistaken." He laughed a little harder.

"Put a sock in it Jones," Sawyer said to the Sheriff, who he never liked anyway. "When's your re-election up?"

"Not before yours," the Sheriff responded quickly, proud of himself for it. "And maybe you should tap your boy up there to run your campaign." The Sheriff and his deputy shared a hearty laugh.

Sawyer shook his head and had no comeback. "Maybe if you'd a' done your job and stopped 'em we wouldn't be havin' this conversation."

"Stop 'em? Now how'm I 'sposed to stop 'em when it was you that signed the permit?"

Sawyer glared at the Sheriff. "I didn't sign nuthin'. What the hell you talkin' about?"

"Hell, I seen it with my own eyes," the Sheriff said. "You signed it. It's your signature on the permit."

"There ain't no such thing. I signed nuthin'. He forged my signature. I didn't think he'd do it but he did."

"Well now," the Sheriff said smiling. "That changes everything, now don't it? Whattaya' want me to do?"

Sawyer thought for five or six seconds. "Arrest every last one of 'em."

"You sure?"

"You heard me! Do your job!"

"Don't gotta tell me twice," the Sheriff said, as he reached for his radio to send the message out to his deputies. He also pulled out a piece of paper and pen from his shirt pocket and had Sawyer sign it.

By now the students were marching again. The Sheriff, flanked by his deputies, formed a line to block their path. Sheriff Jones held up both hands to stop them. "Lemme see that permit again, boy."

Noah reached into his pocket and handed him the permit.

The Sheriff pulled the signature Mayor Sawyer just signed from his pocket and studied them side by side, then stared at Noah. "You're good, boy. *Very* good." He studied the signatures again and noticed a difference or two. "Yep. I see it now."

"See what?" Noah asked.

Sheriff Jones showed Noah the signatures side by side and pointed to part of the forged signature. "See right there? See that? That's where you made your mistake, son. See, when your father signs his name he leaves a slight opening on top of the o. You see that. You closed the o entirely. Bad mistake. Oh, oh, and see the t. See it? Your daddy crosses his t's at the top and not the middle like most folk would. And I'm sure there's other mistakes you made. But all in all, you done a good job. I mean you had me fooled for a little bit anyway."

Noah knew it was over. They'd been caught. And it was over.

"You see, son. What you done wasn't just wrong. It was illegal. Do you understand that?

Noah and Billy Ray looked at each other, both unsure of what they should say or do.

"Don't look at each other. It's a simple question."

"Yes, sir," Noah answered. "I take full responsibility. But I knew there was no way he would ever sign it so I just did it."

"No, sir," Billy Ray chimed in. "I was the one that signed it. I'm the one that broke the law, not him."

Sheriff Jones sighed. "Well ain't this heartwarmin'. Both takin' the blame. I think I might cry. I reckon that means I gotta haul both of ya' in and charge you both with forgery and the rest with unlawful assembly."

Two fire trucks rolled to a stop adjacent to the marchers. Sheriff Jones saw the large red trucks, puffed out his chest and pulled his sunglasses down just a bit below his eyes. "Now we gonna do this orderly. You understand?"

"Sheriff," Noah pleaded. "Don't arrest everybody. They didn't know about the forged permit. It ain't their fault and ain't none a' their doin'.'"

Sheriff Jones looked over his shoulder at Mayor Sawyer who kept his distance but was close enough to hear. He nodded his head.

"Aight'," Sheriff Jones shouted so everyone could hear. "Here's what we're gonna do. Everybody listen up. All of you, just turn on around and march on back to the school and nobody gets in trouble 'ceptin maybe by your parents, but I got no control over that. What I do have control over is haulin' you into jail and chargin' you with unlawful assembly. I don't want that to happen."

"Whattaya want us to do, Billy Ray?" Red yelled from the crowd.

Billy Ray and Mayor Sawyer locked eyes. "You just gotta win don't ya'? Win at all costs. That's what you've always said. Losin' just ain't in your nature. But it ain't about winnin' or losin'. It's about doin' what's right. And you just can't see that, can you?"

Mayor Sawyer walked toward Billy Ray and stopped when he was chest to chest. "I done told you once, boy. Since when you think you got the right to address me? Huh? No more warnins'. Haul 'em in Sheriff." Sawyer turned and started walking back toward the courthouse.

"Wait!" Noah cried out.

Mayor Sawyer stopped and turned around.

"We ain't done nothin' wrong, and you know it!" he shouted at Mayor Sawyer.

Mayor Sawyer took a few steps toward the crowd. "You forged my signature. That's against the law, and then you drug all these unsuspecting kids down with you. Now I'm seein' fit to give these others a break if they leave now. But you two are gonna pay for what ya' done."

"We ain't goin nowhere!" Billy Ray shouted. "What we are doin' is the right thing, and if we end up in jail then so be it. But I ain't goin' nowhere. Let's finish what we came here to do!"

The marchers threw their fists in the air and cheered. Slowly, they pressed forward toward the line of men who blocked their path.

The firemen, already dismounted from their rigs and holding water hoses pointed at the students, waited.

The Sheriff looked at Sawyer. "Just give the word, Mayor. One word."

Joshua watched as his defiant son and the others moved closer. "Do it," he said, turning his back on them and walking toward the courthouse.

The TV cameras, poised at strategic positions, clicked and began rolling. Sheriff Jones motioned to the firemen. Like a hail of bullets, the tremendous force of water knocked Billy Ray, Noah and the first several lines of marchers into the air and onto their backs. Others dropped to their knees and buried their faces between their legs to avoid the powerful current. Time and time again, students would try to get up only to be knocked down by the blast. Racial slurs and other derogatory names were shouted by onlookers as they got caught up in the frenzy.

Noah, already knocked down a half dozen times, tried to crawl toward the Sheriff, who was enjoying the show immensely. Out of breath, bruised, and soaked, Noah rested on his hands and knees. "You win. You win. Turn it off."

"I'm sorry, Billy Ray. What'd you say? Can't seem to hear you over these here water hoses," Sheriff Jones laughed.

"We'll go! Just turn off the water!" Noah shouted.

"Smart move, boy." Sheriff Jones raised his arm and the torrent of water ceased.

Slowly, the wet, sore and embarrassed students rose from the pavement.

Mayor Sawyer stood on the courthouse steps with his good friend Judge Stevens who had come out to watch. "You know they won, don't you?"

"Yep," Judge Stevens replied.

"Those cameras," Sawyer said to Stevens while pointing outward. "Those cameras just turned every one of 'em into heroes."

"Uh-huh".

Billy Ray, Noah and the throng of students tried as best as

they could to pick themselves up and wring the water out of their clothes while all the onlookers gawked and laughed. "Let's go," he said to his friends.

"Hold on there, son. You and your friends ain't goin' nowhere. You're all under arrest," Sheriff Jones ordered.

"But you said..." Noah started.

"What I said was for you and your merry band of misfits to move on, but you chose to defy my order. Therefore, every last one of ya' is under arrest." Sheriff Jones then ordered his deputies to arrest the entire group.

The deputies spread out and corralled the marchers like a herd of cattle. Noah begged the Sheriff to arrest just him, explaining that it was his idea. Billy Ray pushed toward Noah also taking responsibility. It didn't matter to the Sheriff. He was about to make more arrests in one day than he had in the last eight years as Sheriff. This would look great at re-election time.

Walking two by two, the deputies led the entire group up the courthouse steps. Mayor Sawyer stopped Noah and Billy Ray as they reached the top. He held up two fingers. "Strike two, boys. Strike two." As they started into the courthouse, Mayor Sawyer stopped Noah by placing his hand on his chest. "As for you, don't bother comin' home evah. You ain't welcome no more."

The Webber County Jail was built in the mid 1800's and had not kept up with the times. It had been renovated on a few occasions, mainly to keep up with sanitation standards. Located in the basement of the building with no natural light, the jail more resembled a medieval prison than it did a county jail. But the jail held a maximum of 15 prisoners when it was built and that number had not changed in a hundred years. It was impossible to accommodate the 200 or so students hauled in, so the Sheriff seated them all in the courtroom to let them think about their actions and to maybe scare some sense into them when the Judge appeared. But Billy Ray and Noah were exceptions. Sheriff Jones found them both damp, cold cells side-by-side.

Upstairs in his office adjacent to the courtroom, Judge Stevens decided the best medicine would be to let the students sit quietly for several hours before he made any decisions on their punishment. His bailiff had already informed the students that their parents had been called and would be making their way to the courtroom shortly. For most, this was punishment enough. The punishment at home would be far worse than anything the court could dish out. Judge Stevens also figured they would all blame Billy Ray and Noah for their troubles and this would have huge negative effect for any future radical activity. Two deputies guarded the students, one in the front and one in the back of the courtroom. Students were ordered to stay silent or face banishment to a cold jail cell. None dared test the order and for a little over three hours, a pin could be heard if it had been dropped. One by one and sometimes two by two, parents began arriving and taking a seat themselves. When the seats ran out, they began lining the edges of both sides of the courtroom. Parents stares could have burnt holes. But no student had the nerve to look their parent or parents in the eye.

In the dark level below, Billy Ray and Noah laid on the metal cot attached to the bars. Neither was outfitted with a mattress. Noah covered his face with his hands and thought about everything that had happened. Billy Ray stared at the dank ceiling above the bars that made a perfect square around him.

"Plan C?" Noah asked.

"What?" Billy Ray countered.

"What's plan C? Are we ready to move on to plan C?"

Billy Ray sat up on the side of the uncomfortable cot and smiled. "I'm glad one of us still has a sense of humor." Billy Ray paused and rubbed his eyes. "I'm all outta plans, man. I got nuthin' else."

Noah sat up on his cot. "How long you think they'll keep us in here?"

Billy Ray drew a deep breath and blew it out. "They ain't gonna make it easy on us. You gotta know that. We're the troublemakers. We're the ones been goin' around stirrin' up all kinds a' trouble. I know my daddy well enough and the Judge. They gotta set bail but they'll make sure it's high enough that we won't be goin' nowhere too soon. So best just get used to your surroundings."

"What about school?" Noah asked.

Billy Ray laughed. "School? You're kiddin' right? Man, I told you when we started all this that we better be ready. Son, if we ain't expelled by now we will be by the end of the day. I'm tellin' you, school is the least of your worries right now. I tried to tell you what the man is capable of, but you didn't wanna listen."

"Me!" Noah interrupted. "So now it's just me."

"Not sayin' that, Noah. I'm as guilty as you are. I'm just sayin' I tried to warn you. That's all." Billy Ray rubbed his head and leaned back against the bars. "Look. It ain't gonna do us no good to squabble amongst ourselves. We got ourselves into this mess because of something God's tryin' to tell us I guess, and for the life a' me I still don't know what God wants from me. If this is His lesson, I sure as hell don't get it."

"So now it's God's fault?" Noah asked.

Billy Ray thought. "Yeah. Reckon it is," he said as he laid back down on the cot. "Reckon it is."

When it looked like most every student was represented by a parent or two, Judge Stevens entered the courtroom decked out in his full length black robe. His bailiff asked all to rise.

"You can be seated," Judge Stevens said, waving his arm across the courtroom. "Ladies and gentlemen. First and foremost let me apologize to all the parents for draggin' you down here in the middle of the day. I know you have work and other more important things you deal with every day. And I am certain you don't want to fuss with, nor have the time, to deal with some of the antics that your children have caused you to be here for this afternoon. But I am a fair man and believe in fair and just punishment. By now I am sure that each and every one of you know what occurred in our fair town earlier today and what your children got mixed up in. But at the same time, your sons and daughters are not totally responsible. The activity was perpetrated by two individuals, and your children here were deceived into coming along. Based on that, I have decided to release each child into the custody of their parents and leave any punishment up to you. However, let me add," he said, pointing directly at the students. "If I see any one of ya' in here again, I won't be so easy. Is that understood?"

A collective "yes, sir" echoed through the courtroom.

"Okay, then. Parents. Take your children and deal with them."

Students slowly rose from their seats and joined their parents in fear of what lay ahead of them when they got home. Judge Stevens grinned sheepishly knowing he had hit a home run. Parents would greatly appreciate him turning their children back to their care so they could dole out their own punishment. But most importantly, he had successfully laid the blame on Billy Ray and Noah. Parents would now demand their child cut any relationship with the two of them. By successfully placing the blame purely on the heads of Billy Ray and Noah, both would become outcasts and therefore scorned. Stevens retired to his office feeling very good about himself.

Long after the other students had gone home and commenced their punishments, Billy Ray and Noah both lay on their respective metal cots. Neither knew what time it was or how many hours had passed because of the darkness in their cell. One light bulb illuminated each cell. Both figured it was close to supper time because they were both hungry, but neither felt like eating.

"You boys awake?"

Both sat up and observed Mayor Sawyer standing at the point where their cells met.

"Couldn't listen to me could ya'?" he said to Noah. "Had to go and get a social conscience all of a sudden."

"Is that such a bad thing?" Noah shot back.

"I don't know. You tell me. Look where you are and then

look where I am. Where would you rather be? See, I'll be goin' home tonight and eatin' a home cooked dinner, sleepin' in my own bed. Matter a fact, I'll be doin' that for days, weeks, months. That's more than I can say for the two of you."

Billy Ray stood and walked to the front of his cell. He pointed to Noah. "I'd rather have his heart and spend eternity in here than walk one minute in your shoes."

"I don't believe I was talkin' to you, boy."

"With all due respect sir, I don't care," Billy Ray said boldly. "You're nuthin' but an oversized, grown up bully. You pick on those that got nuthin' and I guess that makes you feel powerful or somethin'. You run over those tryin' to pick themselves up and make somethin' of themselves and then get some sick satisfaction out of it."

Mayor Sawyer edged closer and stood face to face with Billy Ray, the veins popping on his neck.

"I ain't done talkin', so you listen to me," Billy Ray interrupted.

"Don't do it," Noah tried to stop Billy Ray.

"That's the best advice you'll get all day, boy. Better listen," Mayor Sawyer added.

"Like I said. I ain't done. Not by a long stretch," Billy Ray continued. "For years you been runnin' around all powerful and all mighty like, pushin' around folk like they're no better than dogs. You walk around with your nose all high in the air like you're better than everybody else. Lemme tell you somethin'. You ain't. As much as you wanna think it and believe it, you ain't no better than me or anybody else. Matter a fact, you ain't worth the dirt you walk on. You may have more money and more prestige and live in a bigger house and have all kinds a' high falutin' friends and eat in fancy places. But in the end we all end up on a slab a' metal with no detectable heartbeat. On that day your money, your power, your house, none a' that matters no more. You ain't no different than that poor slob layin' on the slab beside you ceptin' your toe tag'll have a different name on it. You ain't takin' nuthin' with ya' ceptin' maybe your soul, which I am fairly certain of at this time you are lacking."

Mayor Sawyer paused, then pulled a handkerchief from his lapel pocket and wiped his brow. He then placed it back in his lapel and stared at Billy Ray. "Strike three, boy. Strike three." He walked away from the cells and shouted, "Enjoy your accommodations boys. Make yourselves comfortable. You're gonna be there a while."

Noah and Billy Ray watched Mayor Sawyer disappear up the stone stairway.

"That was a big help," Noah said.

Billy Ray lay down on his metal cot. "Yeah, but it felt awful good."

Billy Ray and Noah stood shackled, hands and feet, in front of Judge Stevens. The Public Defender stood between them. The District Attorney was seated at his table and Mayor Sawyer stood at the back of the courtroom by the huge doors, his arms crossed.

"Alright gentlemen, let's get this over with. I'm late for dinner and it's gettin' cold and the missus' don't appreciate it when that happens," Judge Stevens said with a slight chuckle. "The both a' you boys have been charged with forgery and unlawful assembly. Now this ain't no plea hearing so I ain't gonna ask you how you plea. This is nuthin' more than a bail hearing where I set your bond. Do the both of ya' understand that?"

"Yes, sir," Billy Ray and Noah said in unison. Noah knew in an instant the voice he heard in Mayor Sawyer's office was Judge Stevens. He lost any hope of this hearing ending with anything positive.

"Mr. Latham," Judge Stevens motioned to the Public Defender. "Anything you wish to say?"

"Your honor," Latham started. "I request you release both these boys on an O.R. bond. They're both tied to the community, and are not a flight risk. The crimes they are charged with are minor in nature, and at most a misunderstanding. I'm sure both sets of parents will assure they show up at any and all future hearings."

"Mr. Siler," Stevens motioned to the District Attorney.

"No objections your honor," Siler said.

Noah and Billy Ray glanced at each other thinking this wasn't going to be as bad as they thought.

"Thank you, gentlemen," Stevens started. "I've given this a lot of thought. Mr. Latham, and with all due respect, the crimes they are charged with are not so minor in nature, sir. What they did was put this community in danger and they did it with deception and falsehoods. Furthermore, they convinced two hundred or so of their fellow students to break the law with them. I find that not to be minor in nature. That said, I am setting bond at $15,000 each."

"Your honor!" Latham pleaded.

Stevens raised his arm to stop anything Latham said. "Stop right there."

"Your honor. With all due respect sir, there is no way either of these boys can come up with fifteen hundred dollars to make bail."

"That would be their problem," Stevens said, and banged his gavel hard on his desk.

Mayor Sawyer left the courtroom as the gavel echoed inside.

"Bailiff, take these boys back to their accommodations," Stevens said, smiling.

"This way, boys," the bailiff ordered, pulling their arms. "Your yummy suppah' will be served in an hour. Betcha' can't wait."

Billy Ray and Noah both sat on their cots which now had been outfitted with a very thin feather mattress. A plate with unidentifiable meat, some peas and carrots and a slice of white bread, sat uneaten on a dirty tray on the floor.

"Fifteen hundred dollars?" Noah muttered.

"Yeah. Bail's always ten percent," Billy Ray said.

"You know and I know you can get out of here," Noah said. "I've seen the balance in your bank account. You can at least get yourself out of here."

"Nah. Even if I wanted to, he's frozen the account or transferred it into his name. His name's on the account too. He'll make sure I can't get my hands on it. Besides, I'd be bailing you out, not me." Billy Ray looked at Noah and laughed.

"Guess I didn't think of that."

"We're in this together. Alright?"

"Alright." Noah pushed the plate of food underneath the bars to the other side. He wouldn't eat, not here.

Three more hours would pass by before the doors of the Sheriff's office were pushed open by a small but determined black woman who boldly walked up to the front desk. The Sergeant sat on a makeshift podium, making himself a fraction higher than the person in front of him.

"Can I help you, ma'am?" the Sergeant asked.

"I'm here to bail my boy out, sir," Emma explained standing, unflinching before the Sergeant.

The officer chuckled. "By boy, I assume you mean the colored kid down there. Noah Franklin, I think is his name."

"That would be correct, sir. I'd like to post his bail."

Several deputies milling about snickered.

"Ma'am," the Sergeant said. "I don't think you understand. I'm afraid you never seen that kind of money."

"How much is it?" Emma asked.

The Sergeant double checked his clipboard. "Bond was fifteen thousand dollars, ma'am. That means the bail is fifteen hundred dollars. But I tell you what, I'll give you the special of the day which is three thousand for the both of 'em."

Several deputies laughed out loud.

"Both of 'em?" Emma questioned. "Billy Ray still in there?"

The Sergeant grinned. "I'm afraid that boy's a lost cause. As far as the Mayor's concerned, he can rot in there." The Sergeant paused, leaned forward and spoke slightly above a whisper. "Look ma'am. I'm sure you mean well and all, but there ain't no sense in embarrassin' yourself here. A little jail time'll do both these boys world a good."

"I respect what you're sayin', sir. But neither one of them boys belong in there, and I'd like to get them out please."

"Ma'am. You don't understand."

"No, sir. I do understand." Emma lifted her purse and pulled out a small brown grocery bag. Slowly she opened it and began counting out three thousand dollars starting with twenties, then tens, then fives and then ones. It took her almost ten minutes to count it all out and when she was finished, she had a handful of one dollar bills left over that she put back in the grocery bag and then into her purse. For twenty years she worked at the Sawyers for meager wages. But every week she was paid, she managed to put back a little for emergencies. This wasn't something she expected, but it was certainly an emergency and something she considered worthy of using it for.

The Sergeant stared dumbfounded at the large pile of money littered across his desk.

"I'd like to get the boys now if that's alright with you."

"Yes, ma'am. Just need to get their paperwork in order and I'll have 'em right up."

Emma sat down to wait and tried mightily to hold back a grin.

~ 24 ~

Sweat poured from their brows as they split log after log. Their punishment began the next evening. Emma didn't have the heart to make them work the same night they got out. Both accepted their punishment with dignity. It was almost ironic because they both knew they'd be chopping wood for the upcoming winter whether they had been arrested or not. Since living at the Franklin's, Billy Ray had all but perfected the art of splitting wood. With the two of them working in unison, log after log fell like clockwork to the ground below where the pile grew larger and larger. Billy Ray put the ax head on the ground and leaned the handle against a log as the sunset gave way to dusk. He pulled a soiled, frazzled handkerchief from his back overalls pocket and wiped the sweat that glistened as it ran down his face.

The sound of the ax beating against the wood was like music to Emma's ears as she put the finishing touches on her meat loaf. Meat loaf was considered a delicacy in the Franklin household. It certainly was not a regular on the menu. But Emma believed that punishment or not, both boys deserved it. Perhaps more than anything, she thanked God above for the relationship that had blossomed between Billy Ray and Noah. One rich, one poor, who through some sort of miracle she was not aware of, had learned to care for one another and work together for something good.

"How long you gonna make them boys work?" James asked, slinging the water off his hands and walking into the kitchen to dry them off.

"'Til they know they been punished," she answered, checking the homemade bread she was baking in the oven. She pulled the finished loaf from the oven and placed it on the table, then wiped her hands on a red checkered dish towel that was draped across her shoulder. "It's not that what they did was so terrible. Good Lord knows their intentions were in the right place. But that don't change the fact that they challenged authority. And no matter what they was thinkin', they gotta be punished for it."

Outside, darkness began to fall quickly. The aroma of the bread wafted outside. The relaxing sound of chirping crickets filled the air. Billy Ray split one more log and left the ax head embedded in the base stump. "You know, Noah. I've been thinkin'."

Noah split a log then rested on the handle. "Yeah. Me too. 'Bout how good that bread's gonna be when Mama finally lets us in."

Billy Ray smiled and shook his head. "Not about the bread."

"'Bout what?"

"'Bout everything, man. Everything we've been through. I still ain't figured it out yet. Don't know that I ever will. I sure figured God would make it a little more clear to us than he has."

Noah split another log, threw his ax on top of the large pile then leaned against the pile now waist high. "I don't know 'bout that. I think He's been pretty clear."

Billy Ray lifted his arms. "How so?"

"Look. I ain't sayin' I'm in God's mind or I'm some prophet or nuthin' like that. But look at us. Look at everything that's happened."

"Uh-huh. Beatins', fruit thrown at us, fire hoses sprayed at us, jail. Yeah. That's real clear. Think I see God's point now. Thanks for the explanation," Billy Ray said facetiously, as he worked the ax back and forth to remove the head from the stump. He placed another log on the stump.

"That's not what I mean. That's not what I'm talkin' about. What I mean is look at us. What we been through, man. How we both changed. How maybe we changed others. Don't you think maybe that's what God was tryin' to do? Tryin' to tell us. You've heard of that sayin', a means to an end. I'm thinkin' that's what he's tryin' to accomplish. Some means to an end. Whatever happens, happens for a reason, and whatever the reason is will justify the end result."

Billy Ray narrowed his eyes and cocked his head. "What the hell'd you just say? Was that some foreign language or somethin'?" Billy Ray split the log.

Noah smiled, then half laughed. "No. Sorry. Kinda confused myself, too. I reckon what I'm tryin' to say is whatever God's reason for all this is... well, I reckon he'll show us in due time. At some point I'm sure it'll come clear."

"I reckon," said Billy Ray. He rested his ax against the log pile and looked up at the stars now beginning to sparkle across the dark sky. "Noah?"

"Yeah."

"Thanks."

Noah looked at Billy Ray who peered at the sky trying to avoid any eye contact. "You, too."

Neither Billy Ray or Noah noticed James when he stepped on the front porch. "You boys gonna make Ms. Emma cry if ya' keep up with all that mushy talk. Now go on and dust yourselves off, put your shirts on and come on in for what looks to be the tastiest dinner we've had in a while." James opened the screen door halfway then stepped back onto the porch. "I done told Ms. Emma if we gonna eat like this every time you boys get in trouble, I hope you keep gettin' in trouble." James paused. "She didn't take to kindly to my stab at humor."

"What'd she say?" Noah asked.

"She said next time you get in trouble you'll be dinin' on bread and water, but it wouldn't be in her kitchen." James laughed at himself and opened the screen door.

Suddenly, Billy Ray and Noah quickly turned toward the dirt road at the same time. The whirring sound of tires crunching gravel was unmistakable. James stopped and turned and observed a dozen or so headlights speeding down the dirt and gravel road toward his home. Nervously, Emma watched from the kitchen window.

"Get inside, quick!" James shouted to Billy Ray and Noah.

But it was too late. Before either could take one step toward the door, at least six pickup trucks sped and spun into the yard, kicking up a huge dust cloud. Every headlight shone directly on Billy Ray and Noah, casting their oversized shadows onto the shack. No fewer than thirty white robed and hooded Klansmen poured from the cabs and beds of each truck. Most were armed with shotguns and aimed them directly at the two boys who stood frozen by the log pile. The staring match did not last as long as it seemed.

Inside, James quickly hid Emma and grabbed three shotguns for himself, Moses and Adam. They took position by the door and prayed Billy Ray could talk the mob out of anything it was planning to do. Outside, the angry group managed to surround Billy Ray and Noah.

Noah lifted his arms to show he was not going to fight them. "Look. We ain't botherin' nobody no more. We're just out here takin' our punishment and movin' on. We're done tryin' to change things. If you just talk to my daddy, I'm sure he'll tell you boys everything's alright. That everybody's okay. That there ain't no point in pursuin' this no further."

"Ain't you we're after, Billy Ray," one hooded Klansman said. "We're here for the nigga'." Noah and Billy Ray looked at each other, realizing what was about to happen.

"Wait a minute," Noah said, trying his best to stall. "Just lemme call my daddy. I'm sure we can fix all this. Straighten out all the confusion and all. Just give me a minute to go call him and I'm sure this'll all get straightened out."

The mob circled a little tighter.

"Look," Noah pleaded. "You don't know what you're doin'. For God's sake! You have no idea what you're doin'." Noah held out his arms. "Take me. I'm the one you want. I'll take his place. Just let him stay with his family. Please don't hurt him. Just take me and be done with it."

"Don't Noah," Billy Ray said. "This is the way it's supposed to be. It's all clear now. Remember what we said? Everything's clear now. It's alright. I'll be alright."

The Klansman walked up to Billy Ray. "What'd you call him, boy?"

"Nuthin'," Billy Ray answered. "Didn't call 'em nuthin. Let's get this done."

The hooded Klansman took one step over and stood face to face with Noah. "Like I said, Billy Ray. It ain't you we want." The Klansman looked around at his hooded friends. "Get him!"

Five Klansmen converged on Billy Ray and forced him hard to the ground. Three held him firmly in place while one tied his arms behind his back and the other hogtied his ankles. Angry, Noah dove head first into the five and managed to throw three of them off Billy Ray before he was subdued by five or six more robed thugs.

"Let him up or I'll blow two or three of ya' to tarnation," James ordered from his front porch. Adam and Moses stood beside him, shotguns aimed squarely in the direction of some of the Klansmen who also leveled their shotguns back at them.

"Wouldn't do that if I were you," said the head Klansman. "I think you're a little outnumbered."

"Don't care," James said. "May be outnumbered, but I'll take a few of ya' out before you get me, so if you're willin' to take that chance, go right ahead."

"You may be willin' to die mister, but how old are your sons there? And your wife, there? Are you willin' to let them die too?"

James looked at his family.

"Don't you worry 'bout us, Pop. I've been waitin' for this day for a long time," Adam said smiling.

"Besides," said the Klansman. "Ain't gonna do nuthin' more

than have a heart to heart with your boy here," he said motioning to Billy Ray tied up on the ground. "We'll have him back in no time."

"It's okay, Pop," Billy Ray struggled to talk. "Don't do nuthin' crazy like. Go on back inside."

James looked at Adam and Moses.

"I'd listen to him, Pops," the Klansman said. "Don't wanna blow this thing way outta proportion. No need makin' it more serious than it is."

"Please, Pop," Billy Ray begged, gasping for air. I know what I'm doin'. Please go back inside."

A few Klansmen racked their shotguns for emphasis.

"We can take 'em, Pop. We can take 'em," Adam pleaded with his father, knowing it was Billy Ray he was now fighting for. "You know they got no intention a' bringin' him back alive."

"I'm gonna count to five," the Klansman said. "If the three a' you ain't back inside, I'm gonna give the order to fire. One!"

"Pop!" Billy Ray screamed. "Please go back inside!"

"Two!"

"We can take 'em, Pop," Adam kept repeating.

"Three!"

"Mr. Franklin!" Billy Ray screamed and spit out dust. "I'm begging you! Go inside! I know what I'm doing! Please go inside!" He knew what this mob was capable of doing.

"Four!"

"Alright. Alright," Confused, James relented to the dissatisfaction of Adam and Moses. He knew he was outnumbered, and wasn't willing to lose his whole family. He would think his way out of this mess. "We're goin' inside." James, Adam and Moses, guns still pointed at the Klansmen, backed their way into the house.

Several of the Klansmen jerked Billy Ray to his feet that were unbalanced because of being tied so tightly. Noah pleaded with the Klansman once more. "I'm begging you, sir. You are taking the wrong guy! It's me you want!"

The main Klansman who had done most of the talking placed the barrel of his shotgun against Noah's throat. "What's become a' you, Billy Ray? You willin' to take a bullet for this nigga'? You willin' to die for 'em?"

Noah swallowed hard and nodded his head. "Yeah. I am."

Billy Ray forced a smile at Noah. "Ya' see? It's clear now ain't it?"

The Klansman smiled at Noah. "That's mighty noble of ya' Billy Ray. But I got my orders," he said turning away. "Let's get outta here."

Two of the Klansmen each grabbed an arm and swiftly dragged Billy Ray toward the bed of one of the trucks. He was tossed head first into the dirty bed where four Klansmen sat, more than eager to ride along.

The two hooded men holding Noah shoved him to the ground, ran toward one of the trucks, and hopped quickly into the bed, as did the rest of them. Slinging dirt, mud and gravel into the air, the trucks fishtailed, spun their tires and headed off down the dirt road.

The truck holding Billy Ray was the last in line. As it spun its tires, Billy Ray lifted his head and shouted to Noah. "Go tell my father! He can stop it!"

"Shut up, boy!" one of the Klansmen said, slamming Billy Ray's head into the metal bed, leaving a large bloody gash on his head. "Didn't you see what your daddy did back there? He gave up without a fight. Nobody's gonna help you now."

Helplessly, Noah stood by as the tail lights dimmed and faded from view. Then as quickly as it all had started, one truck slammed on its brakes and reversed its direction. Noah wondered if they changed their minds and were coming back for him. The truck spun 180 degrees as it turned into the driveway. One gunman jumped from the bed and began shooting all four tires on Billy Ray's truck. He jumped back into the bed and the truck sped away.

Noah looked toward his shack at his parents inside. He wanted to tell them the truth, that their son had been spared. But there was no time. He began running at half speed away from the house, periodically glancing back at the window where James and Emma stood watching.

When he could no longer see his family, his half speed turned into a full sprint. Thunder rolled in the distance as a cold front neared. Noah ran past the shacks of his neighbors as they all watched him and wondered what terrible thing had just happened. He ran as hard as he possibly could. But he knew it was at least five miles to the Sawyer's home and figured it would take at least forty-five minutes. That was if he could keep up his current pace. But by then it might be too late. He veered off the dusty road and went headlong into the dark woods. There was just enough illumination from the stars that he could run and not bump into trees, but there were ruts and briars and thorns to deal with. He paid no attention because he knew that it was nothing compared to what his friend was enduring. Taking this shortcut would shorten the distance over two miles. Precious time he needed.

The crickets were strangely silent as Noah bolted through the woods. Even though it cut a significant distance from his journey, the uneven lay of the woods took a toll on his legs. He quickly tired from the hills that he had climbed, but he refused to stop even to rest for a minute, though his thighs began to burn.

Noah knew the woods like the back of his hand, but it seemed forever since he'd started. He tortured himself, wondering if he'd taken a wrong turn or maybe was doing nothing but going in circles. He refused to let his mind or body defeat him. He had to finish. He had to save his friend. Something inside him made him go harder and faster. His lungs burned with every stride he took. Suddenly, in the distance was a dim light. He froze, but for only a second. He took off like a sprinter toward the light, and within seconds was thanking God at the sight of a streetlight at the other side of the woods.

Noah knew now he was only minutes from the Sawyer mansion. On the flat pavement, Noah could run full speed and compared to the woods it was like running on air. He jumped a few fences and cut through several yards.

The thunder grew louder and the sky began to be lit up by lightning far in the distance. The clouds glowed as if the lightning was trapped within them. Noah rounded the corner of a street and spotted the Sawyer home ahead about a hundred feet away, lighted from the inside like a beacon. Two houses away, he saw a car backing down the Sawyer driveway. His stomach turned sour thinking he'd come all this way only to lose his one chance of saving his friend. Noah caught the car as it backed into the street and started pounding on the trunk and yelling at the occupant inside. Because of the darkness, Mary Edith did not recognize him. Frightened, she floored the accelerator and sped off down the road. Noah stopped. He knew he couldn't catch her now, but was relieved it wasn't Mayor Sawyer. Hopefully, he was inside. Noah leaned over and grabbed his knees to catch what breath he had left in him. He turned and ran up to the steps of the Sawyer mansion and started pounding on the door to no avail. There was no answer. In the heat of the moment, he had forgotten his appearance. He tried the doorknob and mercifully it was unlocked. He opened the door and stepped inside to a quiet, partially lit home.

The wind had picked up significantly and whistled crossways across the porch. Besides the eerie whistle of wind, the only sound Noah heard was the methodical ticking of the 150 year old grandfather clock in the foyer. He called out for Mayor Sawyer first, but corrected himself and then beckoned for 'Daddy', a term he had never gotten used to. He checked the downstairs, but there was no answer. Thinking he might be in the kitchen drinking his favorite night time drink of coffee with a shot of bourbon, Noah stepped quietly through the swinging doorway of the kitchen. The Mayor was not there. Moving into the foyer from the kitchen, Noah noticed a sliver of light sneaking out from underneath the door of Mayor Sawyer's secret office. Noah hoped Mayor Sawyer had closed himself inside and had been unable to hear him pounding at the door or hear his calls. He bounded up the staircase three steps at a time, rounded the oak banister and kept his eyes focused on the light under the door. Noah crept slowly past the bedroom where he lived after this strange act of God had entered his life. Thunder echoed outside as he approached the padlocked door to the private office Mayor Sawyer had been so protective of.

Noah knocked, but there was no answer. He knocked again and a third time, but there was still no answer. He looked down. The padlock normally keeping everyone out was in the hasp but not locked. He reached slowly for the silver padlock and lifted it. Cautiously, he opened the door that creaked with every forward movement. He fully expected to see Mayor Sawyer slumped over his desk, maybe despondent over everything that had happened and what it might mean to his political career. Maybe that was why Mary Edith had driven away in such a hurry. Noah opened the door just enough to poke his head inside. The office was empty. There was a huge mahogany desk with leather chair to match, but no Mayor Sawyer. He took one step back and was going to leave, maybe find another way. Time was slowly running out. But something hastened him back. He leaned over the desk and switched on the desk lamp. He was immediately overwhelmed by what he saw. Covering every wall were photographs of Ku Klux Klan members. On another wall were framed documents verifying his lengthy years of membership and the offices he had held within the Klan. Noah backed away into another wall. There, plastered across it were photographs of the Mayor himself, dressed in full white garb, his white veil pulled up over his head, smiling proudly and shaking hands with the Grand

Wizard who had also autographed the photo. A framed photograph sitting on the desk that Noah at first missed showed a beaming Mayor Sawyer and Judge Stevens in their traditional Klan garb holding a noose.

Noah became nauseous at what he saw. A feeling of despair overwhelmed him for the moment. He sat down in the leather chair and rested his forehead into the palms of both hands. Attempting to regain his composure, he noticed several newspaper clippings on top of the Mayor's desk along with more photos of his cohorts dressed in white robes and standing by burning crosses. He reached for and thumbed through the clippings, hoping for any clues as to where Billy Ray might be.

Noah picked up a sheet of paper torn from a spiral notebook and noticed several names scribbled on it. It was hard to read in the dim light inside the office. He brought it closer to his face. His blood ran cold. On the paper were four names, three scratched out with red ink. Was this the list the Mayor had referred to? Noah read and recognized the names of the three that had been redlined. They were friends or acquaintances of James' and all had gone missing in the last six months or so. All had bravely spoken their minds, at one time or another, at town hall meetings. Speculation was that they had just run off. Only one name remained on the list that was not scratched out. Noah Franklin. An even smaller note beside his name said 'Ned Turner Farm'.

Noah tossed the list back on the desk and charged out of the office, causing the doorknob to smash through the drywall. He jumped four or five stairs at a time and his heart was beating double time as he pulled open the majestic front door, not bothering to close it behind him. He knew where he was going, and prayed to God it was not too late.

Outside, a bolt of lightning struck a nearby pine tree as thunder rolled in the distance. The wind began to pick up and a light but chilling rain began to fall as Noah ran full tilt toward Ned Turner's. The farm was a few miles away by road, but only about three quarters of a mile through another set of woods adjacent to the Sawyer property that led eventually to the high school...the very woods where this strange adventure had begun.

———————————

Billy Ray's head bounced up and down off the bed of the truck as it traveled down a bumpy road that was not a road at all. It was a rocky path carved over the years by tractors and trucks tending to cattle, goats or sheep. His heart pounded as he was forced to listen to the hooded men in the bed of the truck discussing his fate while they kicked and prodded him. Somewhere along the way he had been blindfolded and gagged with silver duct tape across his mouth.

His mind had somehow shut out the physical pain, but he couldn't help but sense his life flashing before his eyes. He thought of his mother bringing him a cold glass of lemonade to ward off the heat of the summer. The cheering of the crowd as he made another touchdown. He remembered riding on his father's shoulders and pretending he was a giant. He recalled being a four year old pancake. "I'm done!" he would shout, and his dad would flip him. He thought of pitching the baseball or throwing the football in the backyard with his dad. But he also recalled his father preaching hate against anyone different and how, over time, he had accepted and believed it.

The thunder was more frequent now. Cold rain splattered across his face as the truck came to a stop. Droplets of rain streamed down Billy Ray's bare chest that pounded so hard he could feel it in his throat and in his head.

"Is this it?" one Klansman said, standing up in the bed of the truck beside Billy Ray.

"Can't tell," said another. "The rain's causin' the road to wash out. I can't tell if this is it or not." He looked around then knocked on the cab window. "This ain't it. Go on a little further. I'll let you know when we're there."

Behind the school and running like a deer through the woods, Noah knew exactly where he was going, but the cold wind and rain exploding against his face slowed him down. Still, his aching, burning legs refused to fold. His calves churned as hard as they could up steep hills and through shallow creek beds that were beginning to rise from the rain. Soaked and dirty, he swatted at thorn branches that tore at his flesh with almost every stride he took. The more he ran, the more he thought of the irony of it all. That it was supposed to be him in the bed of that truck. That this act of God would save his life and possibly take Billy Ray's. His thoughts tortured him but also inspired him to move as quickly as he could through the thickets and briars toward Nat Turner's farm.

Noah pushed hard up the steep hills. He tried as best he could to keep his footing, but it seemed the harder his heels dug into the waterlogged clay, the more his legs were knocked out from under him. Soaked and dirty, he pulled himself up over and over again and made his way to the farm step by agonizing step.

As jagged branches slapped and stung his cheeks, a bolt of lightning struck nearby. The force of the blast catapulted him through the air and back against a long ago fallen tree. The pain it caused was immense and as he tried to stand, an excruciating pain shot through his gut, doubling him over and knocking him back to the ground. The pain subsided momentarily. Again he tried to stand when a second jolt pierced his abdomen like a hot sword. Amidst the pain, he rose again and had taken no more than twenty steps when the pain hit his gut a third time. Noah fell to his hands and knees and, like a wounded soldier, had to crawl to keep moving.

Like a twin, Billy Ray lay doubled over in agony in the soaked bed of the truck. He felt as if his guts had been ripped out. The Klansmen poked at him with their shotguns wondering if he would die before they arrived at the pre-determined location.

"What's wrong with 'em?" one asked.

"How the hell should I know?" another answered. "Let's just get 'em there first. We don't want 'em to die before we get there."

It took all the energy he could muster to rise a third time. Noah used the overhanging branches of a half-fallen tree to pull himself up. Three steps into the driving rain, the indescribable pain knocked him to the mud soaked ground one more time.

He cried out to God as his body rolled into a muddy ravine. "What do you want from me?! Huh? What do you want?!" he screamed, lying flat on his back, fists raised in the air. "Maybe Billy Ray was right!" Noah yelled at the top of his lungs. "Maybe he was right about you all along! Maybe you are just bein' cruel 'cause I don't know what you want. I don't know what you want me to do!"

"This is it! This is the place!" a Klansman in the cab of the truck yelled, banging on the back window to alert the rain-soaked men in the back. Each truck slogged to a soggy stop, spewing up mud in the process. Gangs of white sheeted hoodlums poured from the trucks and into ankle deep mud. Beams from flashlights danced through the downpour and toward the pickup where Billy Ray lay captive.

"Get his ass outta the truck!" ordered a muffled voice, obviously the leader. "Somebody pick up that no good nigga' and get him over here."

"Cut his ankles loose!" another shouted.

Several sets of rough hands snapped him off the truck and drug him on his back across the muddy ground. He was pulled to his feet first and lifted up on an old wooden sawhorse which had been placed under a tree. A rope was tossed without ceremony over a heavy branch and then a noose was placed around Billy Ray's neck. The Klansmen gathered around him, laughing and joking as Billy Ray teetered back and forth on the sawhorse, trying to keep his balance.

"Take his blindfold off," the leader ordered.

"Why?" one of them asked.

"Take it off, I said!" the leader shouted.

One of the Klansmen got a wooden crate from one of the truck beds and placed it by the workhorse where Billy Ray wobbled slowly back and forth. He removed the bandana from Billy Ray's eyes then stepped down from the crate. Like a river and its tributaries, blood ran down Billy Ray's face in multiple streams as he stared down at the jubilant hooded thugs.

The leader stepped up on the crate and ripped the tape from Billy Ray's mouth.

Billy Ray stared at the hooded man. The pelting rain stung his eyes. "Why?" he pleaded.

The leader grabbed Billy Ray by the neck and pulled him closer. "Cause sometimes you gotta take out the trash."

Billy Ray was frozen. He knew those words and who was speaking them.

Mayor Sawyer lifted his veil for Billy Ray to see. "I want you to see who's sending you to hell."

"You can stop this," Billy Ray pleaded. "You have no idea what you're about to do. Please stop before it's too late."

"Shoulda thought about that long time ago. Before you got my boy all involved in your radical ideas. But you won't be botherin' him no more."

Less than an eighth of a mile away, Noah struggled to his feet. Somewhere in the distance he heard voices, but the thunder and lightning made it difficult to pinpoint. The eerie voices grew stronger as he inched his way through the darkness.

Noah's heart throbbed in rhythm with his pounding feet. He

had the sensation of his worst nightmares, the ones in which he wanted to run, but his legs wouldn't move. Branches ripped and tore at his face, his arms, and his legs. The sweat, produced as much from his terror as from the dark and humid Alabama night, pooled into his wounds, the saltiness burning deep within his skin. He was smothering. Every breath was a struggle. Mindlessly, his legs churned forward. He knew he had to keep moving. He had to save his friend. He had to save himself.

"Let's get this thing over with," Mayor Sawyer said calmly. "Get a hood. I wanna cover his face up."

Billy Ray grimaced as the same pain shot through his belly again. It was all he could do to keep his balance.

One of the Klansmen pulled a small burlap bag from one of the trucks. He handed the bag to Mayor Sawyer who readied it to slip over Billy Ray's head.

"I forgive you for what you're about to do," Billy Ray said.

Sawyer hesitated and lowered the bag. "What'd you say?"

"I said I forgive you."

Sawyer stared at Billy Ray and moved to within inches of his eyes. He looked deep into his son's eyes and cocked his head slightly. "Why?"

Billy Ray paused. "'Cause I got to."

Sawyer cocked his head the other direction and shook his head. With no hesitation, he lifted the bag and pulled it hard over Billy Ray's head.

Holding his gut, Noah burst through the last hedge and into the clearing where the truck headlights lit up the scene before him. A mist began to slowly rise from the ground as the rain began to subside. Everything was eerily quiet as Noah raced in what seemed like slow motion towards the large oak tree surrounded by the ghostly hooded figures. His scream broke the silence.

Sawyer and his fellow Klansmen turned quickly toward Noah. They watched in stunned silence as the black troublemaker they'd just hung charged towards them. Then Noah froze. He clasped his hands on top of his head and fell to his knees as he watched Billy Ray's limp body swing back and forth.

"No! What have you done?"

In shock, Sawyer and his men watched as Noah struggled to his feet, limped over to the tree and stepped up on the crate. Pulling a pocket knife from his pocket, he cut the rope. Billy Ray's lifeless body fell into Noah's arms. Noah fell to his knees with Billy Ray still cradled in his arms. Ashen faced, Sawyer and his gang gathered around him. Noah laid Billy Ray down gently on the cold ground and removed the burlap bag from his head. He cut the rope from his wrists. Gently, he wiped away the blood from Billy Ray's face. Sawyer fell to his knees beside Noah, tore off his hood and threw it to the ground. He turned and vomited into the rain soaked dirt.

Noah slipped his arms beneath Billy Ray's body and lifted him up. Billy Ray's limp head lay across his arm. Sawyer watched as Noah started to walk away.

"Stop! Wait!" Sawyer called out to Noah.

Noah stopped but did not turn around.

"This can't be! This can't be! What have we done?"

Noah turned to face Sawyer, feeling nothing but disgust.

Tears streamed down the Mayor's face. "My boy! My son! What did I do? What did I do?"

Noah looked at the Klansmen, all still in shock. Noah suddenly felt pity for this horrible man. Billy Ray was his son. He carried Billy Ray to his father but before handing his body over, they stared at each other, saying nothing. Noah gently laid Billy Ray's body beside his father and calmly adjusted his arms across his torso. Sawyer was speechless as he watched his son's body lying before him. It was then that Noah noticed Billy Ray's hands. One was open, the other clinched in a tight fist. Noah knelt beside his friend again.

Sawyer watched him, for once in his life, devoid of hate.

"His hand. There's something in his hand."

Sawyer knelt on his knees on the opposite side of Billy Ray's body.

Noah struggled to open Billy Ray's tightly clinched fingers, but when he opened his hand, the silver cross Noah had given him lay in the middle of his palm.

"What is it?" Sawyer asked, wiping away tears.

Noah stared at Sawyer, looked around at the Klansmen and back at Sawyer. "It's his way of sayin' everything's alright. He's alright." Noah pressed Billy Ray's fingers back into a clinched fist, covering the cross.

Sawyer collapsed across his son's body and sobbed. Noah stood up and took one last look at his friend. He then turned and walked away back into the woods.

~ 25 ~

The third trial ended just like the first and second, with a hung jury. Eighteen months had come and gone since that night. Joshua Sawyer sat stone faced staring into the wall behind the Judge. Three times a jury could not come to a unanimous decision that he had intentionally murdered his own son. His attorneys successfully argued that he had indeed intended to hang Noah Franklin, but that Noah Franklin had not been hung. The prosecution said it didn't matter who he killed. The facts showed he murdered his own son whether he meant to or not. Whatever the reasons, part of the jury agreed with the prosecution and part of the jury agreed with the defense. The prosecution gave up and dropped the charges, knowing he would endure a lifetime of regret whether behind bars or not. His supporters would say he had suffered enough, that he would never be the same after that night. This was true. After resigning his position, Joshua became a recluse, and died five years later a broken and pathetic shell of a man.

Within weeks of the lynching, Mary Edith packed her bags and went to live with her sister in Decatur. She returned occasionally to visit Billy Ray's grave, but only offered token gestures of support to Joshua. Sometimes she would drive by the home, park out front for a few minutes and leave. Joshua would see her from inside but never came out. She learned through the TV evening news that Judge Stevens and the other Klan members present that night had plead guilty to civil rights violations to avoid lengthy prison sentences for conspiracy to commit murder. Ten years and a few days after that night, she met a preacher from Tennessee and moved close to the Smokey Mountains. Her trips to Alabama to visit her son's grave decreased to once a year, then once every three or four years, and then none at all. She would never forget, and she would never forgive.

Neither James nor Emma ever knew what happened that fall of 1965. The only thing they knew was they got their son back that night and somewhere in the middle of it all, the town had changed. People seemed nicer, more understanding, and more tolerant. Adam and Moses promised Noah they would never speak of it again and they kept their promise. Time passed on and that short intervention into their lives soon became a distant but always painful memory.

Noah never talked to anyone about what happened. Whatever God had done, He did it in his own time and in His own way. There was nothing more Noah could add. He had been a tool in God's work and hoped he had done right. He would question God from time to time in prayer about why it had to end the way it had. If He answered, Noah never heard it. He knew the purpose, the reason for what had happened. His and Billy Ray's eyes had been opened.

Noah left Webber in August of the next year. An anonymous donor provided a full four year scholarship to the college of his choice. He chose the University of Tennessee in Knoxville, and graduated with honors. He still believed God had a purpose and a plan for his life, but he couldn't stay in Webber and relive the memories every minute of every day. He stayed in close touch with his family. And when he visited his hometown and his family, he never failed to visit the grave of the best friend he would ever have. The bond they shared was sealed with their strange and mysterious secret.

Years later, Noah returned as the state's first black senator. Noah was respected and loved by his constituents, black and white. He purchased the old Sawyer mansion for his mother and father. The house Emma worked so hard in was now her own.

No one ever knew for sure the reason for what happened in Webber, Alabama that fall of 1965. Maybe it was for Billy Ray's salvation. Maybe it was to change his father, or the townspeople. All would speculate. Everyone had an opinion. People that had no connection to the people involved questioned if anything happened at all. It was just a story, a myth. For the people involved, they knew better. They knew something had happened and it was not a natural occurrence. Maybe it came from God, maybe it didn't. But whatever happened, happened. And there was no arguing that their town was caught up in the middle of it. Whatever the cause, whatever the reason, it changed people, it changed a community and it changed a state. Billy Ray and Noah knew exactly what God's purpose was. And in the end, that was all that mattered.

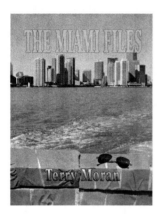

- Title: *The Miami Files* ™
- Series: Miami Files Series™
- Author: Terry Moran
- Price: $27.95
- Publisher: TotalRecall Publications,
- Format: HARDCOVER, 6.14" x 9.21"
- Number of pages: 340
- 13-digit ISBN: 978-1-59095-727-1
- Publication: 2012

Jack Armstrong, an up and coming young businessman in Atlanta, has paid his dues at Marlowe Plumbing and Supply. He finally gets the well-deserved promotion he has sought after years of fourteen hour days and thankless nights. A misdirected shipment of supplies reveals billions of dollars-worth of cocaine which could devastate the company and Jack's good name. Doing what he thinks is the right thing by contacting the FBI backfires and places him squarely in the crosshairs of the FBI Agent investigating and the mob who wants their cocaine returned. Jack races against the clock trying to evade the FBI and the mob, all while trying to prove his innocence. Trekking through the southeast, he finds information which could implicate the FBI Agent chasing him and who may have more at stake than just apprehending Jack. Jack lands in Miami where he finds the information he needs to clear his name, but it may be too little and too late to save him from either side.

CPSIA information can be obtained at www.ICGtesting.com
Printed in the USA
LVOW070027070112

262462LV00002BA/2/P